W9-BGO-620

RAVES FOR THE NOVELS OF
KAREN E. QUINONES MILLER

PASSIN'

"Living a lie has never been so fascinating! Ms. Miller is sure to receive top honors for her work."
—Heather Elitou, Infinite MagaZine, www. infinitemag.net

"A book that is long overdue and bound to leave readers wanting more."
—Miasha, *Essence* bestselling author of *Mommy's Angel, Sistah for Sale*, and *Never Enough: No Secret's Safe*

"An engaging read that brings the age-old issues of race, color, and accepting who you are to light."
—Daaimah S. Poole, *Essence* bestselling author of *All I Want Is Everything*

SATIN NIGHTS

"Don't miss."
—*USA Today*

"A silky-smooth tale filled with drama, humor, and sensuality."
—Urban-Reviews.com

"Blending themes of friendship and romantic angst with tough, independent female characters, *Satin Nights* captures the edginess of urban grit and celebrates the strength of sisterhood."
—*Seattle Skanner*

more...

"[Miller] is the Woody Allen for a black New York. If you know Manhattan, you'll immediately feel at home with the author's uncanny sense of place, and if you're not familiar, you will be after taking in Miller's vivid descriptions . . . You'll almost hear the trains roar into the 145th Street stop."

—*Birmingham Times* (Alabama)

SATIN DOLL

"Gritty, haunting, and hypnotic . . . powerful and provocative . . . Will keep you on the edge of your seat for days to come."

—*Essence*

"In addition to its fast pace, drama, sizzling sex, and domestic fireworks, *Satin Doll* raises deeper questions about class issues."

—*Virginian-Pilot*

"Energetic, fast-paced, and provides intriguing action."

—*Black Issues Book Review*

"A real page-turner . . . Karen Quinones Miller navigates this dilemma of two worlds with skill and passion."

—*Albany Times Union*

"A literary asset; an inspirational, gutsy story with a tough and endearing main character."

—*Philadelphia Tribune*

"Marvelous . . . A skillful blend of romance, violence, and family bonding."

—*Booklist*

IDA B.

"A spunky, speedy read."

—*Publishers Weekly*

"Miller has crafted yet another realistic, poignant, and gut-wrenching tale about the trueness of life on the streets of Harlem. She continues her honest, no-holds-barred style of presentation, where she shares all the ups and downs of life in what some would say is the lower echelon of society: where unemployment is high, hustling is a way of life, and government assistance is a reality."
—Brenda M. Lisbon, reviewer for RAWSISTAZ Book Club

USING WHAT YOU GOT

"You couldn't ask for a more flowing, fast, or satisfying summertime read."
—*USA Today*

I'M TELLING

"An urban fairy tale, a rollicking and robust tale of incest and love, sister and mother bonds, career success, and the lure of the streets . . . a fast read with lively and likable characters. The Freeman women are hot-blooded in every way."
—*Philadelphia Inquirer*

"From the first page, the reader will be pulled in and never let go. This story is an action-packed emotional ride. There are no lulls in this book, so get comfortable because you will read it all in one sitting. The characters jump off the page because of rich dialogue and pertinent flashbacks . . . a compelling story about facing the truth and forgiving oneself."
—*Romance in Color*

Also by Karen E. Quinones Miller

Satin Doll

I'm Telling

Using What You Got

Ida B. (Uptown Dreams)

*Satin Nights**

*Published by Grand Central Publishing

A NOVEL

Karen E. Quinones Miller

NEW YORK BOSTON

This book is a work of fiction. Names, characters, places, and incidents are the product of the author's imagination or are used fictitiously. Any resemblance to actual events, locales, or persons, living or dead, is coincidental.

Grand Central Publishing
Hachette Book Group USA
237 Park Avenue
New York, NY 10017

Printed in the United States of America

Grand Central Publishing is a division of Hachette Book Group USA, Inc.
The Grand Central Publishing name and logo is a trademark of Hachette Book Group USA, Inc.

ISBN: 978-0-7394-9305-2

Maferefun Olodumare
Maferefun Egun
Maferefun Oshun
Maferefun gbogbo Orisha

I lovingly dedicate this book to the memory of my parents,
Marjorie Bayne Quinones
and
Jose Quinones

And also to my dear friend, Mayme Johnson

prologue

1984

Didn't I tell you, Mama? Her skin is so thin and light you can see her little blue veins. I'm telling you, she's gonna have skin as white as Meryl Streep's. And look at that blond hair. That ain't no hair that's going to be napping up!"

The woman's eyes danced as she spoke, her hands softly clapping in delight as she looked at her newborn niece greedily suckling. God had answered her prayers, and the prayers of her mother who were on their knees figuratively, during the nine months of her sister-in-law's pregnancy.

"Ain't that the truth, Evelyn! And her eyes," Cecilia said, every bit the proud grandmother as she hovered over mother and child. "You know, chile, I told Peter when he first started talking about marrying Rina, I said, 'Well, her skin might be a little too dark for my taste, but at least she ain't no ink spot. And if even only one your kids get them blue eyes Rina's grandmother had, it'll all be worth it.' Their first child didn't get 'em, but they lucked up with this one. Oh, they really lucked up with this one."

Rina didn't bother to even fake a smile for her mother-in-law and sister-in-law, since they didn't bother to acknowledge her but instead focused all of their attention on the two-day-old baby at her breast. She wasn't surprised or even hurt—her relationship with her in-laws had always been, at best, strained. Truth be told, the relationship was horrible. Mother Jenkins had never forgiven her for marrying precious little Peter, the matriarch's youngest son. The Jenkins were all light-skinned—in fact, what they called light-bright and damn near white—and made it a point of marrying people with matching complexions. Peter, who was the color of ash wood and with thick, curly hair, was expected to bring home a woman in keeping with that Jenkins tradition. Instead, he brought home Rina. The coldness in Cecilia's eyes were even chillier than her voice when she was introduced to her prospective daughter-in-law. After twenty years of marriage, there'd not been a thaw, even after the birth of Cecilia's one and only grandchild. Joseph was a beautiful child, but the copper tint at the top of his ears indicated from day one that his complexion would be lighter than Rina's, but darker than Peter's. And that, to Cecilia, was unacceptable.

"Yes sir, we got a good-looking baby here," Cecilia said with a satisfied smile. "A real good-looking child. Don't you wish your child came out like this, Evelyn? I thought for sure you was gonna have a good-looking one as fair as you and your husband is, but your boy came out looking like a tar baby, God bless his soul."

"Now, Mama, Booby's a good-looking child in his own right," Evelyn started.

"Of course he is. Just dark as sin," Cecilia said abruptly. "That's not his fault, though, God bless him."

Rina tenderly lifted her newborn child to her shoulder and

began gently rubbing her back. She'd been shocked and terrified when she found out that she was pregnant. She was forty-eight and thought her childbearing years were over. Joseph was already thirteen, and she wasn't sure she had the patience and strength to go through diapering, potty training, and all of that again. But looking at the baby, it all seemed so worth it. There was no doubt about it, this was a beautiful baby. Not because of her complexion, or hair or her eyes, but there was something about her features that was just striking. Delicate, but striking.

Cecilia pursed her thin lips, then said sharply, "Careful, Rina, can't you see that sweet child is fragile?" She reached her spindly sixty-nine-year-old liver-spotted hands out toward her daughter-in-law. "Gimme that baby. I'll burp her for you."

"I think I know how to burp a child, Mother Jenkins," Rina said with a deep sigh. "Like you said, I've already had one child. I've had practice."

"But Joseph wasn't as delicate as this one," Cecilia answered, her arms still stretched out, her manicured fingers wiggling in eager anticipation.

"Why? Because this one's skin is lighter?" Rina said softly as she switched the baby to the shoulder farthest away from Cecilia. "Because she's the one born with blue eyes and blond hair?"

Cecilia slowly pulled her arms back to her sides and fixed a stony glare at the younger woman who had the audacity to challenge her. "How dare you, Rina," she said in a voice as stony cold as her dark brown eyes. "You know I love my grandchildren no matter what color they are." She turned to Evelyn. "Don't I love Booby? Dark as he is? And I love Joseph, too. I don't show any favoritism."

Rina ignored her, choosing instead to kiss and coo at the baby, who had just oozed a bit of breast milk from her mouth. She then put the baby on her stomach and pushed the black button on the side of the steel hospital bed to bring it to a reclining position and closed her eyes.

"Mama," Evelyn said in her irritatingly shrill voice, "come sit down. Rina's just tired, is all. She wasn't trying to insult you. Was you, Rina?"

Rina wearily opened her eyes and looked up at the clock on the wall. Two-fifteen. Thank God the afternoon visiting hours would be over in just fifteen more minutes. She carefully picked up the now sleeping baby and lay her across her chest and began softly humming a lullaby.

"So, Rina," Evelyn said, her always nervous hands fluttering in her lap, "have you and Peter decided on the name for your beautiful little girl? It's bad luck not to have a name by the third day born, you know."

Cecilia sat up straight in her chair and patted her tightly wound bun of bluish gray hair as if to make sure it was in place. "I've already talked to Peter and we've decided to name her Victoria, after her great-grandmother," she said in her no-nonsense voice before Rina could answer Evelyn. "She was the most beautiful and most well-respected woman in Beesville, Mississippi." She paused and looked at Rina meaningfully. "Carrying her great-grandmother's name will always remind her of what a great family she's come from—on her father's side. Something to aspire to."

"Not like my family, right?" Rina said wearily.

Evelyn's eyes darted from her mother to Rina and back, before she cleared her throat. "Now, Rina, Mama wasn't trying to say that—"

"It's not our fault that your family is from the wrong side of the tracks," Cecilia interrupted.

"Mother Jenkins, it's interesting how you seem to forget you lived right next door," Rina snapped.

"But we didn't start out there like your family did, a dirt-poor bunch of low-life good-for-nothings," Cecilia said, her lips curling into a gleeful smirk. "Our family had money and property until—"

"Until white folks strung up your father like a piece of ham and burnt and stole everything you had, right?" Rina laughed softly. "And then you ended up on Chewbacca Road right along with us dirt-poor low-life good-for-nothings."

"Now, Rina, what Mama meant was—"

"You think a lynching's a laughing matter, do ya, missy?" Cecilia broke in with a hoarse voice. Her eyes squinted to the point of almost disappearing as she leaned forward in her chair. "You think that me, a five-year-old child, seeing my father swinging from a tree is funny?"

"No," Rina said in a cold voice. "But what I do find so hilarious is that same five-year-old child growing up to worship white folks and trying her best to be just like them. Even hating African-Americans as much as them. Calling them the niggas while referring to herself as colored." Rina snorted with disgust. "I don't know how you and your high-yaller clan missed the word, Mother Jenkins, but black is beautiful. And black comes in all shades. And this baby mighta been born with blond hair and blue eyes like my grandmother, but she's still an African-American. Not a nigger and not colored, but African-American."

Cecilia jumped up from the chair and quickly strode toward the hospital room door, her back straight and her nose in the air. "Come on, Evelyn. It's time for us to leave. Peter's low-life darkie wife has obviously lost her mind, so there ain't no use in us staying and listening to her hateful rambling."

"Coming, Mama," Evelyn said, quickly rising and giving Rina an apologetic glance before hurrying after her mother.

The two women departed so quickly they almost bumped into a nurse entering the room.

"They seem to be in a rush, don't they?" the nurse said as she walked over to Rina's bedside. "Aw, look at her sleeping like a little angel. Do you want me to take her back to the nursery so you can get some rest?"

"No, I'm fine," Rina said while softly tracing her fingers over the child's face. She was beautiful, so beautiful it almost took her breath away. So beautiful that it made almost six months of morning sickness and twenty-four hours of labor worth the trouble. But there would be trouble ahead, Rina knew. Cecilia and Evelyn, only to a slightly lesser degree, would do their best to ruin her baby. Make her feel the same way they did about her African heritage. Make her feel that she was better than others of her race because of her coloring. It was up to her to put a stop to it, and to do it soon, before their poisoning could take hold.

"I haven't seen your husband today," the nurse said while tidying up the room. "Guess he had to work? Well, I suppose he'll make the evening visiting hours."

Rina said nothing. Chances are Peter was off getting drunk, using the birth of his newborn baby as an excuse for another binge. Better for her to think that than to imagine him laying up in another woman's bed while she was laid up in the hospital. Twenty years of marriage and Peter still hadn't settled down. But she loved him. It wasn't his fault that he was so handsome that women just threw themselves at him. If only he could be a little stronger.

"Maybe he'll bring that son of yours. Most polite teenager I've ever seen. What is he? Like sixteen? What does he think of having a little sister?"

Rina smiled. "Actually, he's only thirteen, and he's thrilled to death to have a sister."

"Thirteen? That big boy? Oh my, he's got to be six feet tall!" the nurse exclaimed. She poured Rina a fresh glass of water. "But then both you and your husband are on the tall side. Wonder how big this pretty baby's going to get."

Rina looked up at the nurse. "Miss Jeffries, will you let whoever it is that needs to know that I've finally decided on a name for the baby?"

"Oh, good. What is it?"

Rina paused. Peter was going to have a fit, and his mother would likely have a stroke, but . . .

"Shanika," Rina finally answered with a wide smile. "S-H-A-N-I-K-A. My little angel's name is Shanika."

chapter one

May 2007

The car never breaks down unless there's somewhere you really need to go. The washing machine never breaks down unless the laundry is piled to the ceiling. And the air conditioner never breaks down unless it's the hottest day of the year.

It was 105 degrees that dismal day in the Motor City, the warmest temperature recorded for May.

Twenty-three-year-old Shanika sat on the wooden steps of the decrepit frame house and fanned herself with the folded copy of the *Detroit Free Press*. She had thought the red halter top and cutoff jeans she put on that morning were a good idea considering the heat, but they gave her no protection from the sun's vicious rays, which caused both to stick to her skin. Maybe, she thought, she should go change into a sundress—and maybe even lose her underwear while she was at it. She looked up at her mother who inexplicably seemed content and cool sitting on the porch sewing a hem in an old pair of gray work pants.

"Mama, when is the repairman going to get here? I'm going to sweat to death out here," Shanika complained. She stuck out her bottom lip and tried to blow air up to cool her nose, but her breath was just as hot as the summer air. This, she decided, is what hell must be like. It was almost enough to make her decide to go to church more often to make sure she didn't face the grim possibility of enduring such heat for eternity. Almost.

"I had to call him back and tell him not to come," Rina said calmly, her eyes never leaving the small, neat stitches her wrinkled hands were producing. "I looked in the cookie jar and we can't afford him, after all. You know your father ain't been able to find work lately." The truth be told, Peter hadn't worked in months, but it was too hot to go into unnecessary details when everyone knew them, anyway. Peter Jenkins was an alcoholic who simply wasn't motivated to find work.

"Oh God!" Shanika let her head loll back and her eyes roll up in her head. "We're all going to die."

Rina lowered her sewing into her lap and quietly chuckled as she looked at her daughter sprawled out on the steps. Even now, after all these years, she couldn't look at her daughter without marveling at her delicate beauty, not that there was anything delicate about her personality. Shanika was assertive, headstrong, and always determined to get her way. But still, Rina thought as she picked up her sewing again, so lovely. A little spoiled, and a little flighty at times, but all in all, a lovely child.

"Stop being so dramatic, Shanika," Rina said in a firm voice. "We'll be fine. Go in the house and get some of the iced tea I made out of the refrigerator. It should be cold by now."

Shanika sighed as she stood up and wiped perspiration

from her brow. She pulled her long, curly amber-colored hair into a thick ponytail; then realizing she didn't have a rubber band on her wrist to keep it in place, she let it cascade back down over her cream-colored shoulders.

"Child, you'd better be glad your Grandmother Jenkins isn't here. She's probably sitting up in her grave now trying to yell at you to get out the sun. Look at your tan." Rina laughed. "She was always screaming at me to keep you out the sun so you wouldn't turn."

"Yeah, well, I like the sun," Shanika said. "And I didn't like Grandmother Jenkins."

Rina frowned. "No need to be saying all that. Show some respect for the dearly departed."

"Dearly?"

"Now, Shanika, be nice." Rina snapped the thread with her teeth. "By the way, your aunt Evelyn called this morning from Mississippi. Your cousin Booby's getting some kind of award from his lodge and she wants us to all come down and celebrate with them."

"Cousin Booby." Shanika snorted. "Now, that's someone who they shoulda kept out the sun."

Rina looked up. "Shanika Ann Jenkins," she said sharply. "I raised you better than that. Don't make me raise up out this chair."

"Oh, Mama, you know I'm kidding," Shanika said quickly. "It's just that it's so funny that Aunt Evelyn has the darkest grandchild in the family with her being the most color-struck in the family. At least now that Grandma Jenkins is dead."

"That ain't no way for you to be kidding."

"Mama, I've heard you say it yourself."

Rina frowned and looked away. "Well, I shouldn't have.

And you need to follow what I say, not always what I do. You ain't that grown, you know."

"Yes, Mama." Shanika shrugged and readjusted the halter top, which barely covered her ample chest, then let out another sigh and headed to the kitchen. She paused in the doorway of the living room to look at the unshaven man sitting in front of the television with just a dingy T-shirt and polka-dot boxer shorts and a stocking cap on his head. "Papa, you want some iced tea?"

Peter Jenkins let out a belch and picked up the sixteen-ounce can of Miller High Life. "I'm good, Nikkie. Thanks, though." He clicked the remote, and the television obediently switched from *Wheel of Fortune* to sports on ESPN.

Shanika nodded, then resumed her slow walk into the kitchen. *God, I hope I get that PR job in New York next week,* she thought while pouring two tall glasses of iced tea. *I should never have come back here after graduation. I should have gone straight to New York and started my job hunt there. Or maybe Chicago, or even Los Angeles. There ain't no damn jobs here in Motown.*

Life had seemed so promising her senior year at Delaware State University. True, she hadn't done any internships, but she had a 3.6 GPA, and she'd been so sure all of the big PR firms would be eager to snatch up a motivated and energetic young woman like her. She was sure it was only a matter of time before she was handling public relations for the likes of Paris Hilton, Nicole Richie, Kimora Lee Simmons, J. Lo, and the other jet-setters she read about in *People* magazine. And she was sure that she would soon make friends with them—after all, she made friends so easily—and pretty soon she'd be dating a billionaire and living the jet-set life herself. And then

People would be featuring her on its covers. That had been her master plan.

But here it was more than a year after she'd finished school, and after sending out more than two hundred résumés, she still hadn't landed a job. She hadn't even gotten to the interview stage. Not until now.

"I've got to nail this job in New York," she said out loud while walking back onto the porch.

"What's that, baby?" her mother asked, setting the newly hemmed pants to the side.

"Nothing, Mama." Shanika bent down and gave her mother a quick peck on the cheek before handing her the glass. "Mama, can't we just call Joe and see if we can borrow the money from him to get the air fixed? Please?"

"We can't keep asking your brother to help us out. He's got his own family to worry about—especially with Ayoka being pregnant." Rina paused, then shook her head. "No, we can't keep burdening him like that. Ain't right."

"Mama, can't we just ask?" Shanika pleaded. "He's a grown man. If he can't afford it, he'll just say no. No harm done."

"You know your older brother, and you know he wouldn't turn us down even if he had to borrow the money from someone else." Rina took a sip of the tea. "Especially once you started batting your blue eyes up at him."

"I promise I won't bat my eyes," Shanika said, quickly holding her fingers up in a Boy Scout salute. "In fact, I'll ask him over the telephone."

"Lotta good that'll do." Rina chuckled. "You're the only one I know who can bat her eyes so hard people can hear it over the phone."

"Mama, please—"

"No," Rina said firmly. "And we're ending this conversation right this minute. Now, you need anything mended before I put my sewing kit away?"

Shanika poked out her lips, then sat back down on the steps. "Mama, can't we at least go to the movies? They've got air there. We've got to get out of this heat."

"You can go if you want, baby. I got too much work to do around here." Rina took another sip of her drink. "I gotta start dinner in a few minutes."

"Oh, Mama, it's too hot for you to be trying to cook up in here," Shanika cried. "What are you trying to do? Give yourself heatstroke?"

"No, just trying to make sure we have something to eat this evening, is all."

Shanika looked at her mother and shook her head. "Mama, you're . . . what? . . . seventy-one years old? You've worked hard all your life and you need to be taking it easy. You know what? As soon as I get a job and hit it rich, I'm going to get you a maid and a cook so you can just be a lady of leisure. And I'm going to buy you a new air conditioner, too. Heck, I'm going to buy you a new house."

Rina smiled at her daughter's verbal daydreams. "That'll be nice, baby."

"You don't believe me, do you?"

Rina chuckled and stood up. "It's not that I don't believe you, but you still sound like a little girl. But that's okay, you're still my little girl. You go ahead to the movies and enjoy yourself."

"I tell you what, Mama. How about I cook tonight? What you want me to make?"

"Girl, please. What you gonna make? Your famous Rice-A-

Roni?" Rina laughed. "You go ahead and get outta here and go to the movies. I'll have a nice cool pasta salad waiting for you when you get back."

Shanika hesitated. "Mama, is there enough money in the cookie jar for me to borrow for the movies?"

"Hello, beautiful ladies!"

Shanika turned around, then bounded down the stairs like an eager puppy and into her brother's arms.

"Joseph!" she shouted. Even though she was five-ten, she had to stand on her tiptoes to give her brother—who was six-five—a kiss on the cheek. Except for his height, he was almost the spitting image of their father when he was young—maybe a little darker, but they had the same dark wavy hair and dark brown eyes that twinkled when they smiled. The other difference between Joseph and his father was that Joseph didn't mind keeping a job. He'd been working at the city's largest real estate firm for eight years. And no matter what Rina said, Shanika had already made up her mind to hit up her brother for some money. She hugged him around his waist and walked him up the porch steps.

"Whoa, what I do to deserve all this?" Joseph looked at his mother. "What's she wanting now, Mama?"

"Nothing you need to be giving her," Rina said, eyeing Shanika up and down. "And you'd better not be trying to get anything, either, young lady. And I'm meaning that," she said, with narrowed eyes.

"Oh, Mama—" Shanika began.

"Oh, Mama, nothing," Rina said firmly. "Don't try me now, hear?"

"Yes, ma'am," Shanika answered sullenly.

"Come on inside with me, Joseph, and don't pay that

sister of yours no never-mind. I'll get you some iced tea." Rina walked into the house.

"What you do to get Mama riled up like that, White Girl?" Joseph teased as he and Shanika followed their mother inside, passing the living room, where their father was letting out loud, wet snores.

"Shut up, Black Boy," Shanika snapped in response.

"Mama, Nikkie just called me 'Black Boy,'" Joseph said as he settled in a kitchen chair.

"Uh-huh," Shanika said from the kitchen doorway. "Don't forget to tell her you called me 'White Girl,' buddy."

"Joseph, you're too old to be calling your sister names," Rina said, placing a glass of tea on the table in front of her son. "And, Shanika, same goes for you." She sat down next to him. "Y'all are both grown now and too old to be acting like that to each other."

"Well, he's older than me and he started it," Shanika said defensively. "He always starts it."

"Stop whining, White Girl," Joseph said, throwing a spoon at her.

"See, Mama?" Shanika said after successfully dodging the flatware.

"Joe, stop it now." Rina gave her son a soft slap on the hand. "You're thirty-five years old and acting like you're five. And here you're about to be a father. How's my daughter-in-law and that grandbaby of mine she's carrying?"

"She's great—finally getting over her morning sickness, thank goodness." He took a sip of his tea. "Mama, can't nobody make iced tea like you. I shoulda married you."

"Stop being silly," Rina said with a giggle.

"But why is it so hot in here? I thought you were supposed to call the repair guy."

"Oh, she called him, all right," Shanika said, giving her mother a playful look. "Twice in fact."

Rina shot her a dirty look, then said, "He'll get here when he gets here, and we'll be fine until he does." She turned to Joseph. "You staying for dinner? I'm about to make some pasta salad."

"Mama, it's too hot for you to be cooking," Joseph said.

"That's just what I told her," Shanika added.

"Y'all hush now. If it's not too hot to be hungry, it's not too hot to cook," Rina said as she started filling a pot with water. "Joseph, you and Ayoka missed a good sermon yesterday. Pastor Reynolds read from Psalm sixty-two of the Good Book. All about learning patience, because good things will come to those who wait."

"We wanted to make it, Mama, but Ayoka wasn't feeling good," Joseph said as he fingered a yellowing hole in the white plastic tablecloth that covered the kitchen table.

"I know, baby. I managed to drag your sister down there. First time in months. But all she did was fall asleep as usual."

"Mama, I'm sure the Lord understood I was just tired."

"Hmph, if you hadn't been hanging all night with your friends, maybe you wouldn't have been so tired. You don't have to go worship but one day a week and you can't even manage to do that without me threatening to throw cold water on you to get outta bed."

"Mama, the Lord knows I love Him, even if I don't make it to church all the time," Shanika grumbled. "I honor Him in my heart."

"I know you love Jesus, baby, but you know how they say,

'Jesus is present whenever two or more gather in His name.' You need to do more than just worship Him in your heart." Rina turned to Joseph. "Your aunt Evelyn called. Said Booby's getting some award from his lodge and she wants us to come down. Sometime in September, she said. I got the date written down."

Joseph's eyebrow shot up. "I know you're not planning on actually going all the way to Mississippi for that, Mama. For some lodge award?"

Rina shook her head. "Stuff like that's a big deal down South, Joseph. I might be thinking of going."

"I'm not," Shanika broke in. "She didn't come up for my college graduation, why should we go all the way down South just so her son can get some award? Besides, I hardly remember Booby. 'Cept that him and Joseph was always pulling on my hair when we went down there when I was a kid. And that he always called me 'Nika' instead of 'Shanika' or 'Nikkie.'" She made a face. "I hate that name."

"I saw him a couple of years ago when I went to New Orleans for a convention," Joseph said. "He's not the same since he came back from the first Gulf War. I think he must be suffering from shell shock or post-traumatic stress, or whatever it is they're calling it now."

Rina wiped her hands on a dish towel and sighed. "And if that ain't a shame. He was always such a nice boy, too. If it wasn't one Bush president getting us into a war, it's another. And it's our boys who have to suffer."

"What do you mean he's suffering from shell shock?" Shanika asked. "Does he go off on people for no reason or something?"

"No, at least I don't think so. He just seemed a little slower than usual, mentally. He didn't get things quite so fast." Joseph shrugged. "Maybe he'll get over it, but it's been like fifteen years, so it's not likely."

Joseph stood up and stretched. "Changing the subject, if I stay in this hot house any longer, I'm going to melt into a puddle of water. How about I treat you two to dinner at Applebee's?"

"Works for me," Shanika said before her mother could respond. "Should I wake up Papa?"

"Is he in his usual drunken stupor?"

"Joseph, don't you be talking like that about your father!"

"That's all right. Leave the boy alone," Peter said as he shuffled into the kitchen. "Wake me up for what, Nikkie?"

"Joseph's taking us to dinner, Peter." Rina walked over and kissed her husband on the cheek. "He wanted to know if you'd like to come."

Peter turned to Joseph. "You want me to come, son?" he asked in a hopeful voice.

Joseph paused before answering, but when he finally opened his mouth to speak, his father's mouth opened simultaneously—forced to do so by a large belch that filled the kitchen with the stench of beer.

Peter looked down at his feet just in time to avoid the look of disgust that enveloped Joseph's face. "Sorry. Um, excuse me, I mean." Peter forced a laugh. "Didn't know that was coming. You know, on second thought, think I'll stay here. Don't wanna miss the baseball game. Bring me back something, won't you?" He shuffled back into the living room.

"I love you, Papa," Shanika called after him.

"You hurt his feelings," Rina told Joseph in an accusing voice.

"I didn't even say anything, Mama. He decided not to go on his own."

"You could have insisted, Joseph. You know that's what he was waiting for." Rina shot her son a dirty look before she followed her husband into the living room.

"Why you always gotta be so mean to Papa?" Nikkie said while pouring another glass of iced tea. "You'd think you hated him or something."

Joseph shrugged. "I never said I hate him. I do hate what he does. Or what he doesn't do. Like take care of his damn family."

"Joseph, that's not fair. The man's seventy years old. What kind of work is he really going to find?"

"Spare me. If he actually kept a job more than a year or two when he was in his prime, he'd have a pension right now, instead of just his measly Social Security checks. But no, he was too busy thinking he was a Billy Dee Williams look-alike to—"

"Billy Dee who?"

Joseph sighed. "You know, the guy who played in *Lady Sings the Blues* with Diana Ross." When no sign of recognition crossed his sister's face, he said, "He played in *Mahogany*? You know, the black guy in the *Star Wars* Jedi movie."

Shanika cocked her head. "I thought that was Samuel L. Jackson."

"The other black guy, Nikkie."

Shanika wrinkled her nose in thought. "Oh yeah," she said finally. "He played Lando. He was kinda cute for an old guy. Papa used to look like him?"

"He thought so. And so did most of the women in Detroit. If he'd spent only half the time working that he spent drinking and bedding every woman who threw herself at him, you and Mama wouldn't have any financial problems."

Shanika shrugged. "Still, he's your father. And like Mama said, you should show him some kind of respect."

"To get respect, you earn respect; and maybe some money along with it. I don't have any respect for a man who chases women instead of chasing a dollar."

Shanika shook her head, then emptied her glass and put it down in front of her. "You're too judgmental, Joseph."

"Shut up, White Girl."

"Mama," Shanika said as Rina entered the kitchen. "See? You heard him, right? He called me 'White Girl' again."

"I told you about that already, Joseph," Rina said as she went to the sink and picked up the pot she had previously filled with water.

"Mama, what are you doing? I'm taking us out to eat, remember? You don't have to cook."

"You two go on ahead. I'm going to stay home with Peter. I'll just fix us something light," Rina said while putting the pot on the stove and turning on the burner. "You don't have to worry about us."

"Aw, Mama." Joseph walked over and hugged his mother from behind. "Come on and go. Please? Listen, I can hear Papa snoring all the way in here. He's back to sleep already. Please? Please?"

"Yeah, Mama," Shanika chimed in. "We'll probably be back before Papa even wakes up."

"Well . . ." Rina hesitated. "I don't know—"

"Good! It's decided." Joseph planted a kiss on his mother's forehead. "Just leave Papa a note that you're bringing him a doggy bag. Come on, old woman. Let's get a move on."

"Well, I . . ." Rina hesitated, then smiled. "Okay. I could use a break, I guess. Just let me change my dress."

"You look fine, Mama. Or are you planning on picking up some man, since Papa isn't coming?" Joseph teased.

"Oh, just hush now. It won't take me but a minute," Rina said while walking out the kitchen.

"Okay, so come on over here and have a seat and tell me what's new in your life," Joseph said, waving Shanika over to the table. "How's the job hunt going?"

"Things are looking up. I told you about that job interview I have coming up in New York next week, right? I have a good feeling about it."

Joseph nodded. "Paxon and White?"

"Paxon and Green."

"I knew it was some kinda color. Are they flying you in?"

Shanika shook her head. "I'm taking the train."

Joseph whistled. "Damn, that's quite a haul. Are they paying for the train? Or your hotel?"

Shanika shook her head again.

Joseph looked at her for a moment, then sighed. How could someone so smart be so dumb, he wondered. His sister was smart as a whip, but she was constantly making bad decisions. Quite possibly, he knew, because there was always someone there to bail her out. "Nikkie, I wish you had taken my advice and done some summer internships while you were still in school. You'd have a job by now, or at least agencies flying you in to interview instead of you having to do all this on your own dime."

Shanika cleared her throat. "Speaking of dimes—"

"Don't worry, sis. I'll cover you for your hotel and train fare." He knew it didn't make any sense trying to be coy about

would be featured on the infamous Page Six of the *New York Post*—not because she'd be involved in any kind of scandal, but because she'd be one of the "beautiful people" who deserved mention in the media. She'd probably get more print than her PR clients. In fact, if they were smart, they'd want to hang out with her just to make sure they'd get play themselves. And she'd let them. After all, that's what she would be getting paid for.

"We only have a nine and a half. Will that be okay?" The clerk was at her side holding an unopened shoe box. Shanika headed to the cashier's desk after trying the shoes on.

"I mean, come on, do you really believe she wasn't messing with him while he was still married to Jennifer Aniston?" the redheaded cashier asked another clerk, a Madonna look-alike, who was standing by the register.

"Well, Jennifer said she believed him when he said he was faithful during the marriage, so who am I to doubt it?" the clerk answered.

"Well, if you ask me, she only said it because it added to her vanilla image," the cashier said with a shrug. "I mean, after all, Jennifer is the new Meg Ryan now. America's latest 'Little Sweetheart.' "

"Ooh, isn't that the truth?" Shanika broke in as she put the shoes on the counter. "America loved ole Meg until they found out she was committing adultery with Russell Crowe."

"Heck, can you blame her?" The cashier laughed as she rang up the purchase. "I'd cheat on my husband if Russell Crowe was trying to talk to me."

"And if I was a man, I'd cheat on my wife with Angelina Jolie," Shanika said with a giggle as she handed the young woman Ayoka's credit card.

"Isn't that the truth?" said the clerk standing by the counter. "I don't even swing that way and I have to say I think she's sexy as hell."

"So exotic-looking," the cashier agreed while swiping the card through the register without bothering to look at the name. Shanika waited until the credit card authorization information appeared on the digital display by the side of the register, then picked up the attached pen and signed Ayoka's name.

"Here you go." The cashier handed her a bag with the shoes inside. "You have a nice day. And don't worry, I won't tell Angelina Jolie you think she's a floozy."

"I didn't say that." Shanika laughed, and the cashier and other clerk joined in. She started to walk away, then turned back. "Oh, I forgot I had these in my hand." She put a large set of ivory earrings on the counter.

"Oh, these are nice!" The cashier picked up the earrings to examine them more closely. "Are they a gift?"

"No, they're for me. They match the shoes."

"Yeah, but . . ." The clerk by the counter hesitated. "I don't know. They look more like something a black person would wear, don't you think? What do they call it? Ethnic?"

Shanika smiled and shrugged. "Well, I'm ethnic."

"Yes, of course, we all are, but I mean—"

"African-American? Well, I'm African-American." Shanika grinned.

The clerk and the cashier looked at her, then at each other, and then back at her.

"I am! Seriously!" Shanika laughed out loud.

"Wow! You could have fooled me," the cashier said finally. She rested her arms on the counter and leaned for a better look at Shanika. "So you're, um, biracial, huh? Is your mother or father black?"

"Both."

"But then . . ." The cashier stared at Shanika, then at the clerk as if for support, before turning back to Shanika. "But then how come you look white?"

"Well, I have white ancestry on both my father's and mother's sides, and I'm what they call a throwback. Both of my parents and my brother are light-skinned, but I'm the only one with skin this light. People mistake me for white all the time." Shanika flashed a satisfied grin at the two women.

"I can see how," the clerk said as she edged closer for a better look. "You just look like you have a tan. In fact"—she stretched her arm out next to Shanika's—"you're fairer than me, girlfriend."

"I know that's right, child," the cashier joined in. "Ain't that right?"

"For real," the clerk answered.

Inwardly, Shanika rolled her eyes, though she kept her smile plastered on the outside of her face. What was it with white folks that once they find out they're talking to an African-American they have to try to use what they thought was African-American vernacular? She picked up the earrings and handed them to the cashier. "So, can I purchase these at this counter or do I have to go to the costume jewelry counter?"

"No, you can buy them here." The cashier rang up the purchase. "That'll be fifteen dollars and ninety-nine cents. Will you also be placing these on your card?"

Shanika nodded and handed her the card.

"I'll need to see some ID, please."

Shanika did a double take. "I beg your pardon," she said slowly.

"It's store policy," the other clerk broke in quickly. "We're required to ask all customers making credit card purchases to show ID."

Shanika stared at her coldly. "She didn't ask me for it a moment ago." Despite the unspoken part of the sentence, they all knew what she meant: "She didn't ask me for it a moment ago when she thought I was white." *Damn, I shouldn't have played my hand until after I bought the earrings.* This wasn't the first time something like this had happened, and she should have anticipated it. She hadn't come to make a scene or to make some kind of a political statement; she just wanted to buy an outfit for her interview. Yes, with someone else's credit card, but if it didn't make a difference when they thought she was white, she'd be damned if they let it make a difference now that they knew she was black.

Shanika turned back to the cashier. "Give me my credit card back, and I'd like to speak to the manager."

"That won't be necessary," the clerk said hurriedly. "Jeannie's a new employee, and she must have forgotten to ask for your ID, but since she didn't ask you before, I agree, there's no reason to ask you now."

Shanika pulled out an emery board from her purse and began to furiously swipe at her nails. It was a habit of hers. Whenever she was angry, or gearing herself up for a confrontation, she'd pull out an emery board and go over her nails. "I'd like to speak to your manager," she repeated without looking up at either the cashier or clerk.

The clerk sighed, and then nodded at the cashier, who

then picked up a telephone near the register and intoned, "Mrs. Wiles, you're needed at the shoe counter."

"I'll talk to you after lunch, Jeannie," the clerk said before hurrying away, leaving the now noticeably nervous cashier to fend for herself.

It took about three minutes, but finally an approaching voice asked, "What seems to be the problem?"

Shanika looked up to see a middle-aged woman with ebony skin, flashing dark eyes, and a purposeful stride nearing them. Shanika wouldn't have been able to hide her smile if she tried, and she didn't. This was in the bag. She dropped her emery board back into her purse.

"Mrs. Wiles—" the cashier started.

"Mrs. Wiles," Shanika interrupted her, "I'm a longtime Nordstrom customer who has now run into a serious problem." She put her hand out for a handshake.

Mrs. Wiles didn't hesitate in physical action, but Shanika felt the familiar rake of the eyes as the woman shook her hand. White people may be normally clueless about her ethnicity, but African-Americans went by the good old "If there's enough of a question for you to want to ask, there's no reason to ask." Still, many—like the woman now in front of her—studied hard to be sure, trying to pick up on clues like her clothing, her tone, or the people who were around her. And quite often, if she was surrounded by white people, they hesitated even longer.

"My name is Ayoka Jenkins"—Shanika paused long enough to confirm the satisfied "I knew it" in the woman's eyes before continuing—"and I made a credit card purchase with your cashier a moment ago and was not asked for an ID. I realize now it's because she thought I was white. But once I happened to mention that I'm black to this same cashier, I'm suddenly asked for credentials."

"Really?" Mrs. Wiles turned and looked at the cashier, her full lips squeezed almost into a tight line. The cashier visibly shivered under the withering look. "Is this true, Jeannie?"

"Mrs. Wiles, I—"

"I'm not trying to cause any trouble," Shanika continued, "but I think it's wrong that I be penalized because I'm openly proud of my heritage, and offered the information unsolicited." Shanika paused, then decided to go ahead and pound nails in the cashier's coffin. "It all started because she thought these earrings were too ethnic."

"It was Rhonda who said they were ethnic," the cashier protested.

"But it was you who all of a sudden decided I needed to show ID when I said I was African-American," Shanika snapped at her before turning back to Mrs. Wiles. "Like I said, I don't want to cause any trouble, but—"

Mrs. Wiles held up her hand. "Ms. Jenkins, you have my most sincere apologies. It is indeed store policy to ask for ID when customers make credit card purchases, but it's an all-around policy, I assure you, not a random policy." She shot the cashier a dirty look.

"If you'll be kind enough to give Jeannie your credit card again, I'd like to have her add one hundred dollars to your account for your inconvenience. I hope that will be okay?"

"That won't be necessary," Shanika answered, hoping the ante would be raised to maybe five hundred.

"Please. I insist," Mrs. Wiles said.

Oh well, one hundred dollars is good enough. Shanika nodded, and handed the cashier Ayoka's credit card again.

"Er, excuse me, Mrs. Wiles," the cashier said nervously. "I had just rung up the earrings—"

"The earrings are on the house, and after you're finished with this transaction, call for someone to relieve you. I'd like to see you in my office immediately. And tell Rhonda I'd like to see her, too."

Mrs. Wiles smiled at Shanika. "Again, Ms. Jenkins, my sincere apologies, and I hope this little incident won't further mar your shopping experience here at Nordstrom."

Shanika nodded absentmindedly. *Now that I'm one hundred dollars to the good, I might as well see if I can find a clutch bag to go with the suit and the pumps.*

She only took a few steps toward the handbag department before she stopped. It would be selfish of her to use the money to buy something for herself. After all, it was Ayoka's card, and she'd already spent about $150 on the suit and pumps. No, the right thing to do would be to give the card back to Ayoka, thank her, and tell her about the hundred-dollar credit to her account.

Or, I could buy a handbag for Ayoka. I know she loves accessorizing, but she's so sweet to everyone that she seldom buys anything for herself. And she always says she loves my taste. I'll buy it for her, that way she won't feel guilty.

It only took her ten minutes to pick out the perfect clutch bag. She marched over, presented the credit card to make the purchase, and then hurried out the store, proud that she had picked out such a wonderful bag for her sister-in-law.

Of course since it also matches my new outfit so well, I'm sure if I ask, Ayoka won't mind me borrowing it for the interview, Shanika thought happily. *All together a very productive shopping day.*

chapter three

The train from Detroit to Chicago took six hours, and that was bad enough, but the second leg of the trip—from Chicago to New York City—was almost twenty hours. As she struggled with her luggage up the steps at Penn Station, Shanika cursed herself for not insisting that Joe spot her an airline ticket rather than a ride on Amtrak. True, she had waited until the last minute and the airfare would have cost $350, which was more than twice the train fare, but she wouldn't be so bone-tired now. And so damn sweaty. And aggravated. Thank God the interview wasn't until the next day. She'd have some time to rest up at the hotel room her brother had reserved for her.

"Excuse me. Can you tell me where the taxi line is?" she asked one of the many police officers milling around the depot. "I was told it was right outside the station, but I don't see any signs."

The officer—a beefy dark-haired man of about forty, with a bulbous red nose—looked her up and down before answering. "They closed it down because of the president. You'll have to walk down the street and hail a cab."

"The president?" Shanika's shoulders sagged, and she

placed her two suitcases on the platform floor. "They closed the taxi line because of President Bush?"

The officer nodded. "He's in town so we're taking extra security precautions. Just walk a couple of blocks in any direction. You'll be able to catch a ride."

Shanika looked at her luggage and chewed her lip while the officer strode away without a backward glance. *Damn,* she thought, *why did I have to pack all this stuff? I shoulda listened to Joe. Now I gotta haul all this crap while I look for a cab.*

"Excuse me, miss. You need some help with them bags?"

She turned to find an African-American man, about her own age, standing in front of her. A set of earphones sat on top of his designer cornrows, and by the way he was bopping his head, he was probably listening to music even while addressing her.

"Yeah, bro. I can use some help," she said with a gracious smile. "Thanks."

He looked at her quizzically, removed the earphones, and stared even more intently, then gave her the rake of the eyes. "Oh shit," he finally said with a loud laugh. "You a sista! Damn, you got that Mariah Carey thang going on for real, yo. But damn, shortie, even Mariah ain't got them baby blues like you." He stepped back and rubbed his chin while taking a better look at her. "Yo, ma, you really had me fooled. What? Your daddy white or you moms?"

"Neither. They both have white blood and they passed a lot of it on to me," Shanika said, her hand on one hip as she appraised him.

His lightweight New York Knicks jersey and his baggy jeans—which looked like they were about to fall off his skinny hips any minute—were clean even if they weren't expensive, and his Air Jordans were at least three years out of date. His mocha-colored face was clean shaven, and his eyes were bright. He didn't look like someone trying to rip her off, but then you never know. But hell, she didn't want to be hauling the luggage around on her own. "So you still wanna help me now that you know that I'm as black as you?"

"Aw hell, naw. You may be a nigga, but you sure as hell ain't black as me, shortie," he said with a wide grin that revealed all thirty-two of his pearly whites. "Yeah, I'll carry your bags. And I won't even charge you. I woulda if you was white for real, though." He picked up her bags. "What's your name, shortie?"

"Shanika."

"Oh yeah, you a nigga for real, huh?" He let go another one of his loud laughs.

"What's yours?"

"Jason. So which way you going?"

"I've got to find a taxi."

He nodded his head toward the right. "This way, shortie. And I know you gonna hit me off with them digits, yo. Where you live?"

Shanika had to trot to keep up with him. "Detroit. I'm just up here for a job interview."

"Shit, ma. Well, good luck. It's tight as a mug out here. I been looking for a J-O-B for a minute now."

"Damn, it's just as hot and humid out here as it is in Detroit," she complained as they walked out the station and onto the street. "I'm going to melt out here."

He gave her a sideways glance and chuckled. "Oh, you that damn sweet, you like sugar, huh? I hear ya, shortie. Where you heading now? A hotel? Which one?"

"No, I'm staying with . . . with my aunt in Long Island," Shanika lied as quickly as she could.

"Yeah? Well, I got a crib in the Bronx, but if you gonna be in the city for a while, maybe I can take you out? You ever been to the 40/40 Club?"

"Jay-Z's club?" Shanika's eyes widened. "No. I'd like to, though."

"Well, maybe we can hook up tonight then, yo. My man be working the door and he'll let us in."

"Yeah, Jason. That'd be cool." Shanika smiled to herself. There was no way she was going to waste her time on an out-of-work scrub who cruised the train stations to carry women's bags in hope of tips and had to depend on his friends to get him into clubs for free. But as long as he was carrying her suitcases, she'd play along.

She reached up to wipe some perspiration from her brow and all of a sudden felt a drop of water plop down on her forehead. "Oh God, don't tell me it's going to rain!"

A clap of thunder splitting the air, followed by a sudden downpour, answered her.

"Shit," Shanika muttered while pulling up the collar of her blue linen suit jacket. She tapped Jason on the shoulder. "How much farther do we have to go?"

"The corner of Thirtieth and Eighth, girl. It's the best place to flag a taxi. Right up at the corner."

It took them less than a minute to walk to their destination, but in that short time Shanika was soaked almost to the skin, as was Jason, although he didn't seem to mind. What did seem to faze him was when yellow cab after yellow cab whizzed by him without stopping. Shanika stood under the canopy of a store with her luggage, impatiently tapping her foot as she watched him. When the fifth taxi passed him without stopping, she grabbed her bags and ran over to the now embarrassed and frustrated man.

"Man, I hate these whack racist mofos," he grumbled, averting his eyes from hers. "If we was uptown, I could catch a gypsy cab with no problem."

"Look. Thanks, but I got this, okay?" Shanika tried to keep her voice soothing, but she was just tired and edgy and she knew it came through in her tone. "You can go ahead. I'll catch it myself."

"Naw, shortie, I got this." He tried to wave her off. He put his hand out as another yellow cab approached and it, too, passed without taking a second look in his direction. This time, however, the cab had to stop only three feet away because of a red light. Shanika watched as Jason stomped through a puddle to get to the car.

"Get in!" he yelled as he tried to snatch the door open. The driver was too quick, though, and snapped the automatic locks on. Shanika shook her head as Jason proceeded to kick the tires, then pummel the cab's trunk.

Just then another cab neared her and she quickly put her hand in the air. The cab stopped promptly in front of her and she snatched the door open and struggled to get her two suitcases in the backseat before Jason noticed.

"The Ramada Inn at Thirtieth Street and Lexington Avenue," she hurriedly told the driver.

"Hey, yo!" Jason was tapping on the closed passenger window of her cab. "Whatcha doing, Shanika? What's up with this?"

She waited until the cabdriver put the car in gear before

rolling down the window. "Sorry, I'm running late. Thanks for everything, though."

She didn't bother to look back as the cab pulled into traffic. She supposed she should have felt a little guilty—after all, Jason was trying to help her and she jumped ship as soon as he turned his back. But, she reasoned, it wasn't her fault that taxis don't like picking up black men in midtown New York City. She'd always heard it was so, in the movies and sometimes on television news specials, but this was the first time she'd actually seen it. But then again, this was the first time she'd been in New York. Obviously, they didn't have as much of a problem picking up a woman. The thought that it was because she was mistaken for a white woman suddenly occurred to her, but she quickly pushed it out of her mind.

"Did you know that man, miss?" the cabdriver—an East Indian—asked her in a West Indian accent after a few minutes.

"No. He helped me upstairs from the train station with my bags," she said simply, while still looking out the window.

"Train station. Penn Station?" The driver peered at her through the rearview mirror, sizing her up.

Shanika nodded.

"Where you coming from, miss?"

"Detroit."

"Your first time in New York?"

Shanika nodded again.

"Well, miss," the driver said as he made a hard right turn onto Thirtieth Street, "you should be very careful. You were lucky. Very lucky. A lot of those people make a living hustling nice young ladies that just come in town. It's the way they were raised. To try and rip off people. Easier for them than to try and find work. They want to rob people or sell drugs, the lot of them, miss. And their women aren't much better. They sell their bodies or have babies so they can get on the public welfare. And they spend all of their time in the beauty salon." He smiled to himself, confident that he'd solidified his tip. Out-of-towners always appreciated advice such as this.

Shanika's eyes widened. Okay, she had gotten the cab because the driver thought she was white. It wasn't the first time she'd benefited from looking white and she didn't feel bad about it. After all, she didn't pretend to be white. She wasn't trying to pass or anything; she'd never do a thing like that. Never. But normally, when she was mistaken for white and someone talked negatively in her presence about African-Americans, she would hurriedly—and haughtily—announce her true heritage. But . . . well, she didn't think the cabbie would throw her out of his car, but he just might. And she was so tired, and already rain drenched. And even if he didn't do that, he might do something like trick her and drive all around New York to get to the hotel, which might only be a few blocks away, since she already said this was her first time in New York. No, it was best to be quiet. And of course she didn't have to contribute to the conversation.

"But then there are a lot of them in Detroit, aren't there? In fact, I've heard your city is full of them," the cabbie continued. He had obviously taken her silence for agreement.

"Them?" Shanika asked.

"Yes. Niggers. The blacks"—he waved his hand in the air as if about to concede something—"or African-Americans."

"I call them African-Americans, and, yes, the city is predominantly African-American. But I'm sorry I don't view them the same way as you." As soon as she said it, she was sorry. Not because she now worried about repercussions, but because in defense of her race she had distanced herself from it. Just by using the word "them" instead of "us." She had never done that before. Her face reddened and she quickly looked out the window so that the driver wouldn't notice her expression in his mirror while she silently asked God to forgive her.

"Here we go. The hotel is right in the middle of this block. And, I don't want you to think I'm a bigot. I may have sounded like one, but I'm not. Some cabdrivers won't even pick them up because they're scared. But I will, as long as it's daylight. That's why I pull the day shift on this job so I don't have to play bias against them. I do hate it when they get in and want to go to Harlem, but I'll even take them there," the driver said, hedging his bets since she made that remark about calling them African-American. He was an unbiased driver, as far as he was concerned. He wanted a tip from both liberals and conservatives.

"That's mighty white of you," Shanika said quietly while taking out her emery board and peering at her nails. She glanced in the rearview mirror and noted with satisfaction that the driver had a shocked expression on his brown face. She couldn't resist pushing it a little further. "You're East Indian, aren't you?" she asked innocently.

"I certainly am."

"That's what I thought. But you have a West Indian accent," she said slowly. She suddenly brightened her face. "Oh, I bet you're from Trinidad! You're a coolie!"

The driver's face darkened, and he said nothing for a moment.

"You are a coolie, aren't you?" she pressed further. "My mother was raised in Trinidad," she lied, "and she told me the

East Indians who lived there were called coolies. She even had one as a nursemaid."

The driver pulled in front of the hotel. Was she trying to play him for a fool or was she the fool, he wondered. He cleared his throat before speaking again. "You do know that 'coolie' is not a very nice word, don't you, miss?"

Shanika widened her eyes and put her hand to her mouth in a show of shock. "Really? No, I didn't know. I learned it from my mother. Is it racist, then?"

"It is," the driver said darkly, realizing she'd, indeed, been playing him for the fool.

"Oh, my goodness," Shanika said, continuing her act of innocence as she dug her wallet out of her handbag. "I guess it's like calling a black a nigger, then? I'm so sorry. How much do I owe you?"

"That would be five twenty-five," the driver said sullenly.

She handed him a five-dollar bill and three dimes. "You can keep the change. And don't worry about helping with my bags," she told him as the hotel bellhop opened her door. "Have a nice day."

Even the elevator ride up to the Paxon & Green offices was awe-inspiring. Detroit had its share of skyscrapers, and Shanika had been in a few of them, but never before had she traveled in an elevator to the forty-second floor of a building. The doors opened and she found herself facing a huge mahogany reception desk underneath a large sign that read PAXON & GREEN—PUBLIC RELATIONS. She took a deep breath before approaching the white woman behind the desk, whose suit looked like it cost three times the amount of hers.

"Good morning. I'm here to see Mr. Kadinsky," she told the woman in her most polite voice.

The woman, who could have been Gwyneth Paltrow's older sister, smiled up at her. "And good morning to you, dear. Do you have an appointment?"

"Yes. For nine-thirty. I'm a little early."

The woman looked at the appointment calendar and the smile that had seemed to be a permanent fixture on her face was replaced by a small frown. She flipped a page, then another one, then looked back up at Shanika. "I'm sorry, but your name isn't Miss Jenkins, is it?"

Shanika nodded. "Yes, it is."

The woman's brow furrowed. "Miss Shanika Jenkins?"

Shanika sighed inwardly as she nodded. She'd been through this scene so often that it felt like a time-worn comedy skit. She knew the woman wanted to ask about her name, not her ethnicity. White people always questioned the name rather than the ethnicity, not understanding why parents would give their child such a black-sounding name. However, they were usually too polite to ask. She sure as hell had hoped, though, that the skit wouldn't have replayed at the most important job interview of her life.

"Yes," she assured the woman. "I'm Shanika Jenkins. I sent my résumé to Mr. Kadinsky a few months ago and I received a telephone call from this office two weeks ago asking me to come in for an interview today."

The receptionist found her smile and quickly plastered it back on her face. "Of course. If you'll just have a seat, Miss

Jenkins, I'll let Mr. Kadinsky know that you're here. Would you like some coffee?" Shanika declined.

The table was filled with copies of *People*, *Us*, *Redbook*, *Advertising Age*, *Details*, and *Esquire*. Shanika picked one up and started flipping through it, so lost in her own thoughts that she didn't notice the name of the magazine or the stories inside the issue. Nor did she notice the passage of time.

"Miss Jenkins?"

Shanika looked up, startled. "Yes, ma'am," she said to the tall African-American woman who stood in front of her. The woman looked like a runway model for *Vogue*. Her makeup was flawless, and her permed bobbed hair looked like it had just been cut, not a strand out of place. Her blue suit looked like it was Versace, and the lines fit her as if it were custom made. And perhaps it was. The woman exuded an air of elegance and success. Suddenly, her newly purchased white linen suit seemed woefully inadequate.

"I'm Mrs. Randolph, Mr. Kadinsky's personal assistant." The woman stuck her hand out, and Shanika hurriedly stood up to shake it. "Art . . . Mr. Kadinsky . . . is in a meeting right now, but why don't you come into my office while you wait for him and we can talk."

She's lovely, simply lovely, Libby Randolph thought as she led a smiling Shanika into a large wood-paneled office with a breathtaking view of Central Park. *But so light-skinned, I wonder if that's going to be a problem. Her inexperience could be overlooked—after all, this is a trainee position—but her physical appearance may be a problem.*

"Please have a seat," Mrs. Randolph said, waving her toward a comfortable padded chair. "Would you like a cup of coffee? Or tea?"

"No thanks . . . um, no, thank you," Shanika said nervously. Something told her that this wasn't just another waiting room. The interview had just begun. Maybe it had even begun as soon as she stepped off the elevator. "I had coffee in the hotel before coming over."

"Oh, good. At what hotel are you staying?" Mrs. Randolph asked as she settled herself behind the desk.

"The Ramada Inn at Thirtieth and Lexington." Shanika inwardly cursed herself for not coming up with the name of a more prestigious hotel to impress the woman.

Mrs. Randolph nodded. "That's a sensible hotel. Centrally located and reasonably priced. Did you fly in town this morning or last night?"

"I checked in yesterday afternoon about five p.m.," Shanika said, not bothering to correct the woman by telling her that she'd taken the train. No sense in letting her know how broke she was.

"Is this your first time in New York City?"

"Yes, but I already love the city. I mean, I haven't had much time to look around, but I love the feel of the city. It's like there's a sense of excitement in the air."

"That would be New York," Mrs. Randolph said with a chuckle. "I've been here almost twenty years and I'm still excited about it. I'm originally from Philadelphia. Big city, but not as big as New York."

"I've never been to Philadelphia, but I've always wanted to go. I'm sure it's really nice." *Shoot, I sound like I'm sucking up.*

"Yes, it is." Mrs. Randolph took a sip of her coffee. "I love that shade of lipstick. It looks quite good on you. Is it from the Ebony Fashion Fair line?"

"Well, actually it's Maybelline, but thank you." Shanika

smiled, knowing this was Mrs. Randolph's way of letting her know she realized she was black. And quite a classy way of doing it, Shanika thought.

"Now, let's see. I have your résumé here somewhere. Ah yes, here it is. So you graduated from Delaware State?"

Shanika nodded, then quickly said, "Yes. I majored in public relations and graduated with a 3.6 average. Cum laude."

"Yes, I see. Very impressive," Mrs. Randolph said in a voice that made Shanika hope she might actually be impressed. Shanika smiled and stuck her chest out just a little bit. The next question, however, momentarily took the winds out of her sails.

"But you don't have much of a work history. You didn't do any internships at all while in school?"

No, because I wanted to spend my summers having fun with my friends at home, not working. Not that she could tell Mrs. Randolph that. Shanika sat up straighter in her chair—Joseph had always told her when she felt like sagging, she should straighten up all the more. "Well, no. But I did very well in my PR classes. In fact, I pulled a perfect 4.0 in my major. And I have letters of recommendations from three of my PR professors."

Mrs. Randolph put her cup down on the desk. "But why didn't you do any internships? Didn't any of your professors tell you how important it is to have internships to land a job upon graduation?"

Shanika took a deep breath. "Well, yes, but you see my mother's been ill, and I already felt guilty going away to college, although I did so at her insistence. So every summer I rushed home to be with her." She lowered her eyes, hoping Mrs. Randolph would think she was overcome with emotion, when in reality she was sending up a quick prayer to God to forgive her lie. *But after all,* she thought, *it was Mama who helped me come up with the fib.*

"Oh, I'm sorry to hear that," Mrs. Randolph said hurriedly. "How's your mother doing now?"

"She's much better now, thank goodness. We're all very thankful," Shanika said solemnly.

Mrs. Randolph paused for a moment before speaking again. "Well, I do want to put this delicately, but, well, would you really feel comfortable moving to New York for a job and being so far from your mother?"

Shanika blinked quickly. She and Mama hadn't anticipated that question. "Well, you know she's been in remission for a while now, and the doctors are very hopeful. In fact, I spoke to her physician before I even applied here . . . just to make sure . . . and he assured me that he thought she'd be fine."

"Oh well, fine then," Mrs. Randolph said reassuringly. "I didn't want to pry. And please excuse me if I was too personal."

"Not at all," Shanika said demurely.

"And let me also say that the position you're being considered for is rather like a trainee, so your inexperience shouldn't be too much of a hindrance. You'd be working as an assistant to one of our associates, probably at least for a year or so, and then you'd be evaluated to see how you've done. And if your work is satisfactory you'd be considered for a promotion. How does that sound?"

"It sounds wonderful," Shanika said excitedly. "And you'll find I'm not only a quick learner, but I'm very motivated, I'm a team player, and—"

"—and you're very enthusiastic," Mrs. Randolph said with

a large smile. "I tell you what, why don't we go see if Mr. Kadinsky is free to speak to you now."

Shanika dutifully followed her out of her office and down a corridor past another set of offices.

"Oh, Jeff," Mrs. Randolph said to a middle-aged copper-complected man in a gray suit who was about to pass them. "This is the young lady who's interviewing for the trainee position."

The man looked at Shanika in surprise, then looked at Mrs. Randolph again. "Really? I thought—" he started, then cleared his throat and turned back to Shanika.

"Shanika, this is Jeff Samuels, one of our vice presidents. Jeff," Mrs. Randolph continued pointedly, "this is Shanika Jenkins. I believe you received the memo saying she was coming in today?"

"Yes, of course. My mistake." Mr. Samuels extended his hand. "Shanika Jenkins, is it?"

"Yes, sir." Shanika shook his hand while thinking, *This guy is going to be trouble.*

"Shanika is a recent graduate of Delaware State University," Mrs. Randolph said in a tone that implied "pay attention."

"She just flew in from Detroit," Mrs. Randolph added.

"Delaware State? Really?" he asked in a preoccupied voice.

Oh God, how stupid is this guy? She's already said my name twice, told him I'm from Detroit, and let him know I graduated from an HBCU. Can't he see that she's trying to tell him I'm as black as he is? The freaking idiot.

"I always think it's so wonderful when our young people

choose to go to one of the Historically Black Colleges and Universities. Don't you, Jeff?"

"Yes, of course. Very commendable." He looked at his watch and then cleared his throat. "Well, I'm running late for the board meeting. Nice to meet you, Miss Jenkins. I hope you enjoy your trip." And with that he hurried down the hall.

Mrs. Randolph frowned inwardly, though she tried to keep a pleasant smile on her face for Shanika's sake. Either that idiot Jeff still didn't get the fact that Shanika was black or he had already decided she wasn't going to pass muster because of her complexion. She may not have been what he expected, but the bottom line was she was black, and wasn't that what was supposed to count? It was a damn shame how color-struck some black folks could be—either discriminating because someone was too dark, or, in Jeff's case, because someone was too light. Of course she could see his point, but Shanika should be given the same chance as anyone else, regardless of her complexion. Besides, in just the few minutes since she'd met Shanika, she had decided she really liked the young woman. And she was going to make sure she was hired, Jeff Samuels or no Jeff Samuels.

Shanika glanced over at Mrs. Randolph and noticed the disapproving look she bestowed on the man's back. *Okay, she's not pleased with how that went. What am I missing here?*

chapter four

She nailed it. She was pretty sure of that. Mr. Kadinsky was impressed by her quick wit, and charmed by her personality—and Mrs. Randolph had made it a point to let her know that the position didn't really require experience—so she was pretty sure the job was hers. Heck, Mr. Kadinsky had even walked her to the door himself, and asked when she'd be available to start. Yes, she had made quite an impression. So why was there this little nagging thought that something was wrong? And the something, she was pretty sure, was Jeff Samuels. She hadn't seen him again that morning, but . . . Well, as impressed as Mr. Kadinsky had seemed, he hadn't come out and offered her the job. Maybe they had to hold a conference or meeting about her to make the final decision. And maybe that Jeff Samuels guy was going to gum up the works. But what the hell had she ever done to him?

She tried to push the troublesome doubt from her mind. After all, Jeff Samuels may have been a vice president of Paxon & Green, but he was vice president of accounting. Why would he have anything to do with hiring? No, this job was hers. It was in the bag. Claim it, her mother had always told her. When you really want something, and you know you deserve it, just claim it. The Creator is always listening. She peered up at the sky. *God, Allah, Jehovah, Olofi, Zeus, or whatever, I'm claiming this job. It's mine.*

Her stomach grumbled as she walked down Madison Avenue toward her hotel, reminding her that it was already past noon and she hadn't eaten since shortly after waking up at six. She mentally counted the money in her purse. She should have about eighty-three dollars left. If she spent seven on lunch, and twenty on dinner, that should still be more than enough to pay for a cab to Amtrak in the morning when her train was due to pull out, and also buy a couple of sandwiches and sodas to tide her over on the long trip home. At least she hoped so.

She paused to take a quick look around for someplace where she could stop and get something cheap to eat. As luck would have it, she was right in front of a sidewalk deli.

"Table for one?" the black-leotarded hostess asked as she pulled a menu from the side of the podium where she stood. "Would you like to sit inside or outside?" she asked before Shanika could answer her first question.

"Your waiter's name is Ivan and he'll be with you in a minute," the waitress said after she seated Shanika at a small round table on the sidewalk.

"Thanks," Shanika said with a small nod. She smoothed the white cloth napkin over her lap and picked up the menu, and then almost panicked. How the hell could they get away with charging $19.50 for a pastrami sandwich? She could get a T-bone steak platter for that back in Detroit. There was no way she was going to blow that much money on a lousy sandwich. She looked around at the other tables. None of the people who were sitting there laughing and talking looked rich, but they also didn't look as if they had been fazed by the prices. In fact, there were a couple of people who had put their cigarettes out in their only half-finished meals. Tacky and nasty, but also a statement. They obviously had money to burn. And she sure as hell didn't.

"And how are you today, pretty lady?" a voice said, interrupting the formulation of her escape plan. Ivan poured her a glass of water from the steel pitcher he held in one hand. "Would you like me to read you the specials?"

"No, actually, I just realized I'm really not hungry," Shanika said quickly. She looked at her watch. "Oh, my goodness, look at the time. I'm really late for an appointment. I'm sorry to have troubled you." She refolded her napkin and replaced it on the table. She flashed a nervous smile at the waiter, who in turn glared at her and sauntered off with a swish of his hips. Her smile froze and her face reddened, and she wanted to yell after him, "Well, fuck you, too, you little faggot," but she didn't want to make a scene. People were already looking as it was.

She brushed a stray hair from her face, took a deep breath to steady herself, and then pushed her chair back as she prepared to get up. It was then that the leg of the chair struck something, forcing her to look down. A BlackBerry phone—and a pearl white one at that. She bent down and picked it up, then cleared her throat to call Ivan back over so she could give it to him, but he just shot her an uncaring look and went to check on another table.

Well, to hell with him, Shanika thought as she slipped the gadget into her pocketbook and walked out the café with her head held high. *I tried to do the right thing, but, shit, now I'm keeping this bad boy for myself.*

"How much are your sausages?" she asked a food vendor on the corner two blocks away from the café.

"A dollar seventy-five," came the reply. "A dollar twenty-five for a frank."

Shanika's brow furrowed. "For a what?"

"A frankfurter. A dollar twenty-five." The man noticed the still-puzzled look on Shanika's face and smiled. "A hot dog, miss. We call them frankfurters, or franks, here in New York," he explained. "You must be from out of town."

"Yeah. Come to think of it, I've heard them called that before," Shanika lied. "I just forgot. I'll take a frank and a grape pop."

"A grape soda," the vendor corrected her with a big grin.

"Yeah, that." Shanika didn't bother to hide her smile. Okay, she wasn't going to be able to pull off the seasoned traveler bit.

"Okay, then, what do ya want on your frank?"

"Do you have chili and cheese?"

The vendor looked at her and shook his head. "In New York we mostly just put mustard, onions, and sauerkraut on franks. Some people put ketchup, but no true New Yorker would have it."

Shanika grinned. "Okay, mustard, onions, and sauerkraut it is. Like they say, when in Rome . . ."

"There's the spirit!" the man said. Just a few seconds later he handed her a topping-laden frankfurter. "And since this is your first dirty frank, it's on the house."

"Dirty frank?"

"It's what we call the franks you buy on the street from vendors. Eat it and you'll be a bona fide New Yorker. Now, the grape soda you'll have to pay for, since you've had one, even if you didn't know what to call it. That'll be a dollar."

Shanika giggled and handed him a single. "Thanks a bunch!" she said as she walked away. She took a bite of the frank, then used the napkin he'd given her to wipe the mustard and the onions off her mouth. "Mmm. Now this is good," she said out loud to no one. Her disposition improved steadily as she strolled down the avenue, peering into store windows. The clothing in the boutiques looked exquisite, but none of the outfits had price tags on them. As a lark she went into one.

"Excuse me, how much is the red silk blouse in the window?" she asked the clerk who stepped up to greet her.

"Actually, it's not silk, but it is a fine polyester blend. And it's on sale for one hundred twenty-five dollars," the woman told her. "Would you like to see it in your size?"

"You're kidding! One hundred and change and it's not even silk?"

The clerk gave her an odd look. "Yes. It normally goes for one ninety-five, but as I said it's on sale."

"Yeah, well, thanks, but no thanks," Shanika said. "There's no way I'm spending that much money on polyester."

"A fine polyester blend," the clerk reminded her in a prim voice.

"Uh-huh," Shanika answered. "A fine polyester blend."

The woman's already thin lips thinned even farther, and she looked as if she were going to rebuke Shanika, but she suddenly burst out laughing and motioned Shanika closer to her and out of the earshot of the other clerks who were looking on with surprised expressions.

"Yes, a fine polyester blend," the clerk said as she struggled to regain control. "In fact, the finest."

"Girl, your New York prices aren't to be believed! How do you people afford this stuff?"

"Where are you from?"

"Detroit."

The clerk suddenly stopped chuckling. "What?" She looked Shanika up and down. "That's not exactly the cheapest city in the world, you know. In fact, we have two, maybe three stores out there and the prices can't be that different."

"Yeah, well, they're a lot different in the stores I shop in back home."

The clerk shrugged. "Well, what can I say? You can find cheaper clothes in New York, too. But if you want fine clothes, you're going to have to spend fine money. That's the way of the world, honey, especially the world of Madison Avenue boutiques."

Definitely a world I want in, Shanika thought later as she lay across the bed in her hotel room. *A world I'll be in if I get this job. Scratch that. When I get this job. I'm claiming it.*

She picked up the remote from the nightstand and clicked on the television. *Friends* was on—the episode where Monica and Rachel are battling Joey and Chandler to get their apartment back.

"Let's see," Shanika said as she grabbed the complimentary hotel pen and notepad. "They said the position pays thirty-two thousand to start. I know rents are high here, but if I shop around, I should be able to find a place for fifteen hundred a month. Or maybe I'll get a roommate, and get a really nice place for four thousand a month. Split two ways, I'll be spending twenty-four thousand on rent, which'll leave me with eight thousand for living expenses. I can buy some fly clothes with that. Especially if I bring my lunch to work and have guys take me out to dinner every night to cut down on grocery bills."

Shanika pushed the notepad aside and rolled over on the bed, letting her head loll over the side. "I can just see me now, hanging out every weekend at the clubs, partying with Usher and 50 Cent. Ooh, maybe I'll even get invited out to one of P. Diddy's parties! They say he gives the hottest in town. Yeah, I'm gonna be all up in that mug. I'm going to freaking own New York by the time I'm through."

Her monologue was interrupted by the ringing telephone.

"Hello? . . . Hey, Mama! . . . Ooh yeah, I think it went real well. I think I got the job, Mama! . . . They said they'd call me in a few days to let me know . . . Oh, Mama, isn't it exciting? . . . Oh, my God, yeah! I love New York . . . No, I haven't gotten out to see a lot, but what I've seen I love. I'm going to fit right in here . . . and as soon as I get settled, I'm going to send for you and Papa to come visit with me for a while . . . It doesn't have to be a long while, Mama, but I know you're gonna wanna come and see my new place . . . I'm not counting my chickens before they hatch, Mama. I can just feel it. They're going to offer me the job . . . How much you wanna bet? . . . Chicken! . . . And guess what? They actually pay moving expenses! . . . I know! Isn't that great? . . . Oh, I don't know, I think my train gets in at like midnight. But, Mama, it's such a long train ride. Can't I ask Joe if he'll pay for me to take a plane? . . . Okay, okay, Mama. I just don't see what the harm is in asking . . . No, Mama, I'm not going to misplace my train ticket on purpose . . . I promise . . . Mama, I have it right here!" Shanika sighed and reached for her purse. "It says I get in at midnight, just like I said." As she tossed her purse back on the bed, the white cell phone tumbled out. She picked it up and started scrolling through the numbers in the address book as she continued to talk. "Are you and Papa going to pick me up from the station? . . . Mama, please try. Or at least tell Joe to come get me. I don't want to haul my stuff on the bus. I already—" Shanika gasped and almost dropped the telephone. "Mama," she said urgently, "let me call you right back. I've got to go to the bathroom. Yeah, I promise I will. No, Mama, please, I can talk to Papa when I call back. Love ya."

She hung up quickly and looked intently at the cell phone. Paris? Could it be Paris Hilton's number she was looking at listed in the address directory? She scrolled up in the directory and came across the name Nicky. Paris's sister Nicky Hilton? Or did Nicole Richie's friends maybe call her Nicky? She scrolled farther up. Lindsay. As in, perhaps, Lindsay Lohan? It couldn't be. It must be another Paris, another Nicky, and another Lindsay. There had to be hundreds of all three names in people's cell phones. She scrolled back down to the number listed for Paris. There's one way to find out, she thought as she fingered the send button. Should she? She looked around the hotel room as if expecting someone to tell her to put the damn thing down and stop acting stupid, then closed her eyes, hit the send button and put the BlackBerry to her ear.

"Hello?"

Shanika gasped out loud, then quickly put her hand over the mouth. That was definitely Paris Hilton's voice on the other end of the phone!

"Hello," the voice said again. "Is anyone there? Oh, I'm just kidding. Fooled you, though, didn't I? That's hot. I'm not available, but leave a message and we'll get back to you. If we get around to it. Bye-bye, now." *Beep.*

Shanika quickly hit the end button on the cell phone. *Oh*

shit, I have Paris Hilton's private cell phone number! She started gasping for breath. *I have Paris Hilton's number!*

She started scrolling through the listings again. Abby, Andrea, Angela . . . there were more than 150 girls' names listed in the directory, though none had their last names. Whose BlackBerry had she found, she wondered. She decided to call one of the numbers in the directory and ask.

She didn't think she'd be able to handle calling someone who might be a celebrity, so she settled on the name Vivian, since she couldn't think of a celebrity by that name.

"What the hell do you want?" someone all but shouted into the phone after only three rings.

"Uh, well, I was just calling because I found this phone, this, um, cell phone, at a restaurant and I wanted to return it," Shanika managed to get out through her shock at the reception.

"Oh!" The voice softened. "Well, thanks. That's nice of you."

"Um, do you know, uh, do you know whose cell phone this is?"

"Yeah, it belongs to my friend Cindy. Hold on, let me call her on her cell phone and see where she is."

This Cindy girl has two cell phones, she marveled, after Vivian put her on hold.

Vivian was back on the line in about forty-five seconds. "Hang up, she's going to call you. She didn't even know she lost the damn thing, the idiot."

The phone rang less than a minute after Vivian hung up.

"Hello," Shanika said hesitantly, not sure if Cindy was going to be as abrasive as her friend.

"Hi. This is Cindy. Vivian just called me and told me you found my phone!" the young woman said in a cheery voice.

"Yes, I found it in a restaurant on Madison Avenue. It was on the sidewalk."

"Now, isn't that something? I didn't even know I'd lost it. It must have slipped out of my purse. Where are you right now?"

"I'm at a hotel on Lexington Avenue."

"Lexington and what?"

"Um, Lexington and Thirtieth Street."

"Oh, good. I'm not far away. Would you be a sweetheart and bring it over to me? I'm with some friends at Sangy's."

"Sangy's?"

"The Sangria Club. I'll be here until about ten. Do you think you can make it before then?"

Damn, this chick got some nerve. Here I'm doing her a favor by trying to return her cell phone and she wants me to come to her? Shanika wanted to tell the girl to go to hell, but at the same time she didn't want to. Going out to the Sangria Club might be fun, she'd get to see a real New York club and maybe meet some interesting people. Of course she couldn't stay too long, since she had to catch the train early the next morning. But the girl just said the club wasn't far.

"Sure," she heard herself telling Cindy. "I can leave right now. Where exactly is the Sangria Club located?"

There was a pause. "You're kidding, right? It's the Sangria Club. You know, on Sixty-seventh and Park."

"Oh, I'm not from here. I'm just visiting New York, but, yeah, I'll be there in a couple of minutes. How will I know you?"

"I'll be in a VIP area with two other girls right by the stage.

I'm wearing a white summer dress and I have long red hair." Cindy started giggling. "You'll know me, I'm the most beautiful girl in the place."

Shanika could hear some girls laughing in the background.

"Oh, shut up, you jealous bitches," she heard Cindy say.

"Okay, I'm on my way," Shanika said, trying to regain Cindy's attention.

"Good. I'll be waiting."

She didn't even ask me my name, Shanika thought after the girl hung up. She probably doesn't care. I guess she's just used to people doing what she wants.

Wow, the VIP section. Boy, she really sounds like she's going to be interesting, Shanika thought as she grabbed her pocketbook and hotel key and headed out the door. *I bet this is going to be fun.*

chapter five

The Sangria Club, which Cindy had described as "not far," was actually a $7.80 taxi ride from the hotel—$7.80 that Shanika could barely afford to pay. She pursed her lips as she handed the cabdriver a five and three singles, preparing for an outburst since she wasn't planning on giving him a tip, unless you counted the twenty-cents change that is, but he never bothered to give her a backward glance as she got out of the car.

"Ten dollars and ID," a beefy brute of a man with blond hair and a neck that bulged out of his heavily starched shirt collar said when she walked into the club. He gave her a quick look up and down and then, clearly deciding she wasn't worthy of more, turned back to the four security monitors in his little lobby cubbyhole and added, "And a two-drink minimum."

"Ten dollars? There's a cover charge to get in?" Shanika drew back in surprise. "A cover charge on a Monday? And it's not even ten o'clock yet!"

"Ten dollars and a two-drink minimum," the man reminded her. "And it's twenty dollars after ten on weeknights, and thirty-five on weekends." He turned to her again, bestowing on her a polite but insincere smile. "We take all of the major credit cards, but no checks. Sorry."

"Not a problem. I'll be paying cash." Shanika quietly fumed as she fumbled in her pocketbook for her wallet and gave the man her driver's license, along with a ten-dollar bill. Between the cab ride, the cover charge, and her two-drink minimum, it was going to cost her a pretty penny to return the stupid phone. *Chickie better at least offer to pay my expenses,* she thought as she walked into the club's interior.

She'd been in some really nice clubs in Detroit, and also while in school in Delaware, but this was something else.

There wasn't a big crowd in the place, maybe about sixty or seventy people, though the club could easily accommodate four or five times that many, and that didn't even count the balcony area.

Isn't that the girl who plays in that new TV sitcom standing over in the corner laughing with that guy? But wait, is that a margarita she's swigging down? The girl can't be more than sixteen. And the guy at the door had the nerve to ask me for ID. Hmmph!

There were only four couples on the dance floor, and all but one were white. The other was interracial, the guy looked Asian, and the woman was definitely African-American—from her dreadlocks to her cowrie shell earrings. The funny thing was the pretty little dreadlocked mama was the worst dancer on the floor—as loud as the bass was, coming from the large speakers situated throughout the club, she acted like she couldn't find the beat if her life depended on it. In fact, she looked like she was having a seizure there on the floor. Shanika struggled not to giggle. So much for all black girls having rhythm.

She was so busy staring at the uncoordinated woman that

she almost bumped into a tall, willowy blonde who looked like a runway model. "Sorry," she said hurriedly.

The blonde looked her up and down, making Shanika suddenly feel self-conscious. "Whatever," she finally said with a heavy Italian accent and turned to walk away.

"Damn, it didn't have to be all that," Shanika said out loud.

The woman turned. "Did you say something to me?"

"I just said it didn't have to be all like that," Shanika repeated.

"Uh-huh. Well, like I said, whatever." The blonde walked away.

Hmmph, I'd better hurry up and drop off this phone before I have to start getting wild up in this place.

It only took her a few minutes to locate the VIP section, and, sure enough, there were three young women sitting there looking bored, and not even moving their shoulders or bopping their heads to the loud music. Nor were they engaged in conversation. They were just sitting there, and one of them had red hair.

If that's Cindy, she sure wasn't lying, Shanika thought as she neared the table. She was indeed the most striking-looking woman in the club—or at the very least one of them. She was skinny—not bony like Nicole Richie, but soft skinny like Nicole Kidman—with long red hair that hung in loose waves past her bare tanned shoulders. The white summer dress, as Cindy had described it, looked almost exactly like one Shanika had seen in *Vogue*—low-cut, tight around her small bodice, and the material, Shanika was sure, had to be silk.

The woman suddenly looked up and Shanika found herself staring into a pair of feline green eyes, topped by perfectly arched red eyebrows that extended down almost to the outer corner of her eyelids.

Shanika quickened her step, sure that she'd indeed found the party she'd been looking for, but her path was suddenly blocked by a tall, thin man wearing a black suit and dark sunglasses.

"Sorry, ma'am," he said curtly. "This is the VIP section."

"Yes, but—" Shanika started.

"Sorry, ma'am," the man repeated, "but I'm sure you'll find suitable seating elsewhere."

Shanika pointed to the women at the table and said, "But I'm with them."

"Of course you are." The man took Shanika's arm, swung her around, and started walking her away from the stage area.

"Hey!" Shanika tried to pull away, but the man's grip tightened. "Will you please let me go!"

"Tony!"

Both Shanika and the man turned to see the redhead standing up and cupping her hands around her mouth as she yelled again, "Tony! I think she's here with me!"

"You *think* she's here with you?"

The woman gave an exasperated smirk and waved them over.

"I'm sorry, Ms. Statler. You said you *think* she's here with you?" the man asked once she reached the table.

"Yes, yes, yes, that's what I said! Damn, man!" the woman said, her green eyes narrowed into slits. "And you don't have to manhandle her even if she's not."

The man quickly let go of Shanika's arm. "Sorry, Ms. Statler," he mumbled before swiftly walking away.

"Are you okay?"

"I'm fine." Shanika nodded. "Just a little shook-up, but fine."

"I'm really sorry about that. Tony's a real gorilla." The redhead sat back down, and then smiled up at Shanika. "So now, tell me, are you the girl who found my cell phone?"

"Huh? Oh yes!" Shanika quickly dipped her hand in her pocketbook and pulled out the phone and handed it to the redhead.

Cindy put the phone down on the table and gave Shanika a long look up and down. She definitely needed some makeup lessons. Who wore amber lipstick? Maybe black girls, but no one she hung out with. And her clothes were nice enough, but they definitely came from someplace like the Gap or Old Navy. The shoes were especially nice, black stiletto heels, but again, not designer. Probably couldn't have cost more than a hundred dollars or so. In fact, the girl's entire outfit probably cost less than Cindy's underwear. But she was pretty. Very pretty, in fact. She might be amusing.

"Well? Aren't you going to tell me your name? You already know mine is Cindy."

"Oh! Sorry." Shanika reached over the table and extended her hand for a shake. "Nikkie. Good to meet you."

Cindy gave Shanika a limp handshake, then motioned for her to have a seat. "This is my cousin Rachel." She waved her hand in the direction of the petite brunette sitting to her right.

Rachel smiled, revealing small perfectly shaped teeth. "Nice to meet you, Nikkie. Thanks for bringing Cindy the telephone."

"That's why I hate you, bitch. I was going to thank her myself, you know."

"Well, you didn't." Rachel smiled at Shanika again. "Don't pay her any mind. She's just being crabby because her *mommy*"—she looked at Cindy and smirked—"won't let her use the Porsche."

Cindy sucked her teeth. "She's another bitch."

Shanika tried to keep her face expressionless. It was bad enough these girls called each other bitches, but they referred to their mothers the same way?

"Anyway, this is Tina." Cindy pointed to the other brunette. This one was short, not quite on the pudgy side, but definitely bigger than either Cindy or Rachel.

"What's up? How ya doin'?" Tina acknowledged with a nod.

"I'm fine, thanks," Shanika answered, a little surprised. Tina's use of Ebonics seemed to indicate that she was aware of Shanika's ethnicity, but it was unusual for white people to figure it out so quickly. In fact, it had never happened before so quickly. She struggled to figure out what to say to the girls next. "How long have you been here?"

"Been where?" Cindy's arched eyebrow arched even higher.

"Here. I mean, here at the club."

Cindy shrugged. "We don't usually go out until one or so, but we decided to come out early for a change as a favor. Big mistake. The place is dead."

"A favor?" Shanika asked.

Cindy waved her hand and caught the attention of a drink waitress walking through the VIP section. "Terry, would you bring us another round of drinks?" She turned to Shanika. "You want a drink, right? Do you like cosmos?"

Shanika nodded.

"And Terry"—Cindy tapped the waitress on the arm—"make sure you tell Steve to bring his cute ass over here as soon as he walks in. Tell him I need to see him about business."

"Hey, Cindy, how are you doing?" asked a pretty Asian woman who seemed to appear from nowhere.

"Hey, Suki. I'm doing great. Can't you see?" Cindy said dismissively.

"Oh well, that's good." The girl stood at the table for a few moments, as if waiting to be asked to join the group, then finally walked away without saying another word.

"That was rather mean of you," Rachel said after she left. "You could have asked her to join us."

"Bitch please." Cindy rolled her eyes. "I didn't notice you asking her to join us."

"I didn't notice her saying hello to me," Rachel said with a laugh. "It's all about you, darling."

"It most certainly is," Cindy said with a smug smile.

"Yeah, usually clubs are banging by the time we get here," Tina said with a nod of her head. "You can't even move on the floor."

"Like that bothers Cindy," Rachel said. "Give her a couple of cosmos and she jumps up on a table."

"Hell, you're only young once," Cindy said in a disinterested voice. She stood up and looked around the club for a moment before sitting down again. "It's bad enough Steve isn't here yet, but there isn't anyone around that I can get anything from. We should go ahead and leave after these drinks. I'm bored. None of you bitches got anything for real?"

"Damn, Cindy, you just dropped some E. Give it some time to kick in." Tina gave Cindy a small punch on the shoulder, then leaned over her toward Shanika. "Do you want some? I got enough to get you straight, girl."

"Uh, no, I'm cool." These girls were something else, Shanika decided. Especially Cindy. But, hell, like she said, you're only young once. You might as well live it up.

The drink waitress reappeared with the cosmos and placed them down in front of the young women.

"So, Nikkie, Cindy said you're visiting the city? Where are you from?" Rachel asked after taking a ladylike sip.

"Detroit," Shanika answered.

"Really? Oh, I love Detroit," Cindy said after taking a huge gulp of her cosmo. "We were just down there for the Super Bowl game this year."

Rachel furrowed her brow. "Detroit? No, that was last year. It was in Miami this year."

"Miami. Detroit. Whatever." Cindy shrugged.

"Oh? Are you-all big football fans?"

"No, we just like the parties." Cindy took another couple of gulps of her drink, then waved the waitress over again. "Terry, sweetie, listen. Bring us another round, okay? And when you see that round getting low, just bring another one."

"Looks like that E's finally kicking in, huh, Cindy?" Tina tapped Cindy on the shoulder again.

"Will you please stop hitting me? Damn. Every time I go out with you, I wind up black-and-blue. But, yeah, I'm feeling okay. I'm feeling pretty good." Cindy started moving her shoulders to the beat of the music. "So, did you go to any of the Super Bowl parties when you were in Detroit?"

"Cindy, she lives in Detroit, remember?" Rachel said with a giggle.

"They have nice parties," Cindy said, ignoring Rachel and not waiting for an answer from Shanika. "Especially the ones the sports agents give. But there's nothing like the Oscar parties. Those really get wild."

Shanika's eyes widened. "You go to the Oscar parties? Really?"

"Oh yeah. Every year. The Elton John party is the best as far as hobnobbing, but I'm going to tell you that black guy . . . what's his name? Jamie Foxx? He's throws the best party."

Now, see, Shanika thought, *this is what I'm talking about. These girls are living it up. This is the kind of life I'm supposed to be living—flying to different cities just to go to a party and hanging out with people like Jamie Foxx.*

"Don't forget the George Clooney party, that was wild," Rachel added.

"My favorite was the one Will Smith and Jada Pinkett gave this year. That party was da bomb! Now that was really da bomb. Everybody who was anybody was there," Tina chimed in.

Cindy snorted. "You mean everybody who's anybody in hip-hop. But, yeah, it was wild." She started moving her shoulders to the music again. "You should go with us next year, Nikkie. Everybody should make it out to the Oscar-night parties at least once, don't you think?"

"I do, I do think," Shanika said as she took a sip from the new fresh cosmo the waitress placed down in front of her minutes before. She was getting giddy, not just from the drinks, but from the whole experience. Yes, this was the life she wanted to live, and maybe these girls were the ticket. Thank God Cindy lost her stupid cell phone. "Let me know your plans, I'd love to meet up with all of you."

"Good. And then there's always the Sundance Film Festival in Utah," Rachel said. "Now, those I prefer to the Oscars."

"That's because the films are more, how they call it? Um"—Cindy raised her glass up to her chin, tilted her head slightly, and pursed her lips—"more avant-garde."

"The Oscars are so commercial and the Sundance films are independent and more entertaining in my view," Rachel said defensively.

"They're just more snooty. And the parties are, too," Cindy said, waving her hand.

"Now, that's the truth," Tina said with a nod of her head. "Snooty and boring as shit. Everyone putting on airs."

Shanika listened in amazement as the girls argued about Oscar, Sundance, NBA All-Star, and Super Bowl parties, before moving on to the Golden Globe parties, which they finally agreed were the most interesting of all, and singer Prince's party was the best of the Golden Globe bashes. Then the talk moved on to the best hotels, and then back to celebrity parties. And Shanika hung on every word.

Shanika finished her drink—her fifth or sixth, she'd lost count—and took another look around the club. More people were drifting in, and the dance floor was finally getting a little crowded. After another hour or so, Cindy finally got on the floor and started dancing wildly. She wasn't bad, but she wasn't good, either. She mainly moved her shoulders to the music and waved her hands in the air without ever moving her feet. Still, she was graceful, and it was hard to keep your eyes off her.

"Come on out here," Cindy said when the next song came on.

Shanika needed no further encouragement, and soon she, Rachel, and Tina were on the floor with Cindy, each doing their individual thing, not seeming to care how they looked or who was watching. While there were lots of couples on the floor, Cindy and her friends seemed to care less about having a partner, and instead just formed a cluster and did their thing out on the floor. When one man tried to pull Cindy off from the cluster for a private dance, she reached down and grabbed his crotch, then pushed him away and continued to boogie with her friends.

Everybody seemed to know Cindy, and wanted to dance close by her, but she was in a world of her own. She opened her eyes only momentarily when someone tapped her on the shoulder to say hello, gave them a half-smile, and then went back into her reverie.

This girl is wild, Shanika thought. *This whole scene is wild. And I love it.*

They stayed on the floor for six songs, then made their way back to the table, where fresh drinks awaited them. Seven or eight small groups of people stopped by the table to talk to them—all of them young, hip, and beautiful.

She suddenly looked at her watch and saw that it was already 2 a.m. How did that happen? She had to be on the train at 7 a.m., which meant she had to check out by 5:30 or so to make sure she got there on time.

She quickly stood up. "Oh no, I have to get out of here!"

Cindy grabbed her arm and pulled her back down. "Oh, come on, you just got here! The night's still young!"

"I know, and, believe me, I normally party a lot later than this, but I've got to check out of the hotel in just a few hours to get my . . ." Shanika hesitated, then said, "To catch my flight." No sense in letting her newfound friends know she was so broke she was actually taking a train from New York all the way back to Detroit.

Cindy drew her head back in surprise. "What time is your flight?"

"I think it's like seven," Shanika lied.

"Oh, you're insane! Why are you flying out so early?" Rachel asked.

"You know how it is." Shanika shrugged. "I waited until the last minute and I had to take what I could get."

"Well, that's just not going to cut it." Cindy snapped open her cell phone and hit a button. "Hello, Maureen? Did I wake you up? I'm sorry, I didn't realize the time. Listen, can you find out if there's any flights leaving for Detroit this afternoon, and if so, I want you to book a flight for my friend." She paused. "Yes, I do want you to take care of it now—you're my travel agent, aren't you? Look, I don't want to argue. Just get on the computer or whatever it is you do, and book a flight to Detroit for my friend. Call me back when you have the info." Cindy snapped the telephone shut.

Shanika put her hand over Cindy's. "You don't have to do that. I can catch my original flight. Call her back and tell her to forget it."

Cindy shrugged. "Well, she's up now, so it would probably

just piss her off if I called her back and canceled. Besides, this way you can stay out with us longer."

"But how am I going to pay for it?"

"Cindy should pay for it, since she's the one making all of your plans for you all of a sudden," Rachel said with a disapproving look.

"Well, as a matter of fact, I was just going to say the ticket's on me." Cindy flipped her hair and turned to Shanika. "As a thanks for returning my cell phone, okay?"

"Well," Shanika hesitated.

"Well, nothing," Cindy said as her cell phone started ringing. "It's all a done deal, anyway. I'm sure this is Maureen calling back."

"Hello. Yes, I think four p.m. will be fine. What time does it get to Detroit? At seven? That'll be great."

"Good Lord, Cindy, don't you think you should at least consult Nikkie to make sure those times work for her?" Rachel tapped her fingernails on the table as she spoke.

"Her name is Nikkie. I don't know. Hold on, you can ask her yourself. And just charge the ticket to the family account." Cindy passed the telephone to Shanika. "She needs your full name. And move over. I have to go to the ladies' room."

"Hi. It's S-H-A-N-I-K-A and the last name is J-E-N-K-I-N-S." Shanika quickly spelled into the telephone, her head turned away from Rachel and Tina, who were engrossed in their own conversation; probably talking about Cindy now that she'd walked away. "You got it? Great. A window seat will be fine, thanks. You have the seat number already? Oh, good. Seat 3A, did you say?" Shanika had to catch herself from gasping out loud. Wouldn't 3A be in the first-class section? It wasn't enough that she was upgrading from a twenty-four-hour train trip to a three-hour airplane flight, but she was actually going to be flying first class? Wow! "Okay, I've got that. Seat 3A. Wonderful. Thanks so much. Do you want to hold on for Cindy? She went to the ladies' room. Oh, okay, I'll tell her. And thanks, again." Shanika snapped the telephone closed. "Wow. What a night," she said out loud.

"What's that?" Cindy said as she returned to the table.

"I was just saying this is really turning out to be a pretty good night. Thanks for the ticket."

"No problem," Cindy said, taking her seat.

"Hey, here comes Jovanna," Rachel said.

"Uh-huh. I bumped into her in the ladies' room and invited her to join us. She should be good for a couple of laughs. She was telling me a funny story about her trip to Milan." Cindy looked around the table. "How about we go ahead and get a bottle of champagne? I'm tired of cosmos."

Shanika looked up and noticed the willowy blond model she'd almost bumped into earlier approaching their table.

"What's wrong?" Rachel asked when she noticed the expression on Shanika's face.

"Nothing."

"No, there's something wrong." Rachel followed her gaze. "Do you know Jovanna?"

"Is that her name? I don't know her, but I saw her earlier."

Cindy put her arm around Shanika's shoulders in a chummy manner. "Did she try to hit on you? Rumor is she's a lesbo."

"No, but she did get smart with me," Shanika said just as Jovanna reached the table.

"Hey, Cindy!" she said in a heavy Italian-accented voice. "As usual you're the life of the party, eh?"

Cindy withdrew her arm from Shanika's shoulders, then glanced at Rachel and Tina before looking over and addressing Jovanna.

"Why are you over here talking to us?"

Jovanna jerked her head back in surprise, but managed to keep the smile on her face. "What?"

"I asked you"—Cindy picked up her cosmo and took a sip—"why are you over here talking to us?"

"Didn't you invite me to join you?"

"Well, yes. It's just that"—Cindy nudged Shanika under the table—"it's just that we've decided we don't like you."

All the girls at the table burst into loud laughter, while Jovanna stood there, seemingly in shock.

"In fact"—Cindy leaned forward—"I think we hate you." She tapped Shanika on the back. "What do you think? We hate her, right?"

Shanika gave Jovanna the same up-and-down look the model had given her earlier, then nodded and said, "Decidedly so."

The girls burst out in laughter again.

Jovanna looked at them, one by one, then tossed her hair and said, "Whatever" before stomping off.

"Now, see, that's exactly what she told me," Shanika said, pounding on the table with laughter.

She looked at Cindy, who was laughing so hard she was gasping for breath. She was a trip, arrogant and sometimes rude, but she sure was fun. So were Rachel and Tina, but Cindy was definitely the ringleader, and it was obvious—to her, anyway—that Cindy welcomed her into the group. Imagine dissing Jovanna like that on her behalf. Oh yeah, it was juvenile, but it was funny. And Jovanna did deserve it.

"Girl, did you see that look on that stupid bitch's face? I was waiting for her to say something to me because I woulda stepped to her," Tina said as she wiped the tears of laughter from her face.

"Oh, you 'woulda stepped to her,' huh?" Cindy gave Tina a shove, then looked at Shanika. "You have to excuse her. In case you haven't figured it out yet, Tina is our resident wigga."

Shanika stopped mid-giggle. "Your what?" she asked slowly.

"Our resident wigga," Cindy repeated. She leaned in closer to Shanika. "I didn't know what a 'wigga' was, either, until one of my black friends told me. A wigga is a white person who wants to be a . . . you know . . . a nigger."

"Oh please, Cindy," Tina snapped.

"As if I'm lying," Cindy retorted. She turned back to Shanika. "Tina is always trying to act all hip and down, or whatever they call it. Always using black slang and everything. You'll get used to it."

"She used to do it in front of black people, too, but after Jasmine called her a 'wigga,' she stopped that nonsense," Rachel added.

Shanika took a deep breath to try and calm the butterflies that had suddenly invaded her stomach. "Who's Jasmine?"

"Jasmine's our black friend. She moved with her family to Brazil a couple of weeks ago," Cindy answered. "See, we're a diversified group." She giggled. "Me, I'm the spoiled arrogant one. Rachel's the refined sophisticated one. Tina's the . . . well, you know, the wigga. And Jasmine's the black one."

"Well, now that Jasmine's out of the country, I guess we need to get another black," Rachel interjected.

Shanika's breath quickened as her mind raced. So Tina wasn't using Ebonics because she knew Shanika was black, but because she thought she wasn't. They all thought she was white. That is what Cindy was saying, right?

"So," she said slowly, "have you picked Jasmine's replacement yet?"

"No hurry. I was getting tired of her, anyway. She was beginning to act as spoiled as me. She actually thought she was better than me, I think," Cindy said while pouring herself a glass of champagne. "Nope, no hurry at all." She raised her glass, spilling a bit of its contents onto the table. "Drink up, everybody! The night's still young!"

Shanika snatched up her glass and raised it high above her head. "That's right. The night's still young, and so are we. Young and beautiful, and the world is ours!"

"Girl, you're too much." Cindy slapped her on the arm and then turned to Rachel. "Isn't she too much?"

"Yep." Rachel nodded. "She's too much."

"You know what?" Cindy slapped Shanika on the arm again. "You should come up with us to Cancun this weekend!" Cindy looked around the table. "Oh, my god, that's such a great idea!" she said as if she hadn't come up with it herself. "Nikkie should come with us to Cancun!"

Shanika giggled. "Just like that? You want me to go with you to Cancun?" She shook her head. "Girl, you are such a trip."

"No, I'm not a trip, but Cancun is," Cindy said as she took a long slurp of champagne.

"But I can't just pick up and fly to Mexico anytime I want," Shanika protested. "I mean, I'm not rich or anything."

"So what? I am." Cindy giggled. "The trip's on me, okay? Let's just say I'm still paying back for the cell phone thing, okay? Like you said, we're young, beautiful, and the world is ours. So let's enjoy!"

chapter six

It had been one whole week, and still no word from Cindy. Not that she could really have jetted to Cancun with them, but it would have been nice to think they were serious when they told her they wanted her to do so. The ten hours she'd spent with them had spoiled her, as did the first-class flight to Detroit. Now she was back in her hometown and it was as if she'd never left. Well, the air-conditioning was finally working, thank goodness, but all else was the same. Her father was still half-drunk from beer and sitting in front of the television, her mother was still cooking and cleaning, and she herself was still lying on the worn green shag carpet in the living room, bored as all hell with nothing to do. Nothing but think of her time in New York, and try to figure out a way to get back and resume the new life she'd so briefly and wonderfully experienced. She was young and beautiful, just like Cindy, Rachel, and Tina. Why shouldn't she be having as good a time as they? Of course they were rich, and she wasn't, but she'd let them know she wasn't and it didn't seem to bother them. And so what if they thought she was white? It wasn't like she told them she was; she just didn't tell them she was black. It wasn't like it had actually come up in the conversation.

She pushed from her mind—violently shoved, actually—the fact that although it hadn't come up, there had been opportunity to tell them. Especially when they mentioned Jasmine.

"What are you thinking about, White Girl?"

Shanika looked up from the magazine she'd been absently flipping through. She hadn't heard Joseph enter the room, but there he stood.

"Nothing," she answered sullenly.

"You've got to be thinking of something. You're turning those pages too fast for you to actually be reading." Joseph walked across the room and took a seat in the tattered brown armchair, which was as old as he was. "And the look on your face says that whatever's on your mind isn't too pleasant."

Shanika stretched and pushed the magazine away. "I was just wondering how long I'ma have to wait to find out I got that job in New York."

Joseph studied his sister a moment before speaking again. She'd changed since she'd returned from New York. She was on edge, apprehensive even. Shanika was always a daydreamer—it was one of the endearing things about her—but now she seemed always far away. And when her mind was on the present, she seemed dissatisfied. What could have happened during her trip? he wondered. Did she meet some guy? He couldn't help but notice that she jumped every time her cell phone rang, and rushed to look at the caller ID to find out who was calling her. The look of disappointment that crossed her face when she realized it wasn't the call she was waiting for was also apparent. If Paxon & Green were calling, they'd likely be calling the house phone, so it had to be some guy she'd met, whom she was waiting to hear from.

"You know, Nikkie, you haven't been out since you've been home. Why don't you call Toni or Jenny and see if they want to go to that club you guys like to hang out in."

"That club is lame," Shanika grumbled.

"Well, why don't you call them and see if they want to go to the movies or something. I'll give you some cash."

Shanika grabbed the magazine again and started furiously flipping through the pages again. "Because they're lame, too."

"You've known them almost twenty years and all of a sudden they're lame?"

"Yeah. They're lame. What of it?"

"Fine." Joseph shrugged. "They're lame. Well, how about I take you to the movies? Or am I lame, too?"

"I don't feel like going anywhere. Thanks for asking, though." Shanika didn't bother to look up.

Joseph cleared his throat. "Look, Nikkie, I know you have your heart set on that job in New York, but if you don't get it, it's not the end of the world. Ma said the church is looking for a new administrative assistant since Miss Rose retired. Why don't you just—"

"Paxon and Green are going to call. I *know* I've got the job," Shanika snapped.

"You're just that sure, huh?"

Shanika jumped up. "Yes! Yes, I am that sure! Why is it so hard to believe that they would hire me, Joe? I mean, just because you don't think I'm smart and capable—"

"I never said that!"

"You didn't have to. You treat me like I'm stupid, and you obviously think I am. You don't think I'm smart enough to land a cushy job in New York. You don't think I could survive in New York. You think I'm supposed to just lie around here and maybe get some stupid administrative assistant job at some stupid church!"

Joseph slowly stood up. "What the hell is wrong with you, Shanika? I didn't say any of that. I was just saying . . ."

"I know what you were saying. And don't call me 'White Girl.' "

Joseph drew his head back in surprise. "I didn't call you 'White Girl.' I called you by your name. Shanika."

Shanika put her hands on her hips. "You called me 'White Girl' when you walked into the room, though, didn't you?"

"Well, what if I did? You know I didn't mean anything by it." Joseph stepped back. "What the hell is wrong with you, all of a sudden?"

"For your information"—Shanika started jabbing her finger in his chest—"I'm black. I'm just as black as you."

"I know that—"

"Well, do you know that it's because I'm not considered black enough that I didn't get the job?"

"What!" Joseph said in a hoarse whisper.

"What are you talking about? Who said you're not black enough?" Shanika and Joseph turned at the sound of their mother's voice. Rina stood there, in the middle of the floor, wiping her hands on a dish towel and looking back and forth at them. "What do you mean you weren't black enough for the job?"

"Nothing, Mama," Shanika said finally. She took a deep breath and started to leave the room.

"Girl, get your ass right back in here and finish what you

were saying," Rina said in a low voice that sounded like a growl. "Don't you play with me, hear?"

Shanika turned to face her mother. "Mama, I did get a call from that lady at Paxon and Green that I was telling you about. Mrs. Randolph. She told me—"

"What? You said you hadn't heard from them yet!" Rina clutched the dish towel tightly and sank into the chair that Joseph had vacated. "When did she call?"

"The day after I got home."

"Why didn't you tell someone?" Joseph demanded.

"Because I'm hoping she's going to call back," Shanika said defiantly.

"Well, what did she say, child?" Rina asked.

Shanika took a deep breath. "She said that Paxon and Green were looking for a black to fill the job. They have to keep the numbers up to meet their affirmative action quotas. When the guy in charge of their Affirmative Action Committee, that guy Jeff Samuels I mentioned, when he got my application and saw my name and saw that I went to an HBCU, he assumed I was black. But then when he saw me in person, he assumed I was white."

Rina threw her hands up in the air. "Well, why don't you just tell him that you're black?"

"That's what I suggested to Mrs. Randolph. She knows I'm black. But she said that if we told him, he still probably wouldn't let them hire me, because he'd consider it a slap in the face of the Affirmative Action Committee. They want the position to go to someone who everyone can look at and know they're black."

"Joseph"—Rina turned to her son with pleading eyes—

"they can't do that, can they? Can't she sue them or something?"

"Of course, Mama." Joseph started rubbing his mother's back.

"Oh, Mama, that wouldn't work," Shanika said impatiently. "They'd never admit that was the reason. They'd just point to my inexperience and say they didn't hire me because of that."

"Well, wouldn't this Mrs. Randolph person stand up for you in court? You said she's the one who told you what the real deal is, right?" Joseph asked.

"Do you really think she's going to say something like that in court?" Shanika guffawed. "She'd lose her job and I still probably wouldn't win my case. She told me what she told me on the down low."

Joseph sat on the arm of Rina's chair. "Nikkie, what did you mean when you said you're waiting for Mrs. Randolph to call you back?"

Shanika crossed her arms, a defiant expression on her face. "Mrs. Randolph said—she suggested—that I wait and let them fill that affirmative action position, and that she'd do what she could to hire me in another trainee position in another one of their offices."

"I see," Joseph said slowly. "A trainee position, but not an affirmative action trainee position."

"Right."

"So, basically, a white trainee position?"

Shanika hesitated. This was exactly why she hadn't told them about her conversation with Mrs. Randolph in the first place. There was no way they could understand.

"A white trainee position?" Joseph asked again.

"It's not a white trainee position," Shanika finally said. "It's just a trainee position."

"So let me get this straight. The position you interviewed for was for a black trainee. But since you're not black enough to get that, as you say, you're going to interview for a regular trainee position. Is that right?"

Shanika jutted out her chin. "Basically."

"But if you're a trainee, and you're not a black trainee, wouldn't that make you a white trainee?" Joseph said in a level voice.

"It would just make me a trainee."

"Now, who thinks the other person is stupid, Shanika?" Joseph's voice rose a couple of decibels. "This Mrs. Randolph is saying you should go in there and be white."

"No, she's not!" Shanika walked over to her mother and knelt at her knee. "Mama, all it is, it's like this, in this new trainee position it doesn't matter what color you are, and in the other it does. And I'm not the color they want."

"Yes, but . . . well, I mean . . . I don't understand. One position you have to be black and the other you don't?" Rina started twisting the dish towel in her lap.

"Exactly, Mama. I don't have to say I'm white. I don't have to say anything at all for this other position coming up."

"Then are you going to tell them you're black?" Rina's eyes took on a pleading look again. "I mean, if it doesn't matter, it doesn't matter, right?"

"That's right, Mama. It doesn't matter."

"So you will tell them?"

"Mama, they're not going to ask."

"So, why should you tell, right?" Joseph said in a steely

voice. "It's like the military thing with gays, huh? 'Don't ask, don't tell'?"

"Come on, Joseph. It's not like that! If they don't ask, there's no reason for me to mention it, not until I actually have the job. You know, just to make sure."

Rina grasped Shanika's shoulder tightly. "But as soon as you got the job, you'd tell them, honey? Wouldn't you?"

"Of course, Mama," Shanika said soothingly. "You know I'm not trying to pass or anything."

"Oh, Mama." Joseph jumped up from the arm of the chair. "Who is she trying to kid? That's exactly what she's talking about doing."

"Oh, dear God, Joseph. That's not what the girl is saying."

"Mama, that's exactly what she's saying. Oh, not coming out directly and saying it, but that's what the deal is. Let's call a spade a spade."

"Funny choice of words," Shanika muttered.

"Yeah, very funny." Joseph shot her an evil look. "And on point, too."

"Well, why shouldn't I pass for white if it's going to help me get this job?" Shanika stood up and faced her brother. "All my life I've been made to feel like I didn't fit in as a black."

"Shanika, that's not true," Rina protested.

"Mama, you know it is!" she said, turning to her mother. "How many times did I come home crying because the kids teased me because I was so light? How many times did I come home beaten up and bruised after being jumped by a gang of girls who thought I was trying to act like I was white?"

"Oh, so your solution is that now you're going to be white, huh?" Joseph challenged her.

"No, I'm not going to be white. I'm black, and I know I'm

black, but since I finally have an opportunity for my complexion to work in my favor, why shouldn't I take it? It's not like I'm the first person to do it."

Rina put her hands up to her ears. "Will the two of you please stop shouting?"

"Nikkie, people used to pass because they had to. Because they were discriminated against, because they couldn't get jobs—"

"Oh, for Christ's sake, Joe! Isn't that what I just said happened to me here in this case? Only I'm not being discriminated against because I'm black, but because I'm not black enough!"

"It's not the same thing, Nikkie. You can get a job, you just can't get that particular job," Joseph shouted. "You're just lazy, impatient, and spoiled. You want what you want when you want it."

Nikkie crossed her arms and glared at him. "Yeah, that's right. And I'm going to get what I want. I'm going to get this job."

"By passing for white." Joseph's lips curled. "But then again, you've always figured out some way to get what you want, haven't you? And you've never been called on it, because you're 'our darling Shanika, and isn't she cute?' Well, you know what? You're grown now, Nikkie. And you're not so damn cute anymore."

"I never said I was cute."

"It's not cute to turn your back on your family in order to get a job, and it's downright ugly to turn your back on your race to get one," Joseph continued, ignoring Shanika's interruption. "Turn your back on your race if you want to, but you'd best remember, when you burn bridges like that, you're going to have a helluva time trying to cross back over to the other side when you need to do so."

"I never said I was turning my back on anyone," Shanika shouted. "Don't be trying to twist my words!"

"Well, then, what do you call it?" Joseph shouted back. "If you're going to pretend to be white, you can't very well have pictures of your own mother on your desk, now can you? And I can't just stop by and visit to take you to lunch without you introducing me as someone other than your own brother, now can I?"

"Stop being stupid. I'm going to be in New York. You planning on coming out all the way there to take me to lunch?"

"That's not the point."

"Well, then, what is the damn point?" Shanika challenged him.

"Now who acting stupid?" Joseph threw up his hands. "The point is you going to acknowledge me if I did want to stop by your office."

"Yeah, well, as far as I'm concerned, the point is moot. Like I said, you're not coming to New York anytime soon to take me to lunch, and by the time you did get around to it, I wouldn't have to act like I didn't know you or anything, because by then I'll let everyone know I'm black."

"Well, that's mighty white of you. But don't do me any favors, because as far as I'm concerned, if you go through with this charade you don't have a brother. And I sure as hell don't have a sister."

"So, now, who's turning their back on who?" Shanika poked out her lips. "You talk about me disowning you and Mama, but it sounds like you're the one disowning me."

"Joe, your sister's just . . ."

Joseph bent down and kissed his mother on the cheek. "Mama, I've got to go. I'll give you a call later, okay?"

"But, Joseph"—Rina put her hand on her son's arm—"I don't want you and your sister fighting like this. You know I hate when you fight. And she's not—"

"Mama, she can do whatever she wants. I'm not going to fight with her. She knows how I feel. You know how I feel. And I would have thought you'd feel the same way—"

"But, Joe—"

Joseph held his hands up in front of him. "Mama, I'm not saying another word. I'm not even mad. I just don't even want to talk about it anymore." He kissed her again and headed out the door.

Shanika watched him go, not sure what to say. She'd known she was going to have to have this conversation, and she knew it was going to be tough. She also knew she hadn't handled it well.

"Okay, Joseph," she finally called after him. "I'll see you later."

"Yeah, okay, *White Girl*."

The words stung Shanika like never before.

chapter seven

June 2007

"Why not beat them at their own game?" Mrs. Randolph said as she cut into her prime rib at Morton's Steakhouse. "I do think you should change your name because Shanika really is too Afrocentric-sounding. Eventually, someone will catch wise if you keep it, but otherwise, it's not going to be like you're lying to anyone. Send in your résumé again, with your new name, but otherwise the same information."

"But won't they be able to tell?" Shanika asked nervously. "I mean, my résumé doesn't say that I'm black, but it does have that I attended an HBCU and that I was secretary of the African-American student union."

"Take out the African-American student union thing, but don't worry about your school. Hell, most black people don't know that Delaware State is an HBCU, and I know the white folks at Paxon and Green don't know."

Shanika fingered her napkin as she listened to the composed woman sitting across the table. Two weeks had passed since Mrs. Randolph's first telephone call saying that she wouldn't get the job, and she'd all but given up hope on the second position when Mrs. Randolph called to say she was in Detroit for the National Black Public Relations Society Conference and wanted to meet with her for lunch.

"And you really don't think I'll be caught?"

Mrs. Randolph gave a little laugh. "No, I really don't think you'll be caught. And I don't believe I really have to convince you of that fact. Come on, now," Mrs. Randolph lowered her voice. "Are you going to tell me that most everyone who looks at you doesn't already assume you're white?"

"Well, yes, but . . ."

"And are you going to tell me that when it's to your advantage you don't sometimes let them keep that assumption?" Mrs. Randolph's eyes twinkled.

Shanika's mind flew back to her meeting with Cindy and her friends. "Well, I mean, there have been some occasions, but . . ."

"Well, this would be one time that it would truly be to your advantage. So take advantage, my dear child, take advantage. The only one who might present a challenge is Jeff Samuels, but he's retiring in two weeks."

Shanika nodded and took a sip of her Diet Coke. It sounded easy—too easy, in fact. And why would . . .

"I'm surprised you haven't asked why I'm willing to help you with this little charade," Mrs. Randolph said suddenly.

Shanika smiled. "I was just wondering about that."

"Well, to be honest, it would be like my little private joke on them."

"What do you mean?"

"Shanika, I've been at Paxon and Green for almost thirty-five years now." She paused and smiled at Shanika's expression. "Yes, thirty-five years. I look good for my age, don't I? But like they say, black don't crack."

Both women laughed.

"As I was saying, I've been at Paxon and Green for thirty-five years. I was one of the original affirmative action babies at Paxon and Green, hired back in the seventies when large liberal firms were scrambling to bring in minorities to show just how liberal they were. But even though I graduated summa cum laude from NYU with a marketing degree, the furthest I've ever gotten in the firm is personal assistant. Now, don't get me wrong." Mrs. Randolph dabbed at the corner of her mouth with her napkin. "Personal assistant to the president of a Fortune 500 firm is a very big deal, and the salary and the benefits are better than I ever dreamt about, growing up in North Philadelphia, but the fact is, I had the potential to be so much more. I should be in line for the presidency when Kadinsky retires next year. But I'm not even going to be considered. Now, is that because I'm black? Who's to say? But I will say that in all the time I've been there, and we've already established I've been there for way too long, there's not been one black public relations associate who has even moved into the vice presidency, no less been in a position to take over the presidency."

"What about Mr. Samuels? Isn't he a vice president?"

Mrs. Randolph waved her hand. "Jeff is vice president of accounting. We also have a black vice president of human resources. And a Puerto Rican vice president of labor relations. But there's not one person of color in a prominent public relations position."

"I see."

"Do you?" Mrs. Randolph took another bite of her steak.

"Now, I'm not saying we haven't hired any blacks as public relations specialists, we certainly have. Quite a number. But they're always put in a position where they eventually crack their head on the infamous glass ceiling. They're put under one of the superstar specialists, helping out with large accounts, but never given one of their own so they can shine. The smart ones eventually get tired and leave to start their own firms. And with good reason. They're just not going to get far at Paxon and Green. History has proven that.

"Now, I'm going to be retiring very soon with a big fat pension and I'm going to spend my retirement basking in the glow of the Caribbean sun, but there would be nothing that would give me more pleasure than to have placed a spook inside of Paxon and Green's office door."

Shanika raised her eyebrows in surprise.

"Oh, come now, you have heard of the book *The Spook Who Sat by the Door*, haven't you?" Mrs. Randolph put her fork down. "By Sam Greenlee?"

"Oh! Oh yeah. I had to read it for second-year lit. About the black guy who went to work for the CIA or the FBI or something, and learned all of their secrets and used it against them."

"Exactly. Well, I'd get a real kick out of putting in my own little spook." Mrs. Randolph chuckled. "I'd love to see the look on their face if you moved up the ranks, became president, and then they find out you're actually black."

Shanika paused, trying to take this all in. Was this woman saying that she thought she had what it takes to be the president of Paxon & Green? Wouldn't that just be something? Boy, she could just see her name engraved on the office door.

"That's not to say you'd ever become president, of course. I wouldn't expect for you to pass for that long, just long enough to position yourself in the company," Mrs. Randolph said as if reading her mind. "And when they did find out, it would be my own little joke on them." She reached over and placed her hand over Shanika's. "Our little joke."

It had been just as simple as Mrs. Randolph said it would be. A couple of forms to fill out over the Internet, a thirty-nine-dollar filing fee, and voila! Shanika Jenkins was now Nicole Jensen. There was no hassle to it at all. She took the certification she received in the mail to the Social Security office, and very soon she had a new Social Security card. A trip to the Bureau of Vital Statistics and she even had a new birth certificate. Of course, she hadn't told her family what she was doing, but then again, why should she bother them with minor details? The bottom line was she was going to be an official employee of Paxon & Green, and that was all that mattered. Her dreams were finally going to come true.

Did she feel guilt? Not even a little bit. Or none that she cared to admit to having. It wasn't like she was disowning her family, she reasoned. She wasn't going to be like those people passing for white that she'd read about—people who back in the thirties and forties would walk past their family in the street and not even speak. Of course it wouldn't be an issue, since she'd move to New York and her family was in Detroit, but even if they had been in the same city, she'd never do that to them.

If anything, it was her family that seemed to be trying to disown her. At least Joseph. Rina wasn't happy about the prospect of her passing, and let her know in no uncertain terms that she raised her to be proud of her heritage. In the end, though, she relented when Shanika promised it would only be a temporary passing, and only for the purpose of getting the job. Peter seemed to have no opinion on the matter, but then he seldom had opinions about whatever happened in the household. Joseph, on the other hand, was another matter. He would have nothing to do with her in the weeks before she left Detroit to return to New York. But Shanika was confident that she'd eventually win him over, she always had.

But first things first, it was important that she land that trainee position, or she would have gone through all this trouble for nothing.

A week later the butterflies in her stomach were flying around so furiously she thought she was going to be sick as the elevator door opened and she stepped into the offices of Paxon & Green.

"I have an appointment with Mrs. Randolph," she said, trying to keep her voice as steady as possible. "My name is Nicole Jensen."

It was the same receptionist whom she had met the first time she'd walked into the office in May, but, thankfully, there was no glint of recognition in the woman's eyes.

"If you'll just have a seat, Miss Jensen, I'll let Mrs. Randolph know that you're here. Would you like some coffee?"

chapter eight

Nikkie was sitting alone at a table in the company cafeteria, waiting for her new teammates, Yanna Goldberg and Susan Flanders, who were both still placing their orders, when she saw a beautiful six-two milk-chocolate beauty purposefully striding toward her.

"Hi," she said when she reached Nikkie. "I'm Jenice Hanford." She placed her tray on the table and stuck out her hand. "I'm supposing you're the new girl they hired Tuesday. Nicole Jensen, right?"

Before Nikkie could answer, Yanna was at the table.

"Hey, Jenice," she said as she took a seat. "I see you've met Nikkie. She's going to be working with Susan and me."

A confused look suddenly appeared on Jenice's face. Had she been mistaken? she suddenly wondered. "Yes, I was just introducing myself," she said while taking a closer look at Nikkie. No, she was pretty sure she'd been right.

"Thanks for taking the last apple pie, Yanna," Susan said as she took the seat next to Nikkie. "Hey, Jenice," she said absentmindedly. "I heard you're working on the new Brunson account with Hal. How's that going?"

"Fine. Just fine," Jenice said in a suddenly uncertain voice.

When she'd first seen Nicole at the table, she'd assumed she was by herself, and had also originally thought her to be white. But on closer inspection, she began to have her doubts, then came to the conclusion that, yes, the woman was actually an African-American. It was nothing she could put her finger on, but she just knew. She would have introduced herself either way, but she had to admit that she was elated to find another African-American employed at Paxon & Green. But now, with Yanna's and Susan's actions, she was suddenly unsure.

Nikkie knew that Yanna and Susan had no idea what was going through Jenice's mind, but she knew exactly what the woman was thinking. She'd seen the way Jenice looked at her before walking her way, taking a look, then a deeper look, before approaching her. Jenice was sure, or pretty sure, that Nikkie was black, and had come over to introduce herself to her new compatriot—and while Nikkie had not yet spoken or given any indication of where her head was at, Yanna and Susan were making it clear that Nikkie was one of them. Oh, not in any conscious way, but in a way that any black person would pick up on. Jenice knew that if Nikkie were black, both Yanna and Susan would have made a big deal about introducing them, as if presenting her with a gift. It was just what white folks did. Instead, they acted like Nikkie was no big deal. Jenice now had to reconsider her first assessment of Nikkie.

Jenice reflected that this was Nikkie's opportunity to let everyone know who she really was. After all, she already had the job. There was no reason to continue to let people think she was white.

"It's nice to meet you, Jenice," Nikkie said in a tone she knew was just a little too formal. She couldn't help herself; after all, this was the woman who had gotten the job she'd wanted in the first place—the woman who was so much blacker than she. The woman who, in a way, forced her to pass in the first place. Well, okay, not really, but Nikkie still felt a sense of resentment against the woman. "Why don't you join us," she said with a phony smile.

Jenice's look of confusion was suddenly replaced with an icy squint, and Nikkie felt a sudden sense of panic. She was about to be outed.

"No thanks. I was actually planning to eat in my office. I've got some work to catch up on." She picked up her tray. "It was so very good to meet you, Nicole," she said.

"Please call me Nikkie. All my friends do," Nikkie said weakly.

"Oh well, thank you!" Jenice said a little too enthusiastically. "I'm sure I'll see you around, Nikkie. Yanna, Susan, see you guys later."

Nikkie watched as Jenice marched out of the cafeteria, looking neither left nor right as she exited. *That's one pissed-off sister*, she realized. *I think I've made a stupid mistake.* But how was she supposed to handle it? Should she have grinned and said, "What's up, my sister?" And come on, it wasn't her fault that Yanna and Susan thought she was white. She never told them she was. It wasn't like she was actually "passing," kind of "passing." *Then why was I suddenly worried about being outted?* She pushed the question out of her mind.

"Hmm, does it seem like Jenice had an attitude about something?" Susan said.

Yanna shrugged. "You know how she gets sometimes. Hal's probably riding her too hard. You know how he gets. That boy's a workaholic, and he expects everyone else to be, too."

"Who's Hal?" Nikkie said, now that her nerves were finally beginning to settle.

"Hal Richardson," Susan answered. "You'll probably meet him in the next day or so. He's the company golden boy, and can do no wrong. They even paid for him to go to a sanatorium when he had a nervous breakdown a couple of years ago, right here in the office. They forgave him even after he threatened to kill a janitor."

"Susan!" Yanna said sharply. "You don't know that for a fact. That's just office gossip."

"Well, I'm not the only one who's heard it," Susan said defiantly.

"That doesn't mean you need to spread it," Yanna said reprovingly. She turned to Nikkie. "Actually, Hal did go through a bad spot right after he found out that his brother died, but they were very understanding here. Probably because Mr. Kadinsky just lost his wife and knew how he felt. The bottom line is Hal's been fine since. He's really brilliant and knows his stuff. Jenice should feel lucky to be teamed with someone like him. She'll learn a lot working with Hal."

The words Mrs. Randolph had spoken at their dinner in Detroit suddenly rushed back into Nikkie's head: "They're put under one of the superstar specialists, helping out with large accounts, but never given one of their own so they can shine."

No, Nikkie decided as she took a spoonful of her too-sweet custard pudding, this was not the time to announce her blackness.

chapter nine

"So, have you found an apartment yet?"

"Still looking. I didn't think it would be so damn hard to find a place. I had a hard enough time talking the company into letting me stay in the corporate apartment for two weeks, I can't ask them for an extension," Nikkie said with a frown as she looked up from the classified section of the *New York Times,* which was spread open on her desk. "I was hoping to find a spot in the Village, but some of the places are going as high as five thousand a month. And that's just for a studio. Can you believe it?"

Yanna smiled. "Welcome to the Big Apple. Have you tried Brooklyn? It's still expensive, but not as expensive as Manhattan. I'm only paying twenty-five hundred for my place, and it's a one-bedroom."

Nikkie grimaced. "That's still more than I wanted to pay."

Yanna chuckled. "Well, good luck finding something cheaper."

"Well, have you looked in Harlem?" said a new voice. "There's some inexpensive apartments there."

Nikkie looked up at Jenice, who was leaning against the

wall of the cubicle. "Um, no, Jenice. Actually, I haven't had a chance to check out—"

"What are you talking about, Jenice?" Yanna interrupted. "The prices up there are as expensive as some of the places in the Village."

"Oh, I don't know, Yanna," Jenice said a little too nonchalantly. "Not every neighborhood in Harlem is as expensive as others. I mean, you'd probably have to live in some of the areas that are still predominantly *black*," she said, putting extra emphasis on the word, "but I'm sure that wouldn't be a problem for Nikkie." She pointedly looked at Nikkie. "Would it, Nikkie?"

It was obvious that Jenice was suspicious about her ethnicity, but she was almost certain the woman didn't know for sure. She certainly never came out and asked. But for the past week or so, Jenice's comments had been getting ever sharper.

"No, of c-course not," Nikkie stammered. "I'll have to check it out."

"Cool. I'll bring you in a copy of the *Amsterdam News*. You know about the *Amsterdam News*, right? The African-American paper? They have all the Harlem listings in there."

Yanna suddenly stood up and snapped her fingers. "Wait a minute. What's wrong with me!" She turned to Nikkie. "Do you remember me telling you about my cousin's roommate moving to Israel at the end of the month? Well, Sarah is looking for another roomie. They live on Seventy-first Street between Broadway and West End Avenue. A really good neighborhood. Beautiful apartment, spacious, lots of closet room, parquet floors, and just a half block from the subway. And if I'm not mistaken, I think your share of the rent would only come up to something like sixteen hundred dollars. Let me give Sarah a quick call."

"Seventy-first Street and Broadway?" Nikkie's brow furrowed. "What part of town would that be considered?"

"The Upper West Side," Jenice said dryly. "Don't worry, it's not Harlem. Only two subway stops away, though." She straightened up and pulled the strap of her pocketbook farther up her shoulder. "You have to make it a point to *pass* through sometime. You can do that, can't you?"

"Jenice," Yanna said before Nikkie could answer, "what are you doing this evening? My fiancé just got four tickets for tonight's performance of *The Color Purple* from a client. He's taking me, of course, but he also invited another client of his, this big-shot stockbroker that everyone's talking about. Tyrone Bennett, I think is his name. Wanna come along as a fourth?"

"No, sorry, I have karate class tonight. Thanks for asking."

"You sure?" Yanna walked over and nudged Jenice on the arm. "Jacob says he's very handsome."

"Oh, he does, does he?" Jenice grinned.

"No, don't even try it," Yanna said with a wave of her hand. "My man is secure enough in his masculinity that he can admit another man is handsome."

"Just kidding," Jenice said with a laugh. "But, no, I'm sorry. I'm going up for my purple belt in a couple of weeks, so I'm spending all my spare time in the dojo."

"Okay. Good luck with that," Yanna said with a smile.

"How come you didn't ask me?" Nikkie asked after Jenice left.

"Hmm? Oh. Well, you know, Bennett's black. I was trying to hook Jenice up. You can come if you'd like, though."

Nikkie's mind started racing. She'd love to go see *The Color Purple*. It was one of the hottest shows on Broadway, and prime tickets were going for something like four hundred dollars. And to be accompanying a handsome stockbroker would make it all the more pleasurable. "Well, I—"

Yanna snapped her fingers. "Wait a minute. I bet my next-door neighbor Sabrina would like to go. She's black, and always complaining how hard it is to find a good black man." Yanna walked over to Nikkie's desk, picked up the telephone and started dialing. "Oh, and I'll call my cousin and check when you'll be able to see the apartment."

"Okay," Nikkie said lamely. *Damn. There goes my date.*

"So, does Jenice know or doesn't she?" Nikkie asked in a plaintive tone when sitting in Mrs. Randolph's office a few hours later.

"I assume she does. At the very least, she strongly suspects. But I don't think you have anything to worry about," the older woman answered as she placed a couple of books in the large cardboard box on her desk. "She's not going to out you."

"She told you she knows?" Nikkie demanded.

"Actually, she asked me if I thought you were, and I told her I had no idea, and that I really didn't care." Mrs. Randolph took a framed certificate off the wall, wrapped it in Bubble Wrap, and also placed it in the box. "She pressed the issue, and insisted I had to know, so I asked her what difference would it make if you were. She said it didn't make any real difference, but it just irked the hell out of her that people feel they need to pass in this day and age. I advised her to get over it."

"What's her problem? And it's not like I'm really passing, you know. I never told anyone I'm white. The subject never came up, just like you said it wouldn't," Nikkie said impatiently. "But do you really think she's not going to say anything? What makes you think she won't?"

Mrs. Randolph sighed and sat down. "Nikkie, let me ask you something. How long do you intend to carry out your charade?"

Nikkie leaned back in her chair and crossed her arms. "What do you mean? This whole thing was your idea, remember."

"True, but the idea was for you to use your complexion to get the job, and you have it now. Are you *ever* planning on letting people know your true ethnicity?"

Nikkie fell silent. She'd been wondering about the same question.

Mrs. Randolph strummed her fingers on the desk. "Nikkie, I'm out of here in just two weeks, but you know I'm in your corner any way you want to play it. You wouldn't be the first person in the world to pass, nor will you be the last, but I do think you really need to give some thought to what you're doing. And you need to be honest with yourself."

Nikkie looked up. "What do you mean?"

"Well, don't say that since you haven't told people that you're white, you're not actually passing. You know you are, so be honest with yourself about it, okay?"

"But—"

Mrs. Randolph held up her hand. "Spare me the bullshit, I don't even want to hear it."

Nikkie once again fell silent.

"As I was saying," Mrs. Randolph continued, "you need to be honest with yourself. Honest about why you're passing, for instance. Obviously, it's not just so you could get your foot in the door, because you're now in. So is it so you can climb the corporate ladder? I wouldn't say that's a bad reason. But is that the only reason? For instance, do you pass only here at Paxon and Green, or in your personal life as well?"

"Only here," Nikkie said sullenly.

"Oh? So, do you have black friends outside the job, then?"

"I don't have any friends here in New York. I've only been here a few weeks, remember?" Nikkie said defensively.

"True, but I'm sure you've gone out at least a few times. Do you got out with anyone?"

Nikkie lowered her eyes. "I've gone out with Susan and her friends a couple of times. And I've gone bike riding with Yanna and her fiancé. Just to pass some time."

"All of whom are white?"

Nikkie said nothing.

"So you've managed to find personal time to spend with white friends, but no blacks. Did you have black friends when you were in Detroit?"

"Of course."

"But somehow, you haven't found time to connect with any since you've been here in New York"

"I will. I just haven't . . ."

"Nikkie, it seems to me that you're making a life choice, and if that's the case, you need to fully consider the repercussions. For instance, if you're going to continue passing, what are you going to do about your family? For that matter, how is your family taking it?"

Nikkie sighed. "My mother seems to be taking it well, although she keeps asking me the same thing you are: when am

I going to let people know I'm black? My father . . . well, I'm not even sure he knows. My brother, on the other hand, is furious. He's barely speaking to me."

Mrs. Randolph nodded sympathetically, then asked, "Have you ever heard of Adam Clayton Powell Jr.?"

"The congressman?"

"Yes. Did you know that he passed for white?"

Nikkie's eyes widened. "Really? I thought he was like, you know, a black militant or something."

"He was—though more so as he got older," Mrs. Randolph explained. "But in his first year at Colgate University, he passed for white. Like you, he later explained that he never said he was white, but never corrected the assumption that he was. So even though the university was fully integrated—and this was in the 1920s, you understand—he was part of an all-white fraternity, and lived in an all-white dorm, and even dated a white student from a neighboring university."

"Get out of here," Nikkie said in a low voice.

"He was eventually found out," Mrs. Randolph continued. "He used to boast to his schoolmates that his father headed the largest church in Harlem. Harlem was pretty mixed in the 1920s, so that didn't raise any red flags, but when a group of his friends from school came down to Harlem for a visit, they decided to stop by the church. When they saw that all-black congregation, they couldn't wait to get back to the university and tell what they knew. Powell was asked to leave the fraternity, he voluntarily moved from the all-white dorm into an integrated dorm, and, oh yeah, his girlfriend dropped him."

"Dag!" was all Nikkie could say.

"And then there was Anatole Broyard. He was the book reviewer for the *New York Times* in the seventies and eighties.

He started passing when he was in his late twenties, I think, and he went to his grave passing. Even his children—"

"His children? He had children?" Nikkie broke in.

Mrs. Randolph nodded. "He married a white woman and had two kids. Even they didn't know until ten days before he died of prostate cancer. And even then it was their mother who told them."

"So they didn't look like they had black blood?" Nikkie wondered out loud.

"I've never seen pictures of them, but I guess not. Like I said, they didn't know." Mrs. Randolph paused and took a good look at Nikkie. "Like you, neither Powell nor Broyard were biracial; and like you, they made a decision to pass. With Powell, it was a teenage lark; on the other hand, Broyard went to his death passing."

"And no one outted him in that whole time?" Nikkie asked in an amazed tone.

Mrs. Randolph seemed irritated by the question. "With Powell, it seemed, the black students at Colgate knew but never outted him. It was the white students who eventually brought his charade to a halt. With Broyard, well, I think he was more like you, harder to detect. Usually African-Americans can tell right off, or after a little scrutiny, when someone is passing, but Broyard looked so white that even African-Americans had a hard time telling. There were some who knew, but most, I believe, didn't. I think those that did only knew because they were acquainted with him before he started passing. But that's not exactly the point I was trying to make."

"What was your point?"

Mrs. Randolph shook her head. "Come on, you know."

Nikkie sighed and stood up. "I don't know. I don't know,

okay," she said as she paced the floor. "I only intended for it to be until I got the job, but then I realized that getting the job wasn't the only thing. Remember what you told me about the African-Americans being teamed with superstars and therefore never really making their own mark? Well, look at Jenice. Isn't that what just happened to her? Being teamed with the illustrious Hal Richardson?" Nikkie stopped and faced Mrs. Randolph. "Well, I don't want that to happen to me!

"And quiet as it's kept," she continued, "there are people who talk behind Jenice's back and say she only got the job because she's black. I wouldn't want that said about me."

Mrs. Randolph's eyes narrowed into a squint. "You know what? I'm not your mother, but let me tell you right now if I find out that you're one of the people who are saying that shit about Jenice, I will slap you silly."

Nikkie put her hands up in front of her in a gesture of surrender. "I'm not saying it, but like I said, I can't defend her against it because it's true. Isn't it?"

Mrs. Randolph shook her head. "Nikkie, do you actually think that you're more qualified for this job than Jenice?"

"Well, I don't know, but—"

"Well, you're not," Mrs. Randolph snapped. "And what you're talking about is quotas, or set-asides, as they used to be called. But look around the office. African-Americans make up thirteen percent of the U.S. population, but of the seventy-five PR specialists here, only four are African-American. Now, why is that? Because people tend to hire people whom they perceive to be most like them. When Paxon and Green set aside trainee positions specifically for African-Americans, they're not hiring people who aren't qualified to be trainees; to their credit, they're just making sure they don't inadvertently discriminate against them. But all trainees pretty much have the same qualifications."

Nikkie plopped back down in her chair. "Yeah, but it's the label, I guess. It's just the label. An affirmative action hire. People just automatically assume she's not as qualified."

"Sticks and stones, I guess. And what doesn't kill us, will make us stronger." Mrs. Randolph shrugged. "I can't think of any more clichés that fit, not that those did so well. The bottom line is there's nothing I can say about it. You're right. The label stinks. But such is life." She smiled. "So, okay, I did think of another cliché."

Both women laughed.

"Look, I really don't think you have to worry about Jenice outing you." Mrs. Randolph started adding more items to the box, a signal that the meeting was over. "Black people tend not to out people who they know for a fact are passing, and she'd be crazy to out you when she only suspects."

Nikkie nodded dismally. "I only hope you're right."

Nikkie flipped through the pages of the *New York Post* during the subway trip uptown to look at the apartment she hoped she'd be moving into. There it was on the infamous Page Six, a picture of Cindy. It wasn't the first newspaper photo she'd seen of the young woman since moving to New York, and like most of the others, she was pictured at a club—champagne glass in hand—perfectly tanned and perfectly posed as she gave that delicious half-smile to the camera.

Nikkie read the caption beneath the photo: *Manhattan socialite and real estate heiress Cindy Statler partied the night away at New York's newest hot spot, Dalliance. As usual, she was the last to leave.*

Nikkie sighed as she closed the paper. She hadn't known that Cindy was a minor celebrity when they first met. That night with Cindy and her friends had been one of the best in her life, but it would have been so much better if the paparazzi had been there to snap a picture of her dancing her ass off with one of the wildest party girls in Manhattan. What she wouldn't give to have another night like that night.

She had considered looking Cindy up once she arrived back in New York, but her pride wouldn't let her. The girl had her number and had promised to call and hadn't. She wasn't going to force herself where she wasn't wanted. Still, it would be nice if they accidentally ran into each other. She'd have to see if she could arrange to do just that once she was settled into her new place.

"I just want you to know I know," a raspy voice broke into her thoughts.

Startled, Nikkie looked at the old African-American woman sitting next to her. The woman had gotten on two stops before, and had sat down without saying anything. "I'm s-sorry," she stammered. "You know what?"

"You know what I know," the woman answered with a smug look while pulling her beat-up black leather pocketbook farther up her ample lap. "You know what I know." And as if to make sure to clear up any misconceptions, the woman rubbed her hand over her almond-colored skin. "You know what I know," she repeated again.

Nikkie's mouth dropped open, causing the woman to give a little laugh. She then took a book out of her pocketbook and focused her attention on the written word, ignoring Nikkie's distress.

When the train pulled into the next stop, Nikkie quickly stood up and got off, looking neither left nor right. It was pure coincidence that it was the Seventy-second and Broadway station, only a couple of blocks away from her destination. Nikkie tried to slow her breathing as she walked slowly up the stairs and into the daylight. She didn't know why she was so upset. It wasn't the first time an African-American had approached her to say that they realized she was black. But it was the first time since . . . well, since she started passing.

chapter ten

"Sarah, what are you doing?"

Nicole's roommate looked up from the sink where she was depositing the contents of a pot into the garbage disposal. "I'm throwing out the broccoli you had on the stove."

"But why?" Nicole asked as she placed her grocery bag on the kitchen table.

"I was cleaning up the kitchen and opened the pot," Sarah said as she started running tap water. "I saw it was really overcooked and knew you didn't want it. It was downright mushy. Yech. I figured you didn't have time to throw it out before you rushed out." She gave Nicole an accusing look as she wiped the pot clean. "So what did you buy at the store?"

"Nothing," Nikkie said, trying to hide her frustration. She'd been looking forward to having broccoli with her steak and Rice-A-Roni, and had only run out to the store to buy butter to put on her vegetables.

Sarah took another look at the grocery bag, shrugged her shoulders, and walked out of the kitchen.

It was bad enough Nikkie had to buy a whole set of pots on her own, since her new roommate was Jewish and wouldn't let anything with pork be cooked in her pots and pans, but since moving in, Nikkie hadn't been able to fix herself a decent meal.

It hadn't taken Nikki long to find out that Sarah, and all of her other white friends, steamed their vegetables, and just barely did that. They seemed to like their veggies to crunch when they chewed them. And the idea of putting any kind of grease or oil into the vegetables was also foreign to them.

It was a white thing, Nikkie figured, so she tried to get used to it. *But, God,* she thought, *what I wouldn't give for some ham hocks, greasy collard greens, and rice smothered with gravy.* She'd been excited when Susan suggested they go to Harlem one night for dinner, but instead of going to a soul food restaurant, her coworker insisted on dining at some hoity-toity restaurant that had just opened on Adam Clayton Powell Boulevard. Another meal with almost raw vegetables and bland rice. At least the spareribs she ordered were meaty and succulent, but the iced tea was, of course, unsweetened. And no matter how much sugar you add after the fact, iced tea never tastes as sweet as it does when the sugar is added right after it's finished brewing.

She walked into the living room and found Sarah in front of the television watching *Laguna Beach*, her favorite show, at least since they took *The OC* off the air. How the hell she could watch crap like that and then burst into laughter when she found Nikkie watching *America's Next Top Model*, Nikkie couldn't understand. But still, Nikkie had quickly switched the channel and said she'd been daydreaming and didn't even realize what was on the television. The same thing with the radio. Nikkie was a hip-hop fiend, but she didn't feel comfortable listening to HOT 97, which only played rap and hip-hop. Instead, she listened to Z100, which played a mixture of rock and rap. And she never got a chance to listen to "The Wendy Williams Experience" on WBLS anymore, even though she'd been an avid fan of the celebrity gossip queen back in Detroit. It wasn't that there weren't *any* white folks who liked *America's Next Top Model*, HOT 97, or "The Wendy Williams Experience," but since the shows had a predominantly black audience, she couldn't risk being a fan, just in case it made people wonder. The hardest part was probably not being able to watch her favorite show, *Girlfriends*, anymore—and syndicated reruns of *Friends* was a poor replacement.

Nikkie walked into her bedroom and flopped onto the couch. "This shit is getting too hard," she said out loud to nobody as she began to file her nails.

It was bad enough when she had to play the role at work; well, not so bad, it was actually kind of fun—kind of like playing a role in a movie. But now that she had moved in with Sarah, she felt like she was in a never-ending bad reality show. She couldn't act black at work, and now that she had a white roommate—and a cousin of one of her coworkers—she couldn't even be black in the privacy of her home. She thought back to her conversation with Mrs. Randolph. When does it end, she wondered, when would she be able to resume her life? Or would she ever? She pushed the last question out of her mind. Of course she'd eventually be able to stop passing for white. Right now pretending to be white was just a means to an end. Once she reached the end, everything would go back to normal. The problem was, she couldn't decide what end she was looking forward to achieving. The thought depressed her. Sorely.

She was so deep in thought she actually jumped when she heard the knock on her bedroom door.

"Hey, Nikkie, you wanna go to a club tonight?" Sarah asked through the closed door.

Nikkie got up and let the young woman inside the room. "I don't know. What club? Who else is going?"

"That new club in the Village, Cachet. They have jeans night every Wednesday."

"Who else is going?" Nikkie asked again.

Sarah shrugged. "Me and you, if you wanna go. You've been here almost a month and we've never gone out together. I thought if you weren't doing anything, maybe we'd try out the club. You interested?"

"Um, yeah, that might be nice. What time you wanna leave?"

"I figure about nine—things are going to start early, since it's a weeknight and most people are going to have to work in the morning. We can hop right on the subway and be there in about a half hour."

"Cool."

Nikkie posed in one position and then another in front of the full-length mirror in her bedroom. She looked good, she knew she did. She wore a silk champagne-colored split sleeve that had a high waistline and a built-in bra that lifted her ample cleavage to wonderful heights. And the new House of Dereon jeans she'd bought only a few days before hugged her body just right. She turned with her back to the mirror again and stretched her neck to look over her shoulder at her posterior. Yeah, her ass looked good in the jeans. She may be thin, but she always did have a shapely and full butt.

"How do I look?" she said when she entered the living room. She did a slow twirl in front of Sarah, awaiting the compliment she knew was sure to come.

"You look good. You ready?" Sarah said as she picked up her pocketbook.

"Um, yeah." Nikkie paused, suddenly insecure. "What do you think?" She presented her back to her roommate. "Does my butt look good in these jeans?"

"Well—"

Nikkie swung back around. "What?"

"Well, it does make your butt look kinda big," Sarah said diplomatically.

"Huh?" Nikkie said in a confused voice.

"It might not be the jeans. They're probably fine. But, well, you know you're kind of, well, overly endowed back there. Not that it looks gross or anything, but you do need to be careful of what kind of jeans you wear. But then we all do, don't we?" she added quickly. "What about me? Do these jeans make my butt look too big?" She turned around to give Nikkie a good view.

"No, you look nice and small," Nikkie said, trying to keep the amusement out of her voice.

"Good." Sarah turned back around with a smile. "My boyfriend says it's one of my best features."

Nikkie shook her head as they walked out the door. *These white folks. I'm never going to get used to them.*

chapter eleven

The club was packed—people were dancing, drinking, and making goo-goo eyes at each other. Just the kind of atmosphere that Nikkie liked. She didn't like the fact that it was so crowded that she wasn't going to be able to find a table, but she could get used to it. Hopefully, she'd spend the evening dancing her ass off. She inwardly laughed at her ironic thought.

Sarah had abandoned her shortly after they arrived when she "spotted some friends from work." So much for saying she wanted to hang out with her new roommate. She didn't offer to make any introductions, she just walked off.

Nikkie squeezed into a position at the bar and managed to catch the eye of the bartender, ordered a cosmopolitan, and then made her way around the place. She'd circled the place twice when she heard someone call her name. Someone from the VIP section.

"Oh, my God," she said, almost dropping her drink. There in front of her sat Cindy and Rachel, waving her over. She hadn't expected to run into anyone she knew at the place, but especially not them. Cachet was nice, but was nowhere near as posh as Sangria, where she'd first met them.

"How are you guys doing? Where's Tina?" she said as she sat down with them.

Cindy simply shrugged and made a face, but Rachel answered. "She couldn't make it tonight. It's a long story. But how are you doing?"

"I'm doing fine, thanks. I can't believe I ran into the two of you here. I mean"—Nikkie paused—"I mean, I wouldn't have thought it was your kind of club."

"It's really not, but we had to come," Cindy said dryly. "You know how it is. The owner has a friend, who has a friend, who is a friend of mine, and they insisted we make it tonight."

Rachel must have noticed the puzzled look on Nikkie's face. "Club owners want people like Cindy and me—well, especially Cindy—to come out to their clubs for bragging rights. We get in for free, of course, and all of our drinks . . ."

"And drugs," Cindy broke in with a giggle.

Rachel shot her a dirty look and continued, ". . . are on the house."

Nikkie's eyebrows furrowed. "But we—I mean, you—paid for the drinks at the Sangria."

Rachel jerked her head back. "What? No, we didn't."

"Humph! No, we most certainly did not." Cindy's indignation was evident in her voice and on her face. "We wouldn't have been there if we had to pay for anything."

"But what are you doing in New York?" Rachel asked. "Another job interview? Oh no, don't tell me . . . you got the job?"

Nikkie nodded.

"Oh, that's just wonderful!" Rachel clasped her hands together. "Isn't that great, Cindy?"

Cindy shrugged. "I guess."

"So now"—Rachel took a sip of her cosmopolitan—"what kind of job is it again?"

"Public relations. I'm at Paxon and Green," Nikkie said proudly.

"Wonderful, just wonderful." Rachel turned to Cindy. "I think this calls for champagne, don't you?"

Without answering, Cindy put her hand in the air to signal one of the drink waitresses assigned to the VIP section. "Bring me a magnum of Dom Pérignon. And three glasses."

"Hey, Cindy."

Nikkie looked up to see a younger, but just as tanned, version of George Hamilton. It took her a moment to remember where she'd seen him before, but she then realized she'd seen him in her latest copy of *New York* magazine, in an advertisement for Calvin Klein. He looked as good in jeans as he did in his underwear.

"I didn't think I'd see you here," he said as he took a seat.

Cindy waved the waitress back to the table. "Make that four glasses."

A girl resembling the woman who played Heath Ledger's jilted girlfriend in his latest film pulled a chair from another table and sat down with them. "Okay, bitches, I'm here," she said haughtily. "But I want you to know I'm only staying for like an hour."

Nikkie's eyes widened. It *was* the woman who played Heath's jilted girlfriend.

"Oh, shut up, bitch. You know you owed me." Cindy waved to the drink waitress. "Make that five glasses."

"Brad, Lucia, this is Nikkie . . ." Rachel turned to Nikkie. "What's your last name again?"

"Jensen," Nikkie said breathlessly.

"Right. This is Nikkie Jensen. Nikkie, this is Brad Cooper and Lucia Silver."

"How do you do?" Nikkie quickly extended her arm for a handshake. Boy, oh boy, did she want to reach out and touch them—just to make sure they were real.

Brad flashed her a dazzling smile. "I'm doing fine. Sitting next to three beautiful women."

"Three?" Cindy raised her eyebrow.

"Lucia doesn't count," he said, giving the actress a nudge that almost pushed her out of her chair.

"Pig," she spat as she straightened herself up. "And I was going to tell Steven Spielberg to put you in the new film I'm doing with him."

"Yeah, right. Like you have a part in a Spielberg film." Brad threw back his head and laughed.

Lucia shot him a dirty look. "Well, I have an audition with him, anyway."

"Well, once you get the part, I'll kiss your ass, but until then, you're just another wannabe."

"Oh, shut up, Brad. If you didn't eat pussy so well, I'd throw this drink in your face."

Brad grinned. "Why don't you just throw it on my dick. Then you can slurp it up later when I take you home tonight."

To Nikkie's astonishment, instead of being insulted, Lucia started laughing.

Rachel sighed. "Must you two always be so vulgar?"

Just then the drink waitress returned with the champagne settled in an ice bucket and started putting the glasses on the table in front of the group. She uncorked the bottle and poured the bubbly liquid.

"Okay, everybody, we have to have a toast," Rachel said grandly.

"What are we celebrating?" Brad asked.

"Nikkie's new job."

"Yeah?" Brad turned to Nikkie. "What kind of job?"

"I'm a public relations specialist. For Paxon and Green."

"Really?" Brad flashed that dazzling smile again. "I would have thought you were a model or actress."

Oh, this guy is good, Nikkie thought.

"Paxon and Green?" Lucia frowned. "That's one of the big firms, isn't it? I'm looking to change firms. That bitch doing my PR is lame. You got a card?"

Cindy rolled her eyes. "I know you guys aren't really going to talk shop while we're out at a club having a good time."

"Stop acting so snobbish, Cindy," Rachel said sternly. "Nikkie's a working girl. She's supposed to be looking out for clients." She turned to Nikkie. "Am I right?"

"Most definitely." Nikkie pulled one of her brand-new business cards out of her purse and handed it to Lucia. Thank goodness she had thought to put a few in before she left the house. What a coup it would be for her to land an account after only being at the company a month.

She was still smiling to herself when she suddenly saw a dumbfounded Sarah approaching the table.

"Hey, Nikkie," she said when she reached them. "You look like you're having a good time."

Nikkie grinned in response. "I am, Sarah. What about you?" That'll teach her to just abandon her. What did she think? That she'd be sitting nursing a drink at the bar while waiting for her to return? How pathetic did she think she was? Well, look who was pathetic now, she thought as Sarah stood in front of her, shifting from one foot to another, with a stupid smile on her face.

"Oh, let me introduce you to everyone," Nikkie said grandly. "Sarah Rosenblatt, this is Brad Cooper, Lucia Silver, Cindy Statler, and Rachel . . ." She paused. "Rachel, what's your last name?"

"Riverton."

". . . and Rachel Riverton."

Cindy leaned in close to Nikkie. "Do we hate her?"

Nikkie shook her head. "No. She's my roommate."

"Oh well." Cindy sat back up and took a sip of her champagne, having totally lost interest in the newcomer.

"Miss Silver, I just want to tell you that my friends and I loved you in your latest film. You were just fantastic."

Lucia's face turned into a scowl. She turned to Cindy. "She's got to be kidding."

"Lucia!" Rachel said sharply.

Nikkie inwardly grimaced. Sarah would have to come over and act like a fawning idiot.

Lucia turned back to Sarah and extended her hand. "I'm only playing. I just wasn't expecting to run into any one of my fans here." She shot Brad a dirty look when he started to chuckle. "But it's good to meet you," she continued. "And I hope you and your friends will continue to support my films."

"Heads up. Heads up," Cindy said quickly as a photographer approached them. "Make like I just told a funny joke."

Obediently, everyone started smiling and chuckling, while at the same time posing for the camera shot they knew was coming. The flash blinded Nikkie, but she felt it was the high point of her life. Cindy had actually draped her arm around her shoulder just before the shot was taken!

"Do you mind if I get your name?" the photographer asked her as he pulled out a small notepad.

"Nicole Jensen," Nikkie said breathlessly. "That's J-E-N-S-E-N."

"And who are you?" he asked brusquely.

"I beg your pardon?" Now, how was she supposed to answer that? she wondered. Suddenly, she felt a kick under the table and saw Rachel give a discreet nod toward the business card that Lucia had left on the table. "Oh! I'm with Paxon and Green."

"The PR firm?"

"Yes," Lucia cut in, pushing her shoulders back and her cleavage out. "She's my PR person."

"And also a close friend," Rachel quickly added.

"A very dear friend," Cindy said, not wanting to be left out.

"I happen to be madly in love with her," Brad added.

Nikkie sneaked a peek at Sarah, who was still standing at the edge of the table. She looked appropriately impressed.

The photographer nodded, put the pad in his pocket, and turned to go.

"Um, do you need my name?" Sarah asked timidly.

"Nah. You're not in the shot. I just got Cindy, Brad, Lucia, Rachel, and the new girl."

"Oh" was all Sarah could say in response. "Sorry."

That's me. The new girl. Pinch me, I must have died and gone to heaven. Oh God, please let that photo make its way to Page Six—

"Um, Nikkie," Sarah interrupted her thoughts, "it's getting kind of late. Let me know when you're ready to leave, okay?"

"Oh, don't worry about Nikkie. One of us will give her a

ride home," Cindy said, waving the woman off. "It was nice meeting you, Rebecca."

"Her name was Sarah," Rachel said when Nikkie's roommate slinked off.

Cindy shrugged. "Whatever."

chapter twelve

JULY 2007

"Look, Beverly Rich is one of my clients, and I adore her, but come on, we've got to address the problems she's been creating since she started dating this rap guy, Boss Dawgee. I mean, she's black, and though she's always dated white guys, I don't think anyone would be surprised about her all of a sudden going out with a black guy. But does she have to start dating a"—Hal Richardson put his fingers up in quote mode—" 'ghetto nigger.' "

Nikkie audibly gasped and looked around the table to gauge other people's reactions.

Yanna sucked her teeth. "He's an asshole, but you don't have to call him that, Hal."

Hal snorted. "Yeah? Well, just in case you didn't know, that's the name of his latest CD."

"Well, I bet you wouldn't say it to his face."

Hal shrugged. "Yeah, well, I don't get it. Why is it okay for them to call each other nigger, but then they want to fight a white person for calling them a nigger? Isn't that reverse discrimination?"

"Exactly," Susan chimed in. "And like, black comedians can get up on stage and talk about white people in the audience, and even talk about 'crackers' and all that, and all people do is laugh. But look what happened when Michael Richards called an audience member a nigger! I mean"—she looked around at the other people sitting at the conference table—"I'm not saying what Michael Richards did was right, but I just don't understand why he's being blasted by everyone when people like Chris Rock and Dave Chappelle are called 'comic geniuses.' And they both call black people 'niggers,' as well as white people 'crackers.' Come on, doesn't anyone else see it as a double standard?"

Nikkie rubbed her pulsating temples. She wanted to say something, but wasn't sure exactly what to say. To be honest, what Hal and Susan said actually seemed to make sense; yet it just didn't seem right. And for her to just sit there and say nothing about it was just wrong, she was sure about that. She just wasn't sure about anything else. The right thing to do was probably jump up, announce she was black, and stomp out the door. But really, what would that accomplish? There would be a lot of stunned faces, a lot of people coming over to her cubicle later apologizing and saying that she was right to be offended, but what would that really change? And what effect would it all have on her career? Who would benefit from her throwing the holy fit that she kind of thought she should have? No one—and certainly not her.

And, she further reasoned, didn't Hal and Susan actually have a point? Wasn't there a double standard? She fished an emery board from her pocketbook and started furiously filing her nails. Hell no, they didn't have a point, she decided. "Cracker" did *not* have the same connotation as "nigger," and they knew it. If it wasn't for the fact that she had come to know both of them in the past few weeks, she'd assume they were racist. But, no, they were just more than likely "clueless white folks," as Joseph used to call white people who acted like that. White folks who just didn't, or wouldn't, get it.

"Okay, while we're on the subject, what about the black-only clubs and organizations?" Hal said, tapping a pencil on a yellow legal pad while he talked. "Like, what's the name of that convention that Libby Randolph goes to every year? The National Association of Black PR People or something?"

Hmm, maybe he isn't clueless. Maybe he is a racist.

"National Black Public Relations Society Conference," Yanna corrected him.

"Right. That. She'd be the first one wanting to raise holy hell if any one of us was to announce that he was going to the National White Public Relations Society Conference, wouldn't she?" Hal glanced around with a satisfied expression on his face. "I rest my case."

"That's because you're a bigot."

Nikkie looked gratefully at Yanna for saying the words she'd wished she had the courage to say.

"Spoken like a true-blue liberal," Hal said with a laugh.

"There is a definite need for black organizations, and you know it," Yanna said without missing a beat.

"I don't know any such thing," Hal said in a reasonable voice. "Why is it okay to have black organizations but not white organizations?"

"Just look at the public relations industry. You have to agree that most of the people in the higher echelons are white, right?

Why is that? Because from the beginning the higher echelons have been white, and the people in power tend to put other people in power whom they consider most like them. It's the infamous 'ole boy network' in play. So blacks have developed their own networking organizations to try and help each other move up. I don't see anything wrong with that."

"If the 'ole boy network' is the problem, why don't they have a women's organization in public relations?"

"They do, you idiot. The Women Executives in Public Relations."

"Okay, so then if that's the case, Libby Randolph is a woman, so she doesn't need to join the black organization, since she can join the women's organization. You've made my point." He chuckled, crossed his arms behind his head, and leaned back in his chair.

"You really are an idiot." Nikkie didn't realize that she had said it out loud until she heard the laughter from the other people around the table and saw Hal's face redden. "I'm just kidding," she said quickly as she dropped the emery board back into her purse.

"No problem," he said sullenly. "I was just kidding, too. But let's get back to the problem at hand. How do we spin Beverly getting arrested again?"

Like hell you were kidding, Nikkie thought later as the group began to drift out of the conference room and back to their cubicles. Like her, Hal Richardson was only twenty-something, but he had been at Paxon & Green for almost eight years, having graduated from the University of Pennsylvania at the tender age of nineteen and immediately joining the firm. He was a mover and shaker and was the star rainmaker—meaning he brought more new accounts to Paxon & Green than anyone else. Hal was tall, blond, and handsome, with an athletic build that he kept in shape by coming in two hours early every morning to work out at the company gym. All the higher-ups liked him, and so did most of his colleagues—he was a hard person not to like. He was always pleasant, but never cloying; witty, but never sarcastic. And he was always willing to help others out with advice and tips. In fact, Nikkie really liked him, even if he did have what Joseph used to call the "Master of the Universe" mentality—the expectation that everyone should listen to what he said, simply because he was the one who was saying it; and people should take him seriously, simply because he took himself seriously. You didn't even have to agree with him, but you were supposed to realize his opinion was always at least worth hearing.

"When a young black man walks in the street when there's traffic coming and he doesn't look both ways, he has the attitude that if some car dares to hit him, he's going to get up, drag the driver out the car, and kick his ass. When a young white man walks in the street when there's traffic, he doesn't bother looking both ways because he has the expectation that no one would even consider hitting him, and will just stop because he is who he is," Joseph would say. "Almost as soon as a black man comes into this world, he learns he has to fight his way through. A white man, on the other hand, has expectations that everything is just supposed to go his way, and can't quite understand when it doesn't, because—after all—he's Master of the Universe."

Joe. Just the thought of him made Nikkie feel a bit depressed as she took a seat at her desk. He hadn't called her since she moved to New York, though he was always cordial when she called to see how he and Ayoka were doing. He asked how she was doing, but never specifically asked her about her job, and never brought up his disapproval of her not letting her colleagues know she was black. The disapproval, however, was apparent, and it hurt her terribly. He hadn't even come over to see her when she went home to visit Mama a few weeks back. The ringing telephone interrupted her thoughts.

"Nicole Jensen," she said in the businesslike manner she'd picked up since starting at Paxon & Green.

"Hi, this is Lucia Silver. Remember me?"

Nicole almost gasped. So the actress was serious, after all! After three days without hearing from her, she'd just put it down to one of those things that people say when they're high. But here it was, and she was on the phone.

"Of course I remember you, Lucia. How've you been?" Nicole pulled an emery board from her desk drawer and started swiping at her fingers in an attempt to keep the excitement from her voice.

"I'm fine, thanks. I just wanted to follow up on the conversation we had over at Cachet the other night," the woman said in a bored voice. "I was serious, you know. I would like to talk to you about doing my PR. Rachel says you really know how to handle yourself."

Rachel did? Wow!

"Well, I certainly do what I can." Nikkie picked up some papers and started shuffling them near the receiver so that Lucia would hear and think she'd been busy when she called. "As a matter of fact, I've already come up with what I think are some pretty innovative ideas I'd love to talk to you about. How about we do lunch? Are you free tomorrow?"

"No, I have to fly out to the Coast. I've got a callback on the Spielberg audition."

"Lucia, that's wonderful!"

"So how about next Monday? You can come over here to my spot, if you'd like. I have a wonderful cook, and it wouldn't be any problem for her to whip up something real quick."

Nikkie glanced at her calendar. "That's very doable. What's your address?" She scribbled down the woman's information.

"And, Nikkie, let me just tell you now that the Lucia you met at Cachet is not the same Lucia you'll be lunching with next week."

"What do you mean?"

"Well, I'm actually a pretty levelheaded and intelligent person. What you saw was my club persona; it seems to attract more attention, so I go with it. Actually, I'm a graduate from Sarah Lawrence, and I went there on an academic scholarship. I'm very, very serious about my acting career; so whatever you do, don't play me for the fool you met, and we'll get along just fine."

I've got to call Rachel and thank her, Nikkie thought after Lucia hung up. She picked up the receiver again to dial out.

"So you feel like going spelunking this weekend?"

Nikkie looked up to see Hal sitting on the side of her desk, coffee mug in hand.

"Spelunking?" She wrinkled her brow.

"Cave exploring. A group of us are going to Clarksville this weekend," Hal explained. "We try to get out there at least once or twice each summer."

"Who else is in the group?"

"Just Yanna and her fiancé, Susan and whoever she's dating that week, Sam Epson and his girl, and me."

Nikkie leaned back in her chair. "You don't bring your girlfriend?" she asked with a slow smile.

"Unfortunately, I don't have one at the moment," Hal answered nonchalantly. "But, anyway, there's a lodge that we always stay at overnight. We leave early Saturday morning and then return Sunday evening. It's about a two-hour ride. You in?"

"I've never been spelunking before." Nor had she ever known anyone who had, though she saw no reason to reveal that bit of information. It didn't make sense to her why people would leave the comforts of the city and drive two hours to go explore a cave—but, hey, if that's what these people did, maybe there was something to it.

"Not a problem. I'll teach you the ropes myself." Hal stood up and stretched expansively. "So you in or out?"

"How are we going to get there?"

"I pick everyone up in my Hummer. Just e-mail me your address before you leave today, and be outside your apartment building at six a.m."

chapter thirteen

White folks are crazy. Or maybe just stupid. Nikkie couldn't decide. But there had to be something wrong with people who thought it was cool to spend hours exploring caves that hundreds of people had already explored. But Hal and the rest of the crew seemed to be having a ball, as did the other dozen or so people who had traveled from various parts of the country just to risk sprained ankles and broken arms to go into the cold dank grottos. *It's a white thing*, she supposed, *blacks aren't wired to understand*. Perhaps that's why she was the only black person up at the lodge. She herself had tried to keep an open mind, but after an hour or so, it had all seemed too ridiculous. When one of the explorers from another group said she was heading back to the lodge because she wasn't feeling well, she hurriedly offered to escort the woman to make sure she was okay. When Hal offered to accompany them, she waved him off, saying she didn't want to infringe on his fun and that they'd be okay. If Hal and the others had thought she'd return to the cave after the woman was safely inside the lodge, they were sorely mistaken. When they returned to the lodge the following afternoon, they found Nikkie in the common area watching television.

"I'm sorry you didn't enjoy yourself," Hal said as they pulled up to her apartment building early Sunday evening.

Nikkie shrugged. "I'm just kind of cranky today. Maybe I'll have more fun next time." *Ha! Like there's going to be a next time. They can't pay me enough to waste my time like that again.*

Hal nodded. "It's cool," he said as his Hummer silently idled. "Different strokes for different folks, as they say. I'm still glad you came with us, though."

He stared at her expectantly, and Nikkie wondered what it was that he expected her to say or do next. Get out of the car? That's what she wanted to do, but that wasn't the vibe she was getting. Certainly, he didn't expect her to invite him up, did he?

Hal cleared his throat. "Well, I know we have to go to work tomorrow, but I'm not really ready to call it a night. How about we go get something to eat? You hungry?"

Hmm . . . that wasn't what she expected. She paused, wondering how she should respond. She knew he found her attractive. Women can sense these things, but she'd never thought he'd actually make a move. Or was this a move? Maybe he really didn't want to call it a night and figured eating with a coworker was better than simply eating by himself. Just a harmless dinner. But, heck, she wasn't hungry, and all she wanted to do was get in her apartment and soak in a tub of bubble bath and Epsom salts. Even that little bit of hiking she'd done had her aching. She turned to him. "Well—"

"Nikkie, I guess you know I'm attracted to you," he said, cutting her off, "and I thought we'd have more of an opportunity to get to know each other this weekend, but, well"—he paused—"it just didn't work out quite the way I hoped."

So it wasn't just about having dinner with a coworker in

order not to eat alone, Nikkie happily realized. *It's all about me.* Suddenly, her bones didn't ache quite so much. Not that she was really attracted to Hal. While she could admire their good looks, white men just didn't turn her on. But she'd been in New York for about a month now, and this was the most intimate discussion she'd had with a man. *Good to know I've still got it.*

"I'm usually not this direct with a woman, not that I'm a beat-around-the-bush kind of guy, but I'm usually pretty good with figuring out if a woman is interested in me or not, but I haven't been able to figure you out," Hal was saying. "So how about you let me take you to dinner so I can have more time to try and get a peg on you?" He flashed her his brilliant smile.

"And what if you find out I'm not interested in you?" Nikkie asked in a flirtatious voice.

"Well, then, so be it," Hal said in his usual confident voice. "It would probably be the best thing, anyway, because if you were interested in me, and I was interested in you, well, then we'd be in danger of having an office romance. And you know those things don't ever work out." Nikkie gave him a puzzled look, causing him to laugh. "I'm just kidding. Do you like Mexican? Or would you rather Chinese?"

"Um, can I run upstairs, take a shower, and change first?" She actually couldn't believe herself as she heard her own words. Why was she consenting? She didn't really like him. Not like that. Maybe not at all after that "nigger" crack in the conference room a few days before. Still, it was nice to know that one of the most attractive guys at the firm—the company's golden child, in fact—was interested in her. And there was no danger that anything would actually come of it, because, after all, she wasn't into white guys. But it might be fun just to see what it would be like. Yeah, she decided, that's why she was agreeing.

"Sure. In fact," he asked, pausing, "how long do you think you'll be?"

"Not more than forty-five minutes."

"Good, that will give me enough time to drive home and change myself and grab a cab back over here. I hate driving in the city."

This is a first, Nikkie thought while drying off after a quick shower. *Going out with a white guy. Me. Going out with a white guy.* A wave of guilt swept over her. Joseph would have a fit if he ever found out. For that matter, so would everyone else in the family. But then again, it wasn't like it was really going to be anything between her and Hal. She wasn't interested in Hal Richardson. Not like that. She'd never like a white guy like that. She knew who she was, even if no one else in New York did, and there were some lines she'd never cross, and one was going out with white guys. Well, she was going out with Hal, but she didn't really like him, so that didn't count, she reasoned. She was just going out for the fun of it. Just a lark.

The questions that she hadn't been able to answer for Mrs. Randolph a few weeks before suddenly came back to her. How long was she planning on passing? And to what extent?

"You're kidding, right? You've actually gone bungee jumping?"

Hal nodded his head.

Nikkie looked at him in amazement. "I don't get it. Why

the hell would you want to do something like that? Don't you know people die doing it?"

Hal shrugged his shoulders. "The percentage of people who die in bungee-jumping accidents is really minute. I'm sure it's less than one percent."

Nikkie suddenly wondered what percentage of bungee jumpers were black, certain that this was pretty much another white phenomenon—which led her back to her belief that white folks do the stupidest things. "But can you explain why you would take the chance at all? I mean, what do you get out of it?"

"The rush," Hal answered. "There's a rush you get knowing that you're doing something that goes against the laws of nature. Something that every instinct in your body tells you is dangerous. Being able to ignore that instinct, to overcome your fear, it makes you feel . . . I don't know. It makes you feel like a superior being."

Nikkie shrugged. "If you say so."

"How about you come with me the next time I go skydiving? Then you'll see what I mean."

Nikkie snorted. "I know you're crazy if you think I'm jumping out of a plane."

Hal laughed. "But enough about me, tell me more about you, Miss Jensen."

"There's not much to tell. I'm from Detroit, and since I was a little girl, I dreamt about doing PR, and now here I am."

Hal laughed. "When you say there's not much to tell, you weren't kidding, huh? Care to expand just a little more? For instance, tell me about your family."

Nikkie's heart quickened and she tried to keep her voice steady. No one had yet asked about her family, so this was the first time she was going to use the rehearsed story she'd come up with. "My parents and my older brother still live in Detroit. We kinda, you know, fell out, so I'm not really too much in touch with them." She managed to get through it.

Hal put his hand over hers. "Would it be too personal a question to ask what you fell out over?"

"Well," Nikkie said with a sigh, "it's not really something I like talking about. I hope you understand."

Hal nodded. "No problem. Maybe when we get to know each other better, you'll feel comfortable talking about it."

Maybe by the time I get to know you better, I'll have come up with the rest of the story.

"Well, I hope they know how well you're doing at the job. The way you're going, you'll be getting a promotion pretty soon. You shocked everyone with the Lucia Silver account. I mean, she's not a big star now, but the girl has talent, so she might go far. And then getting the firm's name mentioned in that photo with her and Cindy Statler"—he whistled—"that's good stuff."

Nikkie grinned. "Thanks. But come on, you know when it comes to getting accounts, no one can touch you."

"Well," Hal said modestly, "I've been at it longer."

"I heard you made senior account executive faster than anyone in the history of the firm. And the word in the office is that they're thinking about making you partner," Nikkie said carefully.

"Hah! Don't believe everything you hear."

"Really? I mean, wouldn't you like to be a partner?"

"Sure, but when it comes, it comes. I'm in no hurry," he said too casually. *Yeah,* Nikkie thought, *this is a man with huge ambition. Nothing wrong with that.*

"So what are your future plans? Are you going to eventually open your own firm?"

Hal sighed. "Probably, but not anytime soon. I'm going to stick around Paxon and Green for a while longer, then take some time off, and then maybe hang out my shingle."

"What are you going to do during that time off?" Nikkie asked, not really caring.

"I want to go on a couple of missions."

"Missions?"

Hal nodded. "I'm a Mormon, a member of the Church of Latter-Day Saints. We're required to go on at least one mission. I did one right after my senior year at high school before I went off to college. I worked at a hospital in Somalia. It really changed my life."

Nikkie's eyes widened. "You went on a mission to Somalia? Get outta here!"

Hal chuckled. "Yeah, I don't usually talk about it much. But like I said, that mission changed my life." His tone turned somber. "It's something to work with those people. Many of them were starving, all of them lived in poverty and squalor, but they had such pride about themselves. Do you know that even though they didn't have any money, and the medical care was free, they insisted on giving some kind of payment? Sometimes it was a chicken, sometimes it was just a basket of eggs, or even just one egg. But they always tried to give something. And the ones that didn't have anything else to give gave their time—volunteering at the hospital." Hal shook his head. "It made me feel lousy, the way we take things for granted here in the States."

"Wow."

Hal grinned. "Hey, did I tell you I have two kids?"

Nikkie jerked her head back. "Really?"

"Yep." Hal took his wallet out of his pocket and opened it to show Nikkie a picture of two young Somalian children—a boy and a girl who looked to be about eight or nine.

"That's Abdul and Fatima. They're brother and sister. He's twelve and she's eleven."

Nikkie took another look at the picture. "They're so small."

Hal nodded. "They were malnourished, and actually this is the 'after' picture. The 'before' picture would make you cry. I started sponsoring them about two years ago."

"Wow" was all Nikkie could say. Suddenly, she felt guilty about all the times she'd switched channels when those commercials came on about sponsoring children in underdeveloped countries.

"I'm trying to work it out with an organization now to bring them to the States, where they can get a good education."

Nikkie slowly shook her head. This was a side of Hal she never thought existed. Deep down inside, it seemed, he was really a warm and sensitive guy. Not so much a Master of the Universe as much as a Lover of Humankind. "I woulda never have thunk it of you. Hal Richardson, you are full of surprises."

Hal grinned. "But still an idiot?"

Nikkie blushed. "I told you I was only playing around. I'm really sorry about that."

Hal shrugged. "I guess I did sound like a jerk. Just upset about the whole Beverly Rich thing. I still can't believe she's dating that . . ." He paused to choose his words carefully. "I can't believe she's dating that jerk."

"Oh, Hal. Yanna would be so proud."

They both started laughing.

"But listen, I don't want you to think I'm some kind of racist. I'm not. Some of my best friends are black—"

Nikkie groaned. "I can't believe you actually said that!"

Hal sat back in his chair and laughed. "Okay, but you know what I mean. There are good black people in the world, and there are bad black people . . ."

"There are good white people and bad white people, too," Nikkie hurried to point out.

"You didn't let me finish, but I was just going to say the same thing." Hal smiled. "But, anyway, jerks like Boss Dawgee, well, that's someone I have no problem calling a 'nigger.' "

Nikkie shifted in her seat. She could see where Hal was coming from, but still, it didn't sit right with her, listening to a white person using the "N" word.

"To me, he's a disgrace to his race, his community, and, hell, especially to his parents," Hal said, oblivious to Nikkie's discomfort. "He's not someone I think anyone in their right mind would want to claim as their own. You know he just got arrested again, right? He brought some ten-year-old girl on stage at his last concert and simulated having anal sex with her. The bastard."

"Yeah, he's an awful guy." *And you're at least borderline racist, even if you don't realize it.*

"People like him just need to be eliminated. And I would say that just as fast if he were a white guy, believe me. It's not a race thing; it's a human being thing."

Hal shook his head. "And what gets me is Beverly was with this really great guy, Bob Harris, who loved the ground she walked on, and she dumped him for this guy? I just don't understand some women."

"I hear you," Nikkie said simply. "I hear you."

"You didn't have to escort me home. I'm used to taking the subway by myself," Nikkie said as they stood in front of her building.

"I wouldn't hear of it," Hal said. He reached out and stroked her cheek. "Besides, I want you to think I'm a gentleman."

"Is that right?" Nikkie smiled.

"Yes, that's right," Hal answered softly.

"And why is that?"

"Because I want to make sure you say yes when I ask if I can take you out tomorrow night."

"Well," Nikkie said coyly, "I might if you ask me nicely."

Hal smiled and leaned in and gave Nikkie a small kiss on the lips. "Was that nice enough?"

"Maybe," Nikkie whispered. *Okay, that wasn't so bad.*

"How about this?" Hal put his arm around Nikkie's waist and gently pulled her into him, then planted a tender and lingering kiss on her lips.

A shiver went down Nikkie's spine, and not the good kind. "I'd love to go out with you tomorrow night," Nikkie said quickly as she extricated herself from Hal's embrace. She ran up the steps of the apartment building after he left, wiping her mouth as she did so. No, she decided. She definitely couldn't have a relationship with a white guy. She couldn't even stand kissing one.

chapter fourteen

Either this is the ugliest jelly I've ever seen, or this has got to be caviar. Nikkie looked skeptically at the brownish globby substance in a golden glass bowl nestled in the middle of a golden tray on the buffet table. *I've got to try it.*

She placed her rum and Coke on the table and picked up one of the small pieces of the toast on the golden tray and used the mother-of-pearl serving spoon to scoop a large amount of the glob onto the toast. She glanced around the party to see if anyone was looking her way. There were only about two dozen people in the large ballroom, and most seemed to be engaged in conversation while the small three-piece orchestra played some unknown tune in the corner of the room. Good.

She sniffed the glob. *Kinda smells like almonds.* She mentally shrugged, then popped the piece of toast in her mouth. Her eyes watered and she almost gagged as dozens of little bubbles burst against the roof of her mouth, each one squirting a gooey liquid that she could only describe as fish juice.

Her first instinct was to spit the stuff out, and she looked for a napkin to do it in a ladylike manner, but it was just then that she noticed her smiling hostess gliding her way. She had no choice but to swallow. Now she just had to hope she didn't regurgitate on Mrs. Riverton's beautiful blue chiffon evening dress.

"I'm so glad my daughter invited you, Nicole," Mrs. Riverton said when she reached Nikkie. "Rachel so seldom invites her friends to my little soirees, but I do like to have young people around. It livens up the party, don't you think?" The woman reached out and grabbed a trim middle-aged man who was walking by, while Nikkie swallowed the bile that had crept up her throat. "Henry, have you met Nicole Jensen? She's a good friend of Rachel's." She turned back to Nikkie. "Nicole, this is Henry Finch. He's one of my late husband's law partners."

"How do you do," Nicole said, sticking out her hand. She wondered at the surprised look on Mrs. Riverton's face, but the man graciously shook her hand.

"I'm fine, Miss Jensen," the solemn man said with a small smile. "It's good to meet you."

"The pleasure is mine," Nicole answered politely.

"So how long have you known Rachel?" he asked.

"Just a few months. Cindy introduced us."

"Where is Cindy?" Mr. Finch looked around the room.

"Oh, I'm sure she's not even here." Mrs. Riverton waved her hand dismissively. "You know how that girl is. Nicole, Rachel tells me that you work at Paxon and Green?"

Mr. Finch raised an eyebrow. "Is that so? I just had lunch with Arthur Kadinsky at the club last Thursday. I'll have to tell him I met you." He winked at Nicole. "I'll make sure to tell him to treat you nicely."

A little stuffy, but a nice guy, Nicole decided as he and Mrs. Riverton began discussing a charity function they were cohosting the following week. She picked up her rum and Coke and took a large swallow to wash down the fishy taste that still lingered in her mouth. It only made the taste in her mouth worse.

"Ooh, is that caviar? I've never tried caviar," asked a young woman with overly bleached hair and a voice that was just a few octaves louder than anyone else's in the room. "Is that the Russian kind or American kind?"

"Iranian, dear," Mrs. Riverton said kindly. "Imperial Osetra. Please try some."

The girl nodded, then picked up the serving spoon and dumped a glob only slightly smaller than the one Nikkie had taken on the small piece of toast.

"Oh, wait," Mrs. Riverton said quickly. "You said you've never had it before, didn't you? You might want to try a smaller portion at first, dear." She took the toast from the woman's hand and scraped some of the caviar back into the bowl. "Caviar is, well"—she looked at Mr. Finch—"an acquired taste, wouldn't you say?"

Mr. Finch nodded. "Indeed."

Mrs. Riverton gave the toast with caviar back to the woman. "Here you go, Amy. Now, just take a small bite at first. A nibble."

"What's that you're drinking?" Mr. Finch asked before Amy could bring the caviar to her mouth.

"An apple martini."

"Hmm. Well, you might want to try vodka or champagne. It goes much better with caviar." He winked at her. "We do want your first experience to be a pleasant one."

"Oh, okay." Amy looked around for a place to set down her caviar serving.

"Here you go, dear. You can just place it on this napkin." Mrs. Riverton placed a white linen napkin on the table.

"Thanks! I'll be right back." The girl hurried off.

Wow, I wish they'd been around to give me a few tips, Nikkie thought as the girl headed off to get a new drink. She half-expected Amy's naiveté to be Mr. Finch's and Mrs. Riverton's new topic of discussion, but they immediately went back to chatting about the upcoming charity event. Either they were putting on an act or they were really nice and genuine people.

"Don't wander off too far, Nicole, dear," Mrs. Riverton lightly called after her when she finally decided to drift away. "There is something I'd like to talk to you about."

She was halfway across the large ballroom when Rachel was suddenly at her side.

"Having a good time? I'm sorry to have abandoned you, but I was called to the telephone. Mother doesn't allow the family to use cell phones in the house."

"That's okay. I've just been mingling." That was actually a half-truth. While she'd smiled and nodded at a few people, the conversation she'd just had with Mrs. Riverton and Mr. Finch was the first she'd been engaged in since Rachel left her twenty minutes before. "This is really a nice house," she said, looking around once again. "I've never been in a house that has an elevator." As soon as she said it, she was sorry. She didn't want Rachel to think she was some kind of hick.

"Um-hm, it is nice. If you want, I can give you a tour a little later. That was Cindy on the phone, by the way. She was supposed to be here, but she asked me to tell Mother she has a migraine."

"I didn't know Cindy suffered from migraines. Is she going to be okay?"

"Oh please! Cindy's fine. In fact, she wants us to meet her at Suede's after the party is over."

The young women laughed.

"You know, there's something I've always wanted to ask you," Nikkie said, moving closer to Rachel. "You and Cindy aren't really related, are you? She's your fake cousin, right?"

Rachel cocked her head and looked at Nikkie quizzically. "What's a fake cousin?"

"You know, a close friend who you call a cousin," Nikkie explained.

"Why would you call a close friend a cousin?" Rachel laughed.

Nikkie's mind raced. *Oh God, fake cousins are just a black thing?* "I don't know," she said finally. "I've just heard of some people who do that. And you and Cindy are so different. I mean, you don't look alike, and you certainly don't act alike."

Rachel smiled. "Yeah, Cindy can be a real bitch, can't she? But"—Rachel tinkled the ice in her glass—"she's certainly a lot of fun."

"That she is," Nikkie said, glad to have gotten out of the "fake cousin" faux pas.

"No, Cindy and I are real cousins. My mother and her father are siblings, but they were just as unalike as Cindy and I. Both of them inherited a bunch of money from their grandfather—he was actually a crony of John D. Rockefeller's, and once was part owner of the Empire State Building—and didn't have to work for a living. Cindy's father never got an actual job, but he continued to invest in real estate. That's our family's thing, real estate. When my mother graduated from Sarah Lawrence, she married my father, another old-money family, after a whirlwind romance. It totally shocked her family. What shocked them even more was that Father decided to actually get a law degree and work for a living, while also continuing to dabble in real estate. Uncle Richard just never could understand it. He and Cindy's mother always acted as if they were superior to us, but the truth is—and believe me they know it—is my parents have more than twice the money they have," Rachel said with only the slightest hint of a boast in her tone.

"Really," Nikkie said breathlessly.

Rachel nodded as they continued to meander around the room. "We're not as flashy as they are, and we live more simply, but we're doing quite well." She noticed the look on Nicole's face and laughed. "Believe me, this"—she swept her hand over the room—"is simple compared to Cindy's family's house."

"Wow" was all Nikkie could say.

"When my father died a few years ago, Uncle Richard tried to become the patriarch of the entire family, but Mother wasn't having it," Rachel continued. "She likes Uncle Richard and all, but she made it clear she could handle the family finances. And they have different philosophies of life. It wouldn't have worked out at all."

A thought suddenly hit Nikkie. "Your mother said she wanted to talk to me about something. Do you have any idea what it could be?"

"Probably one of her projects. She's always trying to get young people more politically and socially active. Don't worry. She's aggressive, but she's not too pushy. Just say you're too busy at work to get involved in whatever it is she has in mind."

"Actually, I like your mother. She seems really down-to-earth."

"Rachel! Finally!" said a tall red-haired young man with freckles. "We've been looking all over for you."

"Hey, Ritchie." Rachel kissed the man on the cheek. "Nikkie, this is my cousin Ritchie. He's Cindy's younger brother. And this is Magda, his girlfriend," she said, waving her hand at the stunning raven-haired woman who clung to Ritchie.

"His fiancée," the woman said in a heavy Mediterranean accent.

"Sorry, I didn't know you two had become engaged," Rachel said, looking at Ritchie questioningly.

"We haven't announced it yet," Magda answered while Ritchie averted his eyes. "We're shopping for the ring tomorrow."

"Well, this is my friend Nicole Jensen."

"Hi," Ritchie said without looking at her, thereby not noticing the hand Nicole extended his way.

"Rache, where's Cindy? She's supposed to be meeting us here."

Rachel smiled. "She called a little while ago to say she couldn't make it because she had a migraine."

"That bitch. She has my Ferrari," he snarled.

"Hello, Ritchie. Hello, Magda."

"Hi, Aunt Helen." Ritchie kissed the older woman on the cheek. "Thanks for the invitation."

"Don't be silly. Where's your sister?"

Ritchie's mouth turned into a sneer. "Rachel just told us she called to say she wasn't going to make it tonight."

"Migraines," Rachel said simply.

"Just turn to Page Six of the *Post* tomorrow and you'll see how much she's suffering."

Mrs. Riverton ignored her nephew. "Magda, dear, you look lovely as usual. And how is your father?"

"He's fine, thank you for asking, Mrs. Riverton," the young woman answered in a bored voice.

"Wonderful. Please tell the ambassador I said hello. Well, I'll leave you youngsters to yourselves." Mrs. Riverton turned to Nikkie. "Do remember we have to talk, dear."

"Are you staying until the party is over?" Ritchie asked as soon as Mrs. Riverton walked away.

"More than likely. Why? What do you have in mind?" Rachel asked.

"I'm supposed to be meeting some black guys in Harlem and I was hoping you could give me a ride so I wouldn't have to get a taxi."

"What are you going to Harlem for?" Rachel asked suspiciously.

"Take a guess," Ritchie said with a chuckle.

Rachel shook her head. "Sorry, you're going to have to cab it. I'm not going to have anything to do with this mission."

"What the hell is wrong with you?" Ritchie snapped.

"And who are these black guys, anyway? How well do you know them? And how did you meet them?" Rachel demanded, color rising in her cheeks. "What do they do for a living?"

"What do you mean? They're just a bunch of black guys."

"No, Ritchie! I know the kind of black guys you're talking about. Do you really intend to disgrace your family like that? They're not just a bunch of black guys, and you know it. They're a particular kind. The kind that Kennedy kid hung out with back in the eighties when they found him beat up and mugged after taking an overdose of heroin."

"They're not just a bunch of black guys; they're a bunch

of no-good niggers," Nikkie said in an attempt to side with Rachel. "There's a difference."

"Is anything wrong, children?"

"No, Aunt Helen," Ritchie stammered. "But Magda and I have to leave. I'm so sorry, but we have an engagement uptown." He looked at Rachel and then back at his aunt. "Could you have your driver give us a ride, perhaps?"

"Let them walk, Mother," Rachel said quietly.

"I'm sorry, but the chauffeur has the evening off, Ritchie dear," Mrs. Riverton said without missing a beat. "But Henry is getting ready to leave, and I'm sure he won't mind dropping you off, wherever it is you need to go, on his way to Hartford."

"That's all right, Aunt Helen, I wouldn't want to trouble him. I'll just take a cab. Good night."

Rachel, Nikkie, and Mrs. Riverton watched as he and Magda headed out—heads held high and looking neither to the left nor right.

"Nicole," Mrs. Riverton said after they left, "why don't you take a walk with me. As I said, there's something I'd like to discuss." She linked her arm with Nikkie's. "Would you excuse us, Rachel? I promise I won't keep your friend long."

Nikkie's stomach fluttered as she accompanied Mrs. Riverton out of the ballroom and onto the large balcony overlooking Fifth Avenue. "I was just telling your daughter that you have a lovely home. Have you lived here long?"

"It's been in my family for almost a century. My mother was raised here, in fact." Mrs. Riverton sat down in one of the six or seven chairs on the balcony and motioned for Nikkie to sit next to her. "So Rachel tells me you're from Detroit. How are you enjoying New York?"

"It's just lovely. My kind of town, as they say." Nikkie laughed nervously.

"I'm sure. I know you and Rachel have been out quite often with Cindy at various nightspots." She smiled. "There's nothing wrong with that, of course. I used to go out quite often myself when I was younger."

Nikkie nodded, not knowing what she was expected to say, and afraid to say the wrong thing.

"I'm glad you and Rachel are friends. So many of the young people she knows aren't doing anything with their lives. They're content just having a good time and whittling away at their trust funds. But you work for a living. And I hope you would work even if you didn't have to. But"—she laughed lightly—"of course you have to."

Nikkie nodded again. The butterflies in her stomach now felt like bees, buzzing furiously around and stinging at random.

"Rachel is quite fond of you, and has spoken about you often." Mrs. Riverton's fingers trailed along the arm of the chair as she spoke. "I've only just met you, and I daresay I also found you quite appealing. In fact, I first wanted to discuss you joining . . ." Her voice trailed off. "Well, it doesn't matter. I find it more important to discuss another matter with you."

"And what would that be, ma'am?" Nikkie's mouth was dry, and her voice seemed strange even to her.

"I know you feel uncomfortable, dear, and I'm very sorry about that. In fact, I could see that you've been uncomfortable most of the evening. You're not used to being around a set such as ours, is that right?"

"Yes, ma'am," Nikkie croaked.

Mrs. Riverton sighed. "I'm trying to put this as delicately as

I can, but I could see that you've been worrying about fitting in. Please don't try, you're wonderful as you are."

Nikkie laughed nervously. "Thank you," she said, relieved that this was all the woman wanted to tell her. "It's just that, well, I'm not up on all the social graces, and—"

"By the way, just so you know, a lady doesn't reach out to shake a man's hand," Mrs. Riverton said, patting Nikkie's cheek. "She waits for him to put his hand forward."

Nikkie blushed.

"Oh, look at you. Don't take it as a criticism, take it as loving instruction." Mrs. Riverton put her hand on top of Nikkie's. "That's the sole intent behind it."

"Well, thank you. I—"

"But this you should take as criticism." Mrs. Riverton sat back against her chair. "I overheard part of the conversation you, Rachel, and Ritchie were having. And if I'm not mistaken, I believe I heard you use the word 'nigger.' Am I mistaken?"

Nikkie's mouth dropped open and her stomach lurched. She suddenly felt like she was going to be sick. She stood up, then hurriedly sat back down. She looked at Mrs. Riverton, then quickly looked away.

"I see I'm not mistaken," Mrs. Riverton said quietly. "I wouldn't have judged you as the type of person who would call an African-American a name like that. In fact, I'm quite shocked—"

"Mrs. Riverton, I'm so sorry!" Nikkie blurted out. "I don't normally use that word . . ."

"I didn't think you did, and yet—"

"And I only used it to make a point. I was just trying to say that there's a difference between black people who are trying to do something with their lives and blacks who are just—"

"And there's a difference between white people who would never use racial slurs and those that would—and do," Mrs. Riverton said firmly. "And I prefer guests who are not in that latter grouping." She paused. "I'm sorry, but I'm going to have to ask you to leave, Nicole. That may seem harsh, and I suppose it is. I do hope you'll respect my wishes."

I can't believe it, Nikkie thought as she collected her shawl and stepped outside the huge mansion. She'd heard Cindy and Hal and a number of white people use the word "nigger" and get away with it when they explained that they were talking about a certain class of black folks. *So why is it that I'm wrong for using the word even when using the same explanation? Because I said it at a swanky party? If the explanation is good enough for private functions, why not public ones? If a person saying it in public makes it racist, then it's just as racist in private. I've been taken to task by a white person for calling a black a "nigger." Just how low have I sunk?*

Rachel called her early the next morning. "Mother told me what happened. I apologize."

"No need to, your mother was right. I was out of line," Nikkie said sullenly.

"Well, yes," Rachel said, pausing, "but I don't think she should have asked you to leave. She's just very sensitive, you know."

"So let me ask you something," Nikkie said, suddenly and inexplicably angry. "You're going to tell me that you never use that word? I've heard you use it myself, you know."

"Oh no, you haven't. Granted, you've heard Cindy use the

word, and I didn't tell her she was wrong to do so, but even Cindy certainly wouldn't have used it in that kind of social setting," Rachel said in an annoyed tone.

"I didn't realize that there was a time and a place to call people 'niggers.'" Nikkie exploded. "And let me tell you something else—"

"Oh, Nikkie, I didn't call to argue. Perhaps I should ring you back in a few days?"

The exasperation in Rachel's voice only fueled Nikkie's anger. "Who said anything about arguing? I'm not arguing, Rachel! I'm just saying—" But before she could say anything else, the line went dead. Nikkie stared at the phone a moment, then slammed it down on the receiver. She reached over to the nightstand and picked up her emery board.

There were things in her life she'd felt guilty about, ashamed about even. Everyone had those things in their life. But for the first time she was actually ashamed of herself. Or was it of the persona that she had taken on? Or was there a difference? She wasn't sure anymore. She did know one thing; she was losing it. In fact, she might have already lost.

She picked the telephone back up.

"Mama? It's me, Nikkie."

"Baby! What are you doing up so early on a Sunday morning? Finally found a church up there you like?"

"No, I'm still looking." Nikkie felt a swift pang of guilt. She'd been raised in the church and had promised her mother she'd join one as soon as she got to New York, but she'd never seemed to get around to it.

"Well, I thought about not going myself, today. My old bones are acting up," Rina said in a distracted voice. "I don't know if I have arthritis or rheumatism. Don't matter. My bones be aching sometimes. But bones or no bones, I'm gonna go worship the Lord. It's good to hear your voice, sweetie. You okay? How's the city treating you? You doing okay on that job of yours?"

Nikkie smiled. "I'm doing fine, Mama. And the job is going good. I'm just a little homesick is all."

"Well, now why don't you just come on home for a little bit? Take a long weekend and spend some time with your mama. You know I miss you."

"I miss you, too, Mama. And, God, I miss your cooking. I haven't had a good meal since I've been up here."

"Um-mm-mm. Well, I guess it would be mean for me to tell you that I've got Sunday dinner all cooked up and ready to eat later this evening. I cooked up some greens, potato salad, ribs, and peach cobbler."

Nikkie groaned. "Oh, Mama, why you gonna go and tell me all that when I just told you I haven't had a good meal in months!"

Rina chuckled. "Just being mean, I guess."

"Why you doing all that cooking, anyway? Joseph and Ayoka coming over after church?"

"Yes. They're doing fine, child. Joseph sold a big apartment building downtown and got a big commission. Took me out to dinner to celebrate."

"That's good. You know I've called him a few times, but he never has time to talk to me but a few minutes."

Rina paused. "Well, you know how your brother is. He's still stewing, but he'll be okay."

"Well, I wish he would hurry up."

"He will, baby, he will. Just give him some time."

Nikkie nodded as if her mother could see her. "Okay,

Mama, I'm going to go. I just wanted to call and see if you were doing okay. Oh, and how's Papa?"

"Why don't you ask him yourself? He's right in the other room."

"No, Mama. That's okay. Just tell him I asked about him. You go ahead and go to church. I'll try and give you a call sometime later this week."

"Okay, baby, but when are you going to come home again?"

"Soon, Mama, I promise."

"You've been saying that for the last few months," Rina said in an accusing tone.

"Well, I mean it this time. Okay, Mama. I love you. Talk to you again, soon."

"Nikkie, wait!"

"Yes, Mama?"

"Nikkie. You sure everything's okay? You sure? You don't sound right. You sure everything going okay at the job? They treating you right over there?"

Nikkie gripped the telephone tightly. She wanted to tell her mother everything, like she did when she was a little girl. She wanted to tell her that she was making one mistake after another, and the mistakes were getting bigger and bigger. She wanted to tell her that she was tired of living a lie, and was worried that the lie was becoming her truth; that she wanted to stop, but didn't know how.

"Mama, really. Everything's fine. I'll call you later this week."

Rina sighed into the receiver. "Nikkie, I know you're going to get upset with me for bringing this up again, but you know no good ever came of someone living a lie. Child, the sooner you come clean and own up to who you are and where you come from, the sooner you'll be able to rest easy." Rina's voice now took on a more urgent tone. "Baby, you promised you were only going to pass for a little while—only until you got the job. Well, you've been there for months now. I know what you said about moving up in the firm, but if you can't move being who you are, maybe it's not the type of company you should be in, anyway. I didn't raise you to—"

"Mama, please." Nikkie pressed her fingertips to her temples, as if it would somehow relieve the pressure building up in her head.

"Yes, 'Mama, please.' That's all you say these days when I bring this up. Well, I'm gonna go ahead on to church, and I'll pray for you like I always do. I'ma pray that you do the right thing. Bye, baby."

Nikkie hung up the telephone and cried herself back to sleep.

chapter fifteen

August 2007

"The company skybox? Get out of here! Kadinsky's going to let you use the company skybox?"

"Yeah, they let account executives use it when they're wining and dining clients or as a bonus when one of us lands a big account. I got it for stealing the Rosenfeld account from the Richardson Grecher Agency. It's a three-million-a-year account, you know."

"Yes, Hal, I know." Nikkie smiled. "You only mentioned it twenty times this week."

"Oh, okay. Wasn't sure you knew," Hal said with a grin.

In the month that she and Hal had been dating, she'd become used to his boasting. But then again, if she had as much success as he did, she'd probably be boasting, too, although she soon realized he used his arrogance to mask his self-doubts. It seemed ridiculous that someone as charming, handsome, and successful as Hal had any doubts about himself at all, but somehow he did. He seldom compared his victories to those of others, but he always compared them to his last—as if he constantly had to prove to himself, not so much to others, that he wasn't slipping.

And the good thing about Hal was—and there were a lot of good things—that he celebrated her small victories as heartily as he celebrated his large ones. She'd been surprised when the company put her in charge of the Lucia Silver account instead of handing it off to a more seasoned rep—with her simply being an assistant—but she set out to prove to the company that they had made a good decision. And she'd been doing well. She'd been able to place six or seven newspaper items on the starlet, and even managed to snag her a cover of one of the local magazines. And Hal had been a major help, giving her access to some of his media sources, something that most of the PR reps guarded with their lives.

In fact, Hal was wonderful to deal with at work, and he was also the perfect boyfriend—or perfect *almost* boyfriend. Although they went out at least twice a week, and he called her every evening after work to make sure she got home safely, she still hadn't been able to bring herself to go to bed with him. She liked him—really liked him—but the thought of going to bed with him was just, well, distasteful. And she had no illusions as to why; she just wasn't physically attracted to white men. Oh, they looked great in magazines with their shirts off, but the thought of one taking his shirt off for her was simply a turnoff. Even the kissing wasn't too bad, but when he tried to slip his hand under her blouse to fondle her breast, she always pulled back after a few moments. The touch of his hand freaked her out. It was too soft. Not soft as in feminine, but soft as in smooth—as a matter of fact, as smooth as hers. She wasn't used to it, and didn't like it. It wasn't that her previous boyfriends' skin had been necessarily rough, but they felt like skin, not like silk. She didn't know how to overcome her revulsion, but she also knew she'd better figure out a way fast if she wanted to keep Hal interested in her.

She felt guilty about leading him on, especially since it was so evident that he was into her big-time, and she knew she'd never be able to return his feelings. She'd been foolish and selfish to let things progress as far as they had. But he was good company, and she learned a lot just being around him. She learned things about public relations, but, more important, she learned more and more about how white people acted, and how to emulate those actions. Hal was good for her. She'd worry later about how to let him down easy. Thank God he was a Mormon and wasn't pressing her about having sex, since his religious faith dictated sexual abstinence until marriage. It did irk him, though, that she insisted that they keep their relationship on the down low at work. There were some coworkers who might have figured out they were seeing each other during their off-hours, but not many. Often they would go out with their colleagues—with everyone hanging out and no one pairing off, so she was sure their friendship seemed innocent to most people.

"Shanika!"

Nikkie's head jerked up, and she almost swung around to find out who was calling her by her given name when she remembered she was with Hal. She quickened her pace.

"The box sits like thirty people, and it's all catered." Hal continued, unaware of Nikkie's sudden feeling of impending doom. "The game doesn't start until seven, so you'll have time to go home and change if you want."

"Shanika! Shanika!"

Whoever was calling was much closer, and Nikkie was

about to suggest to Hal that they duck into a restaurant when the voice abruptly became a grasp on her arm.

"Shanika! Girl, I thought that was you!"

Nikkie suddenly found herself face-to-face with a short, coal-black-skinned, muscular man with long, curly hair. Her heart dove into the pit of her stomach. Cousin Booby.

"You ain't hear me calling you? What are you doing in New York, cuz?" he asked with a huge, pearly white grin.

Nikkie tried to keep her voice calm. "I'm sorry. You must have me mistaken for someone else. My name's Nicole."

Booby jerked his head back in surprise, then actually released her arm and stepped back as if to further appraise her. "What are you talking about, Nika?"

"My name isn't Shanika or Nika," Nikkie said frantically. "It's Nicole Jensen. And I'm sorry, but I've got to go."

"Nicole who? What are you talking about?" Booby's face wrinkled into a scowl.

Oh please, please, please, let his shell-shock thingee kick in now and think maybe he did make a mistake.

For a moment she thought it had worked, but he suddenly grabbed her arm again, more roughly this time. "What the hell's going on?" he demanded.

"Excuse me," Hal said politely but firmly, "but I believe my friend has indicated that you're mistaken."

"Yeah, go ahead and excuse yourself, man," Booby said as he tried to pull Nikkie away. "This is my cousin, and I think she and I need to have a conversation."

"Please let go of me!" Nikkie managed to free her arm.

"I believe you're disturbing the lady." Hal stepped between them as people began to slow down to get a look at what was going on. "Why don't you go on your way."

"Man, get the hell out of my face," Booby said as he tried to sidestep Hal to get back at Nikkie.

"Hal, come on." Nikkie tugged at his arm. "We're going to be late getting back to the office. Let's just go."

"Nika, you ain't going no damn where." Booby grabbed her. "What the hell is wrong with you, girl?"

"Let go of me," Nikkie said through clenched teeth. Damn. What the hell was wrong with him? Not shell-shocked enough to be convinced it wasn't her, but too shell-shocked to get the hint she wanted him to make believe they didn't know each other?

"You heard the lady. Let her go!" Hal pushed Booby in the chest.

"What! Who the hell you pushing?" Booby released Nikkie and quickly stepped into a boxing stance. "I'll knock your damn head off."

Hal's lips turned up into a sneer. "I'm not going to stand out here and fight you like some kind of hoodlum."

"Then don't be putting your damn hands on me."

"Is there a problem here?" a new voice rang out.

Nikkie turned to see one of New York's finest quickly striding toward them, his police car—lights flashing—pulled halfway up onto the sidewalk. The officer's hand was on his holstered gun as he continued his approach. Things were spiraling out of control, and fast.

"It's nothing," she said, quickly running up to the officer before he could reach Booby. "Just a case of mistaken—"

"Officer, this man is harassing us," Hal interrupted in his Master of the Universe voice. "He's obviously drunk. He's using profanity, grabbing my lady friend here, and threatening me with violence."

"Man, I ain't do nothing but try and talk to my cousin," Booby yelled. "And I ain't lay a hand on him. He's the one who pushed me, I ain't touch him."

"Where's your cousin?" the officer asked sternly.

"Right there." Booby pointed to Nikkie. "Tell 'em, Nika."

The officer's eyes switched from Booby to Nikkie, then back to Booby as Hal guffawed. "Ma'am, is this man your cousin?"

"No," Nikkie said nervously, "but I'm sure he believes I am, and it's really not a big deal."

"What do you mean, it's not a big deal?" Booby stepped toward her, but was pushed back by Hal.

"Man, didn't I tell you not to put your hands on me again?" Booby pushed Hal back.

"Hold on there!" the officer said, his voice as menacing as the nightstick he was waving in the air.

"Please! Officer, I swear, everything's okay." Nikkie tried to jump in front of Booby, but was stopped by Hal.

"Man, how you gonna act like you gonna beat up on me when you done saw this man push me and you ain't do shit?" Booby demanded of the policeman.

"Sir, I would advise you to back up, turn around, and put your hands on the patrol car," the officer said in a breathless voice.

"What the hell? I gotta assume the position all of a sudden? For what, man?" Booby walked toward the officer, his hands held out at his sides. "I was just defending myself."

"And I was just defending my girlfriend," Hal retorted.

Booby swung around to face him again. "Your what? You fucking white boy . . ."

"Sir, I'm going to ask you again to put your hands on the car!"

". . . she ain't your girlfriend," Booby continued while walking toward Hal. "She's my . . ." Booby stopped, as if it finally dawned on him what was going on.

"Nika"—his eyes took on an accusing stare before narrowing into a squint as he reached out to grab her—"I know you ain't . . ."

Before he could get another word out, the officer pulled his gun and pointed it at Booby's head.

"Oh, my God!" Nikkie screamed before falling into a dead faint.

When she woke up again, she was on a gurney and being lifted up into an ambulance. She sat up, instantly alert. "What the hell is going on? Oh, my God, did they shoot him?"

"Shh, it's okay. Lie back down. They're just going to take you to the hospital to check you out and make sure you're okay," Hal said soothingly. "Don't worry, I'm going to ride along with you."

"Hal," she said urgently, "did they hurt him?"

"What? No. They just arrested him for disorderly conduct. But how are you?"

"I'm fine." Nikkie jumped off the gurney and into the street just in time to watch the last of the police cars speed off. She couldn't see him, but she knew Booby was in the back of one of them. She grabbed Hal's arm.

"Where are they taking him?"

Hal snorted. "Central booking, I guess. We have to go down later to press charges."

"No!"

"What?" The surprised look on Hal's face was almost funny.

Nikkie's mind raced. "Hal, look, neither of us was hurt—I probably just fainted because I hadn't eaten anything all day—and so what harm was really done?"

"What are you talking about?" Hal asked in a confused voice. "We've got to press charges. We can't let some lunatic go around assaulting innocent people."

"He was confused, you couldn't see that? And, anyway, if we press charges, the news media might find out, and how is that going to look for the firm?"

"It's going to look good. It's going to look like we're doing our civic duty," Hal insisted.

"Well"—Nikkie's mind was racing—"maybe, maybe not. Remember, that officer pulled his gun and pointed it at that poor man. And if I'm not mistaken, I saw someone taking a picture with their cell phone."

"So? The officer didn't shoot him. And he only arrested him because he was making a scene and coming after you."

"He wasn't really coming after me, and you know how these things get blown out of proportion. All that has to happen is that one still shot gets taken to the media and it's all about the cops threatening some black guy for no reason. They're going to say it's just another case of racial profiling."

"That's my point! That's why we have to go down and fill out a statement," Hal said in an exasperated voice.

"But don't you get my point? No matter what we might say, that photo might run, and they may start talking about police brutality, and we're going to get caught up in it, and so will Paxon and Green. It might all eventually get straightened out, but why get caught up in all that bad publicity at all? Let's just leave it alone."

"Booby, I'm so sorry. I feel so bad."

Booby grunted. "You feel bad? I'm the one who had to spend three hours in a jail cell. I got a good mind to call your mama and tell her what you did. Why you do that shit, Nika? Why you deny I'm your blood? That's cold, man."

Nikkie looked down at the ground. "I know. I'm the most awful person I know."

Booby raised his head to get a better look at her. "The most awful person you know? Damn, baby, you even beginning to sound like them." He chuckled. "Even taking me to a Starbucks to talk."

Nikkie started chewing her lip. "Been around them too long, I guess," she said sadly.

"Been trying to be one too long, is more like it."

Nikkie lowered her eyes again.

"Look, I ain't even mad about that. You do what you wanna do. But you ain't got no cause to be letting no policeman pull a gun on me. That's what I can't get over."

"I didn't know what to do," Nikkie said as she sipped her coffee. "I kept telling you that you were mistaken, hoping you would take the hint and leave me alone."

Booby snorted. "Look at how you talking. Hinting for me to leave you alone. Now, ain't that nothing."

"Well, you know what I mean. I was trying to figure out a way to wave you off without having to, you know . . ."

"Without having to let your boyfriend know he's dating a

darkie?" Booby laughed. "Yeah, I guess we shoulda come up with some kinda code or something. You say the password and your family will just keep on walking and let you pass."

"You tell anyone in the family yet?" Nikkie asked nervously.

"Get out! They don't know?"

"I mean about what happened to you." Nikkie paused, then said in a softer voice, "What I *let* happen to you."

"Naw, I ain't tell nobody yet." Booby sighed. "You told the police you wouldn't press charges, and I called one of my frat brothers who works in the District Attorney's Office and he made a call, so the police aren't going to charge me with anything on their own."

"I didn't know you knew people in the District Attorney's Office," Nikkie said incredulously.

"Yeah, a brother's got some connects. I'm not just some country bumpkin, you know."

"So," Nikkie began slowly, "you said you haven't told anyone in the family . . . *yet*. Does that mean you're planning on telling them?"

Booby cocked his head. "I just oughta, you know. They know you up here passing?"

"Mama and Joseph know."

"And they letting you get away with this crap?"

Nikki nodded. "They're not too happy about it, though. Especially Joseph."

Booby chuckled. "I wouldn't imagine he would be." He paused and shook his head. "Naw, I ain't gonna say anything, Nikkie. That would just cause more drama, and I think I've had enough of that for a while. 'Sides, you know you're my favorite cousin, even if you don't own up to me all the time."

Nikkie sighed. "This is such a mess, and you just don't know how sorry I am. Is this your first trip to New York? How about I take you sightseeing tomorrow? I'll take the day off from work and we can just hang out—just the two of us. I promise to show you a really good time."

Booby gave her an amused look. "Why, that's mighty white of you, ma'am."

"Oh, Booby!"

"Naw, I'm only playing, Nika. It's all good. And I don't need a tour guide. I've been to New York before. I keep telling you I'm not a country bumpkin." He fell silent for a moment. "You know," he said finally, "I never thought that you'd be one to be passing. I mean, God knows you're light enough to do it, but I never thought you would."

Nikkie sighed. "I'm sure not the first one, Booby."

"Well, you're the first one in our family."

Nikkie waved her hand dismissively. "Oh please. You're going to tell me that no one in the Jenkins family—"

"Not a one," Booby said, shaking his head. "Grandma was the most color-struck person I ever met, and she was proud as hell that she coulda passed, but she was even more proud that she never did."

"And you believe her?"

"Yeah, I gotta say I do. She was a weird old bird, Grandma was. But I do believe she ain't ever try. She was just like that."

"I guess," Nikkie said in a low voice.

Booby picked up her hand. "Nikkie, I ain't trying to make you feel bad, but you gotta tell me, what made you do it?"

Nikkie could feel tears begin to well in her eyes. "Well, it's not because I'm ashamed to be black or anything. It's just that, well, it just made life easier."

She laid the whole scenario out to him: her initial job interview, the night she met Cindy and her friends, being turned down for the job because she wasn't black enough, her lunch date with Mrs. Randolph, and her being accepted once the company thought she was white. "And"—she threw up her hands—"everything's just kinda got out of hand since then. I keep looking for the right opportunity to let people know I'm black, but it never seems to come. And I'm just getting sucked in, further and further. I really don't know what to do."

"And you even went and got yourself a white boyfriend, huh?"

"No. Hal Richardson is simply a colleague," Nikkie lied. "I'm not into white guys."

"Well, thank God for that." Booby's voice dripped with relief.

"And I really don't like being white. At least not all the time, Booby. You gotta believe that. But how am I going to go into my job and announce that I'm black when, for all these months, I've been letting them think I'm white?"

Booby looked at her strangely. "Nika, all you gotta do is go in there and be black. Don't say it, just be it. Go in there and listen to the kind of music you like, eat the kind of food that you like, and, damn it, watch the television shows you like. Don't announce it, just be it."

Nikkie shook her head. "It's just not that easy, Booby."

"Girl, the longer you wait, the harder it's gonna be. But, hey, whatever. It's your life. Live it white if you want."

chapter sixteen

SEPTEMBER 2007

Three cups of coffee, and Nikkie was still barely awake as she flagged down a cab to take her to the magazine for the photo shoot they were doing on Lucia. It was a cold day for September, and Nikkie wrapped her shawl tightly around her after getting in the taxi. She snapped open her cell phone and punched in her client's mobile number.

"Lucia. I'm on my way now. Are you almost ready? I can swing by and pick you up if you'd like."

"I'm here already."

"Oh, good!" Nikkie guiltily looked at her watch. It was only 8:30; they weren't scheduled to arrive until 10 a.m. Lucia must really be excited to get there so early. Or . . .

"Please tell me you didn't go straight there from some club."

"Fine. I won't tell you. But if I hadn't, I wouldn't have been able to get here on time, you know. I'd think you should be proud of me." Lucia yawned. "How long before you get here? I'm getting ready to go into makeup."

"I'll be there in about twenty minutes, maybe fifteen. Just hang tight." *Oh God*, she thought after she'd hung up. *I hope Lucia doesn't look hungover. How can she do this to me when she knows I'm trying to convince them to put her on the cover?*

The traffic was typical for New York City rush hour, and it actually took Nikkie almost a half hour to get to the magazine.

"Hi, I'm Nicole Jensen," she hurriedly told the receptionist. "I'm here to meet my client, Lucia Silver."

She was shown into the photo studio, where the photographer was setting up for the shoot. Lucia was sitting in the corner flipping through an old issue of the magazine, looking simply spectacular. Her long ebony black hair was pulled up and back into a luxurious fall, and diamonds—or maybe rhinestones—were dotted throughout. Her brows were penciled in to extend to the very outside of her eyes, and were perfectly arched to accentuate her startlingly bright violet eyes. She was draped in a snowy white toga-type getup, pulled tight against her bodice, and showing enough cleavage to make the male readers extremely happy.

"You look beautiful," Nikkie said breathlessly.

"I do, don't I? And I bet you thought I was going to look a mess after staying out all night." The women shared a laugh.

"I was all prepared to have to do my own makeup, but they did a good job. I got the woman's number in case I need her again. She does freelance work, too." Lucia yawned. "So, do you know whether I'm getting the cover or not? I look twice as good as Nicole Kidman, and she's made the cover twice, you know."

"Don't worry, I'm working on it." Nikkie patted the woman on her bare shoulder. "But trust me, I have a really good feeling about this. Especially since you landed the Spielberg role. And the interview you did was just great."

"Oh yeah, we got to talk about that."

"Uh-oh." Nikkie's stomach did a flip-flop.

"Don't worry. I have bad news, but I've got good news, too." Lucia hopped off her chair and moved toward the photographer, who was waving her over. "You got time to do lunch after we're through here? How about we do Elaine's? I haven't been there in a while."

It was Nikkie's first photo shoot, but Lucia seemed to be a veteran. The photographer and his assistant were both oohing and aahing over her poses, and even the fashion editor came out to watch the shoot. *Yeah, I'm sure I can land the cover,* Nikkie thought with satisfaction.

She had put her cell phone on vibrate, and she felt it noiselessly buzzing against her suit pocket.

"Hey, beautiful Nikkie."

"Hey, Hal. I forgot to mention I wouldn't be coming in the office until this afternoon. I'm down here at the magazine; Lucia's doing a photo shoot."

"Wow, I'm impressed! You getting the cover?"

"I'm sure as hell going to try."

"What time are you going to finish up? Maybe we can do lunch?"

"We're going to be finished in about another hour or so, but I told Lucia I'd have lunch with her. I'll see you when I get back to the office." She paused. "On second thought, why don't you join us. I'd love for you to meet my first new client."

Hal laughed. "You sure? That girl's hot, you know. I might have to dump you and move up a couple of rungs on the ladder."

"Ha-ha. Very funny. Yeah, I'm sure. Meet us at Elaine's at twelve-thirty, okay?"

Just as she hoped, Lucia seemed charmed by Hal. And just as she trusted, Hal hadn't tried to pull her star client. They chatted about the movie and television industry and just made general small talk while they ate. It was after they were finished, and were sipping their wine, that Nikkie decided it was time to get down to business.

"Lucia, you said you had something to tell me about that interview. It sounded like it was going to be something heavy, so that's actually why I asked Hal to join us. He's been with Paxon and Green for a while now, and we may have to borrow his expertise if it's something really serious."

"Hmph, I may have been at the firm longer, but Nikkie has been outshining all of us of late," Hal said with a smile. Nikkie squeezed his hand under the table in appreciation. "Still, if there's anything I can do, I'll be glad to help."

"Well, here's the thing." Lucia leaned back in her chair. "You know how I told them that I had gotten the role of the chambermaid in the new Spielberg movie? Well, my agent called me last night. I've ungotten it."

"What?" Nikkie's mouth dropped open. "What do you mean? I thought it was a done deal."

"We left it at a handshake, but they hadn't gotten around to drawing up the contract for us to sign yet." Lucia shrugged. "Meanwhile, Spielberg came up with the grand idea that the chambermaid should be black. They said they hoped I would just graciously back out of it without making a fuss, and of course I have no choice. I do want to stay on Spielberg's good side. And he promised me a really meaty role in his next flick."

"Why did they decide to go with a black chambermaid?" Nikkie asked.

Hal broke in before she could answer. "Another example of someone being screwed because of affirmative action." He snorted.

Lucia looked surprised. "How do you figure that?"

"Well, I bet someone brought it to Spielberg's attention that they didn't have enough blacks in his last couple of movies, or something, so he's making this move to rectify it." He paused. "I might be wrong, of course, but I just don't see why else they would dump an actress of your caliber."

Lucia smiled. "That's very sweet of you to say. But I don't think that's the reason. It just so happens that there are layers to the role that could probably be more developed if the character were black. And I'm not into doing blackface." She took another sip of her wine. "But you sound as if you have something against affirmative action? Haven't you benefited from it?"

Hal jerked his head back. "I beg your pardon?"

Lucia gave a short laugh. "It kills me that so many people think only blacks have benefited from affirmative action."

Nikkie was startled. "I guess Puerto Ricans and Asians, and, well, you know, other people of color have also?"

"Uh-huh." Lucia turned to Hal. "Where did you go to college?"

"The University of Pennsylvania."

"Ivy League. I'm impressed. The tuition must have been pretty steep."

Hal shrugged his broad shoulders. "I was able to get by with school grants and student loans."

"Just what I thought," Lucia said with a satisfied smile. "You, my dear boy, are an affirmative action baby."

"What do you mean?"

Lucia dabbed at her lips with the napkin before continuing. "Listen, the whole purpose of affirmative action is to even the playing field, right? It's for people who have been born with a disadvantage to get the same opportunities to prove themselves as those without disadvantages. That's it, plain and simple. Now, with the cost of college tuition these days, most students have to get some kind of financial aid. Well, financial aid is simply a form of affirmative action. It's to make sure that students who can't afford a college education can still get a college education so that they can then compete in the job force. So anyone—black, white, yellow, or purple—who has received student financial aid is an affirmative action baby, whether they want to recognize the fact or not."

She chuckled. "So, yeah, Hal, you're an affirmative action baby."

"Wow. I never thought of it like that," Nikkie said. *And I've got to remember it the next time someone brings up the subject.*

"Well, it's not the same thing." Hal tried to keep a level voice, but Nikkie knew him well enough to see just how upset he was.

Lucia raised one of her eyebrows. "And why not?"

"It just isn't," he protested hotly.

Lucia looked at him and smirked before turning back to Nikkie. "Remember, though, I said I had good news and bad news. I may have lost the Spielberg role, but it just so happens that I landed the lead in Woody Allen's newest movie. Filming starts in two weeks."

"Oh, my God, that's wonderful!" Nikkie clasped her hands in front of her. "So, okay, I'll have to call the writer at the magazine to let her know to take out the part about the Spielberg film, but to add the info about the Woody Allen movie. That'll be a cinch. Lucia, this is just great." She turned to Hal, who seemed distracted. "Isn't it, Hal?"

"Yes, just wonderful," he said absentmindedly. "Listen, I hope you ladies will excuse me, but I've got to get back to the office. I have a conference call coming up in about an hour, and I have to prepare." He pulled out his wallet and withdrew an American Express Platinum Card. "Please let me take care of the bill."

"Is he your boyfriend?" Lucia said after he left.

"Something like that."

Lucia shook her head. "He's nice, but he's got some real issues, and I suspect you know what they are. Personally, I think you can do better."

Nikkie nodded. "I'm beginning to think so myself."

chapter seventeen

"Nicole? This is Mrs. Riverton. Have I caught you at a bad time, dear?"

Nikkie almost dropped the phone. "No, ma'am. I was just getting ready for work. How are you?"

"Oh, I don't want to make you late, so I'll be brief. I hope you don't mind, but I got your telephone number from Rachel. She said you live at Seventy-second and West End, is that right?"

"Seventy-first Street actually."

"Good. Well, I'm working with the Hillary Clinton campaign and we have an office near there. We're looking for some volunteers to come in on Saturday and help stuff envelopes. Boring work, but for a good cause. Are you free?"

"Sure. What time?"

"Whatever time you're available. I should be there around nine a.m."

"I'll be there at nine-thirty, then. Should I bring in some coffee or orange juice?"

"No, no, no . . . we always supply coffee and doughnuts for the volunteers. Just bring yourself, that's all we need. Well, thank you and I'll see you Saturday morning."

Mrs. Riverton cleared her throat. "By the way, I trust you've taken to heart the conversation we had on the veranda?"

Nikkie blushed. "Yes, ma'am."

"Good. I'm glad that's behind us. I'll see you on Saturday."

Mrs. Riverton was right, the work was boring. By 11 a.m. Nikkie figured she'd stuffed five hundred envelopes. There were about thirty other people in the small campaign headquarters, and Mrs. Riverton was so busy supervising, the two barely had time to talk, although the woman had greeted her warmly when she walked in. She looked at her watch. Almost noon. Hal had promised to pick her up at 12:30.

"Well, looky, looky! Look who's here! What's up, girlfriend?"

"Tina!" Nikkie stood up to give the girl a welcoming hug when she noticed the woman's potbelly. "Tina, you're—"

Tina rubbed her stomach. "Yep, I'm with child, as they say. Four months. It's a boy. Ain't that something!"

"It sure is. Congratulations!" Nikkie sat back down. "This is really a surprise. What are you doing here?"

"Same as you. Doing volunteer work. Or are you a paid campaign worker?"

Nikkie shook her head. "No. Volunteering. Rachel's mom got me involved."

Tina took the seat next to her. "Yeah. She's the one who pulled me in, too. Not that it took much pulling. You know

I'm down for getting the first woman elected president of the United States." She paused. "Of course I'm also volunteering for Barack Obama. I'm down for getting the first black man elected president of the United States." She giggled. "I'm torn."

"So who are you going to vote for in the primary, then?"

"Hell, if I know! I'll probably wait until the last minute to make up my mind."

Mrs. Riverton walked over. "You'd better vote for Mrs. Clinton, Tina." She bent down and kissed Tina on the cheek. "How are you doing, dear?"

"I'm fine. And I probably will. You gonna order pizza for us today?"

"Tina, you just got here." Mrs. Riverton patted her on the back. "But, yes, dear, we'll be ordering in another half hour or so. Can you wait that long?"

"Yep." Tina fished down into her pocketbook and pulled out a bag of pretzels. "I got something to hold me down until then. I come prepared, girl."

Mrs. Riverton laughed. "You're going to weigh three hundred pounds by the time that baby is born."

"So you're pregnant. This is so exciting," Nikkie said when Mrs. Riverton went back to her desk. "No wonder I haven't seen you out."

"Girl, please," Tina said with a wave of her hand. "I be going out. I just don't hang out with Cindy. Girlfriend don't got time for me anymore."

"Why not?"

"She's mad because I got pregnant. Well, mostly because of who I got pregnant for. She's pissed because he's black."

"Stop lying." The two women looked up to see Rachel.

"Cindy could care less that he's black," Rachel said as she pulled up a chair next to them. "She's disappointed in you because he's a dope dealer."

"Whoa!" Nikkie's head jerked back in surprise.

"That's not his fault." Tina's nostrils flared. "He's just doing what he's gotta do to survive."

"Uh-huh, okay. Sure." Rachel snorted. "If you say so."

Tina turned to Nikkie. "You guys don't seem to understand what the black man goes through in this country. If they can't get a job, what are they supposed to do? Starve? I mean, I ain't crazy about the fact that Russell's slinging, but I'm not going to dump him because of it. A man's gotta do what a man's gotta do."

Lord, Tina's Ebonics are worse than ever, Nikkie thought. "And your Russell's got to deal drugs, huh? I mean, even if he can't get a job on Wall Street, he could get a job at McDonald's rather than deal crack."

"For your information he doesn't deal crack, he sells heroin."

"Oh, and I guess that's so much better," Nikkie said incredulously.

"I didn't say that, so don't be putting words in my mouth. And so I guess you think it's okay that a black man has to sling hamburgers to make a living?" Tina demanded.

"Know what, Tina?" Nikkie put her hands up in front of her chest in the form of surrender. "My name is Wes, and I'm not in this mess."

"You should stop the crap, Tina," Rachel snapped. "There's plenty of black men out here who have good jobs, but you just wanted to hook up with the most street guy you could find. And as far as supporting his family, you're supporting him.

Remember, I know! And even with all that, he's still out there dealing. That speaks to lack of character, not survival."

"You know what? I'm not even having this argument."

"Fine. I didn't want to have it, anyway. But don't go around lying about Cindy. That girl has a lot of things wrong with her, but don't go around saying she's prejudiced against blacks."

"You guys are so whack." Tina stood up and scooped the bag of pretzels from the desk back into her pocketbook. "Tell your mother I had to go home because I don't feel good. I'm not going to just sit here and listen to this crap."

"No problem." Rachel shrugged. "In fact, you can tell her yourself. Here she comes."

"Girls, I want you to meet a good friend of mine. Tyrone Bennett, I'd like to introduce you to my daughter, Rachel Riverton, her friend Nicole Jensen, and this"—Mrs. Riverton put her hand on Tina's shoulder—"is Tina Ludwig."

"How do you do." The man extended his hand to Tina, but the young woman rudely pushed by him.

"I gotta go, Mrs. Riverton. I'll see you later," she said over her shoulder.

Mrs. Riverton looked first at Rachel and Nikkie with questioning eyes, then took after Tina. "Tina, dear, wait. Is something wrong?"

"Mother's going to have a fit when she finds out that I'm the one who ran Tina off," Rachel grumbled.

But Nikkie wasn't listening. She was looking up at the dreamiest eyes she'd ever seen; and to her delight, they were looking at her with what she hoped was the same interest.

The man cleared his throat. "Well, it's nice to meet you beautiful ladies," he said in a soft baritone while still not taking his eyes off Nikkie.

"It's nice to meet you, too, Mr. Bennett," she said breathlessly.

"Please call me Tyrone."

"All right, Tyrone. And I hope you'll call me Nikkie." He wasn't handsome. He was gorgeous. Joseph was six-five, and this man was a little shorter, so she supposed he was about six-three. Maybe two hundred firmly packed pounds, judging by the huge biceps that were accentuated so nicely by his navy blue fishnet T-shirt. He wore a blue Yankees ball cap on his head, but the hair on the side that it didn't cover was short and neatly trimmed, as were his moustache and goatee—which had a shock of white going straight down its middle. His complexion and skin were Hershey's milk chocolate—smooth, dark, and creamy. But those eyes. Oh, those eyes. Framed by dark bushy eyebrows, they were shaped like those of a doe, with long, thick eyelashes to boot.

"Tyrone Bennett? I've heard Mother talk about you. It's good to meet you," Rachel was saying. "Won't you have a seat? I'm sure she'll be right back."

"Thanks." Forgoing the seat Tina had just abandoned, Tyrone turned around to pull a chair closer to the two women, giving Nikkie a quick but good look at his rear. *Nice.*

"So Hillary devotees, are you? Do you really think she has a chance to win?" he asked after he was seated.

"Hush!" Rachel said with a chuckle. "If Mother hears you, she'll turn you out on your ear. She doesn't allow doubting Toms in the office."

Tyrone let out a melodious laugh. "Yes, your mother has already let her politics be known. She's quite . . . quite ardent."

Damn, those beautiful eyes actually twinkle when he laughs. "I certainly plan on voting for her," Nikkie said, just to insert herself into the conversation. "It would be nice to have a woman running the country for a change."

"Well," the soft baritone said, "I hope you're not voting for her simply because of her gender."

Nikkie blushed. "No, of course not. I happen to really like her politics, and her stance on a lot of different issues. I think she's compassionate without being overly liberal, she seems to have a sharp grasp of foreign affairs, and she certainly has proven that she understands the fiscal concerns of the country."

Tyrone nodded his head. "True. And of course it doesn't hurt that her husband is Bill Clinton, one of the most popular living presidents."

"Oh dear. Excuse me for a moment? The campaign manager is signaling for me to come over," Rachel said as she got up from her chair.

Nicole was too wrapped up in Tyrone Bennett's eyes to even notice her friend had departed. "I love Bill Clinton," Nikkie said breathlessly.

"So do I. But then, how can you not love a man who gets up on a national talk show program and plays the sax?" Tyrone threw his head back and laughed.

"I heard about that," Nikkie said, joining in his laughter. "I mean, I was only like eight years old at the time, so I didn't see it. But I think that won my brother over. He's a big sax fan."

"Really? So am I."

"Actually, I am, too," Nikkie said quickly.

"Then you've got to make it out to St. Nick's Pub in Harlem. All of the great jazz players—"

"So who are you supporting?" Rachel asked as she returned to her seat.

Damn. He was getting ready to ask me out. I know he was. Nikkie had to control herself from shooting a dirty look at Rachel.

"I happen to like Joe Biden, the U.S. senator from Delaware on the Democrat side, and McCain on the Republican side."

"Are you a registered Republican or Democrat?" Nikkie asked.

"Independent."

Mrs. Riverton returned before Nikkie could ask her next question.

"Rachel, I'm going to need to talk to you again before you leave, dear," she said with a disapproving look on her face.

Uh-oh, I know what that *means. Tina must have told her what Rachel said.* Nikkie gave Rachel a sympathetic look, but her friend just winked at her in return. *I guess she knows how to handle it.*

"So, do the two of you work here full-time or are you volunteering?" Tyrone asked.

"Volunteering," Rachel and Nikkie said simultaneously.

"How refreshing." Tyrone looked at Mrs. Riverton. "And they say young people are apathetic."

Mrs. Riverton smiled. "Well, not these young people, anyway. Come on, Tyrone. Let me introduce you to our campaign fund manager. She'd be furious if she found out I had a man of your financial ability in the office without telling her." She linked her arm in his. "I hope you brought your checkbook. And don't worry, we have plenty of pens."

One of the other campaign workers, a petite copper-skinned woman with shoulder-length auburn dreadlocks, scurried over after they left. "Was that Tyrone Bennett?" she asked excitedly.

Rachel nodded.

"I thought so. I've seen his picture in *Ebony* magazine. That man is fine, isn't he?"

"He sure is," Nikkie agreed.

The woman continued as if she hadn't heard her. "He was in that feature they run, 'Most Eligible African-American Bachelors' or something. He's one of the most successful stockbrokers on Wall Street."

That's where I've heard his name before! That's the guy who went with Yanna and her fiancé to see The Color Purple*!*

"Actually, he's a vice president at Merrill Lynch," Rachel said. She then leaned over and whispered in Nikkie's ear, "So much for Tina's theory that black men can only make money selling drugs."

Nikkie barely heard her. Her attention was on Tyrone and Mrs. Riverton, who had emerged from the campaign fund manager's office and were headed to the front door. *Damn.* She was sure she'd seen interest in his eyes when he looked at her, and thought that if they'd gotten a chance to talk a little further, he'd ask her out, but now he was leaving. "Hey, you know what?" she said as she gathered her purse. "I've been here since like nine-thirty this morning. I'm going to go head home. I'll see you later, Rachel."

She hurried to the exit, and her timing was perfect. She reached the door just as Tyrone was opening it to leave.

"Oh. Are you headed out?"

"Yes, I've done my time," Nikkie said with an exaggerated sigh. "And I'm starved. I haven't eaten anything all day."

Tyrone cocked his head and looked at her with those beautiful, soulful eyes. Nikkie gave him her most seductive smile, hoping he'd take the hint and offer to take her out to lunch, or at least offer her a ride home. She actually only lived a few blocks away, but saw no reason to let the dear handsome stockbroker know that. At least not right now.

But seconds ticked away, and he still hadn't asked her. Had she been mistaken about his interest in her? Her heart sunk when she saw him pull a car remote from his jeans pocket. She must have been. But, no, a woman knows when a man is sending off vibes, and he certainly had been back in the office. *That's right, he thinks I'm white, and he's wondering if I'm going to reject him if he tries.* She was just about to drop a further hint of her interest when he gave her a warm smile.

"Well, I'd be glad to—"

Before he could finish, she felt an arm wrap around her waist. Damn her luck.

"Hey, Nikkie." Hal bent down and gave her a quick kiss on the cheek. "I thought you were going to wait for me."

"Hi, Hal. I forgot you were coming," she said quickly.

"How could you forget when you just called me an hour ago?" He looked at Tyrone and stuck out his hand. "Hal Richardson," he said in a brusque, businesslike manner.

"Tyrone Bennett," Tyrone said just as brusquely. The two shook hands.

"Tyrone Bennett?" Hal's face wrinkled as he tried to place the name. "Right." A toothy smile appeared on his face. "We were seated at the same table at the roast honoring the mayor a couple of years ago. We didn't really get a chance to talk, but I wanted to—"

"I'm sorry, I can't say that I remember you," Tyrone said abruptly. He turned to Nikkie. "Well, Ms. Jensen, it was a pleasure meeting you." With that, he clicked the car remote and stepped into a shiny silver Lamborghini.

"Hmph! Was it something I said?" Hal asked as Tyrone pulled off.

"What do you mean?"

"I mean that he was rude to me for no reason that I can see. 'I'm sorry, I can't say that I remember you,'" Hal said, sticking his nose up in the air and mimicking Tyrone's voice. "Whatever it is he needs to get over himself."

There goes the most attractive man I've ever seen and he's hesitant to talk to me because he thinks I'm white, and I'm stuck with a white guy who's crazy about me and for whom I have not the slightest romantic interest.

"Well, shall we head out to lunch? Are you in the mood for some Pakistani?" Hal asked cheerfully.

"No." Nikkie shook her head dismally. "I suddenly don't feel well. I think I'll just head home."

"What's wrong?"

Nikkie turned to him. "I don't expect you to understand, but I'm just not feeling like myself today. To be honest, I haven't really been myself for a while now. I'll just see you in the office Monday."

chapter eighteen

March 2008

It was her second time flying in first class, and the saddest day of her life. A day that she had just never imagined would happen. Could happen.

The call had come in at 3 a.m. "Nikkie," said a sobbing voice she barely recognized as Joseph's, "Mama's dead."

The telephone fell from her hand, and it was almost a full minute before the paralysis that had spread through her body eased enough for her to retrieve it. Joseph was still on the line.

Rina was killed in a car accident, Joseph managed to tell her. She'd won two hundred dollars on a scratch-off lottery ticket and insisted on taking Peter out to eat to celebrate their fortieth anniversary, which had passed two weeks before, along with Pastor Reynolds and his wife. As usual, Peter had too much to drink, but he insisted he could drive. And as usual, Rina gave in to her husband, likely not realizing just how inebriated he was. The icy wintry roads of inner-city Detroit were too much for her drunken husband of forty years.

Peter was hospitalized in a coma. "I hope the bastard dies," Joseph said in between sobs.

Hal called as she was on the Internet trying to find a flight out, and he insisted on buying her a ticket on the very next flight out. He wanted to accompany her, and it took her a good ten minutes to convince him to remain in New York, reminding him that she'd had an estranged relationship with her family and it would be best for her to work it out with them in private.

She cried as she packed her suitcase, and in the taxi on the way to the airport, her grief at her mother's death compounded with intense guilt. She'd known how painful the whole passing thing was for Rina, but she'd continually comforted herself by saying that it wasn't permanent, and that Rina would forgive her once she eventually reverted back to her heritage, but death came before "eventually." Mama was dead, and she died believing that Shanika had disowned her race.

It was right after Nikkie buckled her seat belt and just before the stewardess asked all passengers to turn off their cell phones that Joseph called to tell her the hope he'd verbalized earlier on the phone had been fulfilled. Peter had succumbed to his wounds.

By the time her plane touched down at 1 p.m., it was the cool, calm, and collected Joseph she'd known all of her life who was waiting for her at baggage claim. Only the sunglasses he wore to hide his bloodshot eyes gave hint to his earlier emotional breakdown.

After almost a year of almost no communication between herself and her brother, Nikkie didn't know what kind of reception she would receive, but as soon as Joseph saw her, he opened his arms, and she flew right in.

"It's okay, sweetie," he said soothingly as he rubbed her back while she cried hysterically. "It's going to be okay. I promise."

The two hugged close as they walked to Joseph's car. "Nikkie, it doesn't make sense for you to stay at Mama's"—he paused—"you know, at the house. There won't be anyone there, and you need to be around family. Ayoka and I want you to come stay with us and the baby. How about it?"

"Are you sure you won't mind?" she asked tenuously.

"Wouldn't have it any other way," he said, giving her shoulder a reassuring squeeze. "You know you're my girl."

She looked at him and suddenly she was crying again. "Oh, Joseph. I've been so miserable. I thought you hated me. I thought you didn't want anything to do with me. My heart's just been breaking. And then with Mama now—"

"Shh, shh . . . come on now, it's okay. You should know I could never hate you. Never. No matter what you do." He held her tenderly as she buried her face into his shoulder. "Come on now. Come on. Everything's going to be okay."

She gave him a watery smile. "You promise?"

"I promise." He opened the car door for her. "Now hop in."

They drove for about three miles, both lost in thought, when Joseph pointed out the window. "Hey, Nikkie, what does that remind you of?"

Nikkie looked over at where he was pointing and saw a little girl of about four or five on a playground swing being pushed by a teenage boy. "Well, I would say me and you, but he's not pulling her hair or hitting her upside the head," she said with a grin.

"Hey, that's not fair," Joseph said with a laugh. "I only got mad when Mama made me take you to the playground when

I shoulda been at basketball practice. It was because of your little butt that we lost the city tournament every year."

Nikkie waved her hand dismissively. "Aw, y'all were lousy, anyway. Central always beat your butt."

"Naw, East Detroit High was good. Central was just better," Joseph said wistfully. "And then every time we played, I had to be looking over at the player bench to make sure you were behaving. It's a good thing I was the tallest kid on the team or Coach wouldn't have put up with me always having to bring my little brat sister to the games."

"Yeah, well, it wasn't like I wanted to be there."

"Stop lying," Joseph said, laughing. "You'd have a fit if I tried to play a game without you there. What about the time you decided to get out on the floor with the cheerleaders and shake your little hips and try to do splits and all that? And then when I tried to stop you, I had to chase you all over the court."

"Oh God, I remember that," Nikkie said, putting her hands over her eyes. "I musta been about five, right? Yeah, because I had just started kindergarten."

Joseph nodded. "You were the cutest little thing, even if you were a little brat." He reached over and tugged a tendril of her hair. "And you still are!"

"Stop playing!" Nikkie slapped his hand away. "What about the time I beat that boy up for you, huh? I bet you forgot all about that, huh?"

"What boy?"

"The one who you were fighting in Klienman's Grocery."

"Oh yeah, yeah, yeah. Vincent Wright. The only boy at East Detroit High who was bigger than me. He got mad because someone told him his girlfriend liked me."

Nikkie nodded her head. "I bet you were glad Mama made you take me to the store that day," she said proudly.

Joseph shook his head at the memory. "Boy, I didn't want to fight that kid, 'cause I knew he was gonna destroy me. But I wasn't going to punk out, either, with him calling me out like that. So I sat you on the counter and we got ready to commence thumping, and then when he landed one good punch—"

"I jumped on his back and beat him up for you!"

Joseph laughed. "You yelled, 'Don't you hit my brother,' and then you leaped on his back and bit him on the side of the throat like a vampire and wouldn't let go. I told Mama she shouldn't let you watch all them Dracula movies." They both started laughing.

"Vincent screamed like a little sissy," Joseph continued, when he finally caught his breath, "and he tried to reach around and pull you off him, and I just started whaling on his face. He's trying to get you off his back, and trying to dodge my punches at the same time. Now, that was crazy."

"And you bought me an ice-cream cone on the way home so I wouldn't tell Mama what happened. Double scoop. With rainbow sprinkles."

"Yeah, and then you still couldn't wait to tell Mama." Joseph reached over and smacked the back of her head.

Nikkie grinned. "I was proud. That was my first fight."

"Mama was so scared his family was going to sue us or something, remember that?" Joseph gave a wistful smile. "She went over and talked to his parents, and then came back and made us go over and apologize. Boy, was she mad at us."

Nikkie nodded. "But Mama never could stay mad long. We

were supposed to be on lockdown for a week, but after you put on your long face—"

"And you batted your pretty eyes—"

"We were back out the house and playing and hanging out at the playground three days later."

"That was Mama. She always wanted to be stricter than she really was, but she was just a natural softy. But that was a woman who really knew how to love, huh?" The sunglasses still covered his eyes, but the tears were evident in his voice even before they started rolling down his cheeks. "She was so sweet. Always looking out for us. Working two jobs, and sometimes three to make sure we were okay. It wasn't like Papa ever kept a job more than a couple of months, so she always had to pick up the slack. To her, it wasn't about keeping up with the Joneses, but it was sure about making sure that we had everything we needed to stay ahead of the game. We didn't have PlayStations and Nintendos, but she made sure we had a computer so we could keep up with our schoolwork. And, you know, that woman never did even learn how to send an e-mail on her own." Joseph took a big gulp of air. "It was all about us, never about her. Always about us."

"She was the perfect mom. She couldn't get to all of my dance recitals or all of your basketball games, but she was there in spirit, wasn't she? And always baking a cake when you guys won." Nikkie sniffed back her tears. "Good thing you were so lousy or both of us would have wound up fat as pigs."

"And that woman could bake some cakes. Man, I used to love it when the school had those annual bake sales, because everyone would go crazy over Mama's cakes."

"She always could throw down in the kitchen. And could sew her butt off, too. I was the only girl at the senior prom wearing a homemade dress that didn't look like a hot mess. In fact, my dress got so many compliments that people started trying to get Mama to make dresses for their kids' proms. Remember that?"

Joseph nodded. "But that was her little special something-something she only did for her family, she'd say. She never would do any sewing for anyone but us, and Papa, of course. Not that he deserved it." He pounded the steering wheel. "He didn't deserve her. And he wound up killing her. I hope he rots in hell."

Nikkie said nothing. She didn't have a particularly close relationship with her father—she never felt like she ever got to know him. He was always content sitting in front of the television with a six-pack. She never remembered a really tender word from him, but never a harsh word, either. He was just there. It was Mama who was always the force in the house. And now Mama was gone.

"Hey."

She looked over and saw Joseph wiping his face with the back of his hand. "You know I saw him a couple of months ago," he said in a light voice.

"Saw who?"

"Vince Wright. He still has those bite marks on his throat."

"Stop lying!" Nikkie started laughing again.

"If I'm lying, I'm flying. You damn near took a chunk out that poor kid."

The light banter ended when they got to Joseph's house. Ayoka came out to meet them, holding their five-month-old son, Akinseye.

"Nikkie!" She reached her free arm out to give her sister-in-law a hug. "Good to see you, girl. You okay?"

Nikkie nodded. "The best I could be under the circumstances, I guess. Thanks for letting me stay here while I'm in town."

"Don't be silly. You're family. Where else would you stay?" She turned to her husband. "Hey, babe." She kissed Joseph. "The phone's been ringing off the hook since you left. Oh, and the funeral home wants you to call them back."

"I've already made all the arrangements, I hope you don't mind," Joseph told Nikkie as they settled in the living room. "The viewing will be Wednesday night at Haines Memorial Chapel, and Pastor Johnson will preside over her funeral at Mt. Olivet Baptist. Mama would have wanted it that way."

"What about Papa?"

Joseph was silent for a moment, then said, "I've arranged to have him cremated."

"Cremated? Is that what Papa wanted?"

"Mama would still be alive if it wasn't for his drunken ass. The man's going to hell. I thought I'd give him the proper send-off." He turned on his heels. "I'll take your suitcases upstairs." With that, he walked out of the room.

Ayoka sighed and sat down on the couch next to Nikkie. "I've tried to talk to him about it, but I haven't met with much success. You know how stubborn he can be. Maybe you can try."

Even as Nikkie nodded, she knew there was no way she was going to talk to Joseph about the way he was treating Papa, even though she felt he was wrong. Yeah, Papa wasn't the best father—in fact, he wasn't much of a father at all—but the bottom line was that he was their father. She guessed she loved him, and she always assumed that Joseph did, too, even though he never hid his resentment of him. But to just cremate him . . . Nikkie shivered. Still, no, she wasn't going to say anything to Joseph about it. They were getting along too well, and it had been too long since they did. She wasn't going to put that in jeopardy.

"Here, let me hold my little nephew."

Ayoka beamed as she handed the baby over to Nikkie. "Now, be careful. He moves around a lot and—"

"Oh, come on, Ayoka. I know how to hold a baby." Nikkie started chucking him under his chin, causing him to smile and wave his little hands in delight. "Ooh, look! He's smiling at me! You love your aunt Nikkie, don't you, sweetie? Yes, he do," she cooed at him. "Yes, he do."

"And he's so smart," Ayoka said proudly. "He's always so aware of everything that goes on around him. And he's even trying to talk."

"At five months?" Nikkie asked skeptically.

"I know! Isn't that amazing?" Ayoka said while reaching over and stroking her son's cheek. "I tell you, he's going to be a genius."

"That's cause he's gonna take after his auntie Nikkie. Isn't that right, baby?" Nikkie tickled his stomach. "He's just going to be the smartest little thing." She looked at Ayoka and sighed. "Oh, he's just the sweetest little thing. He almost makes me want to have a baby."

"Yeah? You'd probably make a good mom," Joseph said as he walked back in the room. "You have a good heart even if you do act ditzy as hell sometimes." He took Akinseye from Nikkie's arms. "But we won't hold that against her, will we,

Akinseye?" He lifted the child in the air and gave him a little jiggle. "Look at my big boy."

"Joseph—"

"Oh man!" Joseph said as Akinseye burped out a combination of strained peas and breast milk all over his father's suit.

Ayoka giggled. "I was just going to tell you that you might not want to be doing that because I just fed him."

"That's okay. He just wanted to share his food with his daddy. Ain't that right, little man?" He cradled the baby in one arm, sat down next to Nikkie, then reached over and used a handful of her hair to wipe his shirt.

"Ew! You're so stupid!" Nikkie said as her brother and sister-in-law broke out in laughter. She reached over to hit him, but stopped when she noticed that Akinseye seemed to be chuckling. "Don't encourage him, baby. Your daddy is an idiot."

"Oh, shut up, White . . ." Joseph stopped mid-comment, and Ayoka averted her eyes.

No one spoke for a moment.

When the silence had finally become too uncomfortable for her to bear any longer, Nikkie cleared her throat and stood up. "Well, I guess I'll go upstairs and unpack. I might even lie down for a nap for an hour or so. See you guys later."

She walked out of the room and up the stairs without looking back, while wishing she had a pair of sunglasses that could hide her tears.

chapter nineteen

April 2008

Nikkie stared at her puffy face and bloodshot eyes in the ladies' room mirror at Paxon & Green and reached into her pocketbook for the small bottle of Visine she'd had to carry with her for the past two weeks.

She hurt. Bad. It wasn't the first time a man had broken her heart, but the pain had never been so severe or lasted so long. No man had ever hurt her as bad as her brother did when he dropped her off at the airport for her return flight to New York.

"I love you," she had whispered in his ear as she hugged him good-bye at the security checkpoint. "And I'm going to come back and visit again soon. I promise."

"Nikkie, I love you, too. But I don't think you need to come back until you've got your life straight."

"What?" She pulled back from him in surprise. Her stay with him had been so pleasant, considering the circumstances, and she'd thought that he'd finally forgiven her. What the hell was he talking about?

"I'm sorry," he said when he saw the pain in her eyes. "But as much as I love you, I can't support what you're doing. I'm your brother, and I'll never disown you, but as long as you pretend to be something you're not, I don't think we should be around each other."

"But, I thought, I mean . . ." Nikkie tried to keep the tears out of her voice. "I mean, you know, the whole time I was here, you didn't say anything about it or anything. I thought you'd gotten over it."

"Gotten over it?" Joseph snorted. "No, I didn't say anything about it, but you know as well as I do it was like a big pink elephant in the room that no one mentions because they hate to bring up unpleasantness."

"But, Joseph—"

He stroked her hair tenderly. "Get your head together, girl. And when you do, come on home where you can be real. I'm going to be waiting. And so will Ayoka and the baby. But until then . . ." He paused. "Take care of yourself, Nikkie. It was good having you home."

She started crying again at the memory, the bottle of Visine fell on the floor and she tightly gripped the sides of the sink to steady herself so that she didn't fall down beside it as she sobbed uncontrollably. Mama was gone. Papa was gone. And now the only family she had left in the world wanted nothing to do with her.

"Hey, you okay?"

Nikkie hadn't heard Jenice Hanford enter the ladies' room. "I'm fine, thanks," she mumbled before rushing back into one of the bathroom stalls.

To Nikkie's horror, the six-foot-two beauty was still there

when she emerged from the stall a few minutes later, a concerned look on her usually smooth mahogany face.

"You sure you're okay, Nikkie?" Jenice walked over, gently placing her hand on Nikkie's shoulder. "I wish there was something I could do. I know what it's like to lose your parents."

"I'm fine." Nikkie went to stand at the mirror. Her face looked even worse than before. She retrieved the Visine bottle from the floor, rinsed off the nozzle, and began applying drops to her eyes.

"Maybe you came back to work too soon? I mean, you've only been out two weeks. I think the company would understand if you took another few days off to get yourself together." Jenice stood at the next sink, her arms folded against her chest. "I'm sure if there's anything going on with one of your accounts, Yanna or Susan can take care of it."

Nikkie shook her head. "Actually, being at home is worse. It just makes me feel more alone." She started brushing her hair. "I'll be okay."

Jenice looked at her a moment before shrugging her shoulders. "Well, all right, then. Just let me know if there's anything I can do," she said before disappearing into a stall.

"Hey, Jenice, I didn't know you had such a taste for fine dining. Do you mind if I join you?"

Jenice looked up from the magazine she was reading and used her Big Mac to wave Nikkie into the seat across from her. "Not at all." She watched as Nikkie unfolded the paper from her seafood sandwich and tore open the salt and ketchup packets and spread them on her fries. "So how are you feeling?"

"Much better now," Nikkie said after taking a sip from her soda. "I was just going through a bad spot this morning. I'm sorry you had to see it. But thanks for being so supportive."

"No problem."

They ate in silence for a few minutes.

"You know it's like I'm really alone for the first time in my life," Nikkie said sadly. "Papa and I weren't close, but Mama, well, I always thought that Mama would be there."

Jenice nodded sympathetically.

"Now with her gone, I don't feel I have anyone in the world I can turn to."

"What about your brother? You two aren't close?"

Nikkie's eyes found their way down to the table. "We used to be close. Very close. But he kind of stopped speaking to me last summer. When I went home for the funeral, everything seemed to be cool, but then when he dropped me off at the airport, he made it clear he still didn't want anything to do with me."

"I'm so sorry. I know that must be hard. Especially right now."

"Yeah. I think that's why I was really crying in the bathroom this morning. I mean he and I used to be soooooo close."

"Well, is there anything you can do to repair your relationship?"

Nikkie sighed. "I don't know. I mean . . . I just don't know." She wiped away a tear that was forming in the corner of her eye. "He doesn't approve of my lifestyle."

"What do you mean he doesn't approve of your lifestyle? Doesn't he realize you're an adult?"

"It doesn't matter to him. As far as he's concerned, I'm doing wrong and he can't accept it."

"What the heck is it you're doing that he considers so wrong?"

"Just living my life." Nikkie sucked her teeth. "It's a long, boring story."

The two women fell back into silence.

"Well," Jenice said finally. "Well, at least you have Hal. I'm sure he's been some comfort to you. I know how close the two of you are."

Nikkie raised her eyebrow. "Do you really?"

Jenice nodded. "Or I can guess, anyway. Not that it's any of my business—"

"Hal and I are cool, but that's it," Nikkie said, cutting Jenice off. "He must have called me a dozen times while I was home to make sure I was okay, and he's been extra nice since I've been back, but, if anything, he makes me feel worse."

Jenice averted her eyes and said, "Part of that lifestyle thing you referred to a little while ago, I guess?"

Nikkie said nothing, which said everything.

"Jenice, you said you knew how it felt to lose your parents. When did yours pass? Or do you mind my asking?" Nikkie finally asked.

Jenice shook her head. "No, not at all. It happened when I was a kid. My parents and my brother and two sisters were all killed in a fire."

Nikkie dropped the French fry she was holding. "Oh, I'm so sorry."

"Yeah. It was on my birthday, in fact. I had just turned four.

There was an electrical fire that started in the den. Mommy and Dad let me sleep in their bed, since I was the birthday girl, and we woke up around four in the morning because we smelled smoke. By the time Dad opened the door, the whole upstairs was in flames. They dropped me from the bedroom window to safety; I broke my leg, but otherwise I was fine. Then they went to try and get to my siblings. When the firefighters came, they found them all huddled together in the hallway."

"Oh, my God."

Jenice closed the magazine, which had still been open in front of her on the table. "I didn't have any other family, so I was raised in foster care. All the horror stories you hear about foster care are true, by the way. I managed to graduate high school with honors, somehow, and I got a full academic scholarship to Stanford. And here I am."

"Wow" was all Nikkie could say. "You've had one helluva life."

Jenice laughed. "Don't say *had.* It's not over yet, you know."

"I know, I was just . . ." Nikkie shrugged. "You've really lived quite a life. I don't know how I would have made it."

"Faith in God got me through. I give praise to the Almighty every day." She paused. "And that's who you have to turn to." She put her hand over Nikkie's. "Things may seem bleak right now, but with His help, you can get through it."

Nikkie nodded. "Mama was very religious. I promised her that I was going to find a church as soon as I got to New York, and here it is, I've been in the city almost a year and I've yet to attend one service."

"Well, you're welcome to come check out my church. I go to Abyssinina."

Nikkie's brow furrowed. "I've heard of that. The one that Adam Clayton Powell used to minister, right?"

"Yep. Both senior and junior. Up in Harlem." She paused. "It's a black church."

Nikkie smiled and popped another French fry in her mouth. "I've been in black churches before."

Jenice's left eyebrow lifted. "Okayyyyyy."

"So you went to Stanford, huh? I've always wanted to go to California. What was that like?"

"Different. Very different. I had a good time, though. I made it out to Los Angeles and Hollywood quite a few times, and even made it out to Mexico once."

"Wow. Living in Detroit, of course, I've been to Canada a few times, but I would have loved to go out to Mexico. It seems so exotic."

"I only made it out to Tijuana, which is a lot more poor than exotic. But where did you go to school?"

"Delaware." Nikkie paused, then added, "Delaware State."

"Delaware State? Really? You went to Delaware State?"

Nikkie nodded. The question in Jenice's eyes was unmistakable.

And Jenice also recognized the statement in Nikkie's eyes. She'd gone far enough and would go no further.

"Hey! I've got an idea!" Nikkie slammed her hand down on the table. "It's usually slow on Mondays. Do you have anything big going on in the office this afternoon?"

Jenice shook her head.

"Well, neither do I. How about we play hooky and go shopping?"

"Hooky, huh?" Jenice tapped her fingers on the table for a few seconds. "Why the hell not," she said finally. "I think we could both use a break."

To think, for months now we couldn't stand each other, and after just a half day, Jenice and I are acting like best friends, Nikkie thought as they left McDonald's. *And why the hell not? I could use a new best friend.*

"I tell you, there's nothing like an afternoon shopping at Bloomingdale's to cheer a woman up."

"True, true," Jenice agreed. "Even if we're going to starve for the next couple of months to pay off our credit card bills."

Fifty-ninth Street and Lexington Avenue was bustling that afternoon, as always, and was about to get even busier as the evening rush hour began. Still, the two women took their time, swinging their shopping bags, as they made their way toward 63rd Street to catch the crosstown bus back to the west side of Manhattan.

"I can't wait to try out my new shoes on the dance floor," Jenice said, taking a sip of the soda they had bought from one of the street vendors.

"I can't see how you'll be able to walk in those things, much less dance in them."

"Girl, please. Back in the day I did the Harlem Shake in heels twice as high as these."

"Now, you know what? That's a dance I was never able to master. I mean, I did it, but I know I wasn't doing it right."

Jenice stopped in the middle of the sidewalk. "Please don't tell me you dance like a white girl." She started laughing.

Nikkie sucked her teeth. "I'll have you know I can dance my ass off, thank you very much. I may not have gotten the Harlem Shake down, but I bet I can Chicken Noodle Soup circles around you!"

"Ya think so, huh?" Jenice snorted. "Hmph, bet you can't."

"Bet I can."

"How much you wanna bet?"

"Oh no, you're not challenging me to a dance-off, girl." Nikkie put her hand on her hip. "A'ight, you're on. Whatcha doing tonight?"

"Taking your money, honey. Where do you wanna go?"

"Hmm, you ever been to Doors?" Nikkie asked as the two women started walking again.

"I've heard about it, but I've never been. I thought you had to be a celebrity or something to get in."

Nikkie winked. "Don't worry. I got the hook up. And believe me, the place is nice."

"Yeah, all right, but I don't want to go if it's an all-white club."

Nikkie waved her hand. "Don't worry. It's mixed."

"Mixed meaning what? Three hundred whites, a hundred Asians, and five or six blacks?" Jenice challenged. "And be honest."

Nikkie made a face. "Uh, well, yeah. Not quite that bad, but, yeah, I know what you mean."

"Okay, that might work, but, um, are you planning on having Hal come along?"

"No, no, of course not. Why would I do that?"

Jenice laughed. "Oh please. I don't think most of the

people in the office know what's going on between you two, but you haven't fooled me."

"Well, we're just friends," Nikkie said lamely. "I mean, we go out, but it's nothing serious. Just someone to hang out with sometime."

"Yeah. Okay. None of my business, anyway."

The two women fell silent for a moment, before Jenice finally cleared her throat. "Nikkie, I have to ask you, though. I mean, why would you go out with him at all?"

Nikkie shrugged. "Oh, he's really not a bad guy. In fact—"

"You don't find him a little bit racist?"

"Who, Hal? Naw. I mean, he says some stupid things sometimes, but a lot of white folks do."

Jenice snorted. "Not as often as Hal."

"No." Nikkie shook her head. "Hal's not prejudiced. He even sponsors kids from Somalia. I bet you didn't know that."

"Oh yeah, I know. He's shown me the pictures. But that doesn't mean he's not a racist. Even if he doesn't realize it."

"Jenice, I'm sorry but—"

"Well, well, well. It seems I'm not the only one who was shopping at Bloomie's this afternoon."

The baritone voice made Nikkie's heart skip a beat. She took a deep breath to slow it down before turning and looking into those beautiful eyes.

"Tyrone. How are you?"

"I'm doing fine, thanks. Just finished doing a little shopping. My mother's birthday." He held up a tiny Bloomingdale's bag, which screamed, "I'm very expensive!" At least in Nikkie's imagination.

"Too bad we didn't run into you while we were there," Jenice said with a wide smile on her face. "We could have given you a woman's opinion."

To Nikkie's dismay, Tyrone turned his own bright smile on Jenice. "And I would have appreciated it, although after shopping for birthday and Christmas gifts for my mother and sister for the past thirty-odd years, I think I've learned a thing or two about what a woman likes. When all else fails, just go with jewelry."

"Tyrone, I'd like to introduce you to my coworker, and friend," Nikkie hastily interjected, "Jenice Hanford. Jenice, this is Tyrone Bennett."

"My pleasure, Jenice."

"The pleasure is all mine."

The sparkle in Jenice's eyes was fast getting on Nikkie's nerves, especially since Tyrone hadn't averted his. Her heart plunged at the tragic reminder. In Tyrone's eyes she was the white girl. Jenice was the potential date.

And as if Tyrone were reading her mind . . .

"Well, shopping always makes me thirsty. If you two young ladies don't have to hurry off, why not let me treat you to a drink? Or if you prefer an early dinner, why not let me take you to B. Smith's?"

"We'd love it," Jenice answered almost before the question had been asked. "In fact, I think we almost met before. I believe you know another coworker of ours. Yanna Goldberg."

Tyrone's brow furrowed. "I can't say that I place the name."

"Actually, I think you know her fiancé, Jacob. He's your accountant?"

Tyrone snapped his fingers. "Oh right."

"Well, do you remember going out with them to see *The*

Color Purple? Yanna asked me to come along, but I had to pass. Now I'm sorry I did." Jenice batted her eyes.

"Well, it was my loss, I'm sure. But now I'll have the pleasure of taking both you and Nicole out to dinner to make up for it."

Nikkie took a deep breath. "Actually, I have to rush off, sorry. But you two enjoy yourselves."

The polite thing would have been for Jenice to then say she'd just remembered that she also had something to do, but instead the young woman said exactly what Nikkie would have said, had their roles been reversed.

"Oh, are you sure you can't join us?" If Jenice was trying to sound regretful, she wasn't succeeding.

"Positive. But you two have a good time. I'll see you in the office tomorrow, Jenice. Tyrone, it was good seeing you again. Take care." Nikkie quickly stepped off the sidewalk and put her hand out for a cab. Thankfully, one screeched to a halt in front of her before the tears rimming her eyes overflowed.

chapter twenty

Later that same evening Nikkie sighed deeply as his kisses moved down her throat to the nape of her neck, his hands expertly kneading her back and fingering the snaps of her bra through her silk blouse. If only she could feel the way she wanted to feel, the way she knew he wanted her to feel. But instead, she stood there, pushed up against her bedroom wall, trying to figure one more excuse to push the oh-so-very-patient Hal Richardson away.

"Hal, I'm sorry," she said while extricating herself from his embrace. "I guess I'm just not, you know, into it."

"But why?" Hal's voice had the usual pleading note it took on in these cut-short make-out sessions. "Am I doing something wrong?"

"No, no, I mean"—Nikkie searched for something new to say, but finally came up with the old standard—"it's not you, Hal. It's me."

"Nikkie, please. I mean, what is it?" He sat on the bed, then took her hand and pulled her into a sitting position next to him. "You say it's you and not me. Are you trying to tell me you're frigid?"

Hmm, now that's a convenient way out. But, no, she couldn't bring herself to tell that kind of embarrassing lie. "No, it's just that. Well, I kind of think our time has passed."

"Our what?"

"Well, we've known each other for so long just as friends that I can't imagine going to bed with you at this point. I think it would ruin our relationship."

Hal stepped back and took a long look at her before saying anything else. "Nikkie, you know I'm not trying to get you in bed. I don't want to engage in premarital sex, you know that."

"I do," Nikkie said, trying to come up with a reasonable excuse for her behavior. "But it's just that, well, I mean, you know I'm not a virgin, and with us being so platonic so long, I've just begun to think of you as a friend, not as a boyfriend."

Hal's mouth dropped open and he leaned away from her for a few seconds before bursting out in laughter. "You know, between me and my buddies, I thought I'd heard it all, but this is the lamest excuse anyone can think of."

Nikkie couldn't agree more, but she crossed her arms over her chest and put a hurt look on her face. "What do you mean?"

"Look, we've known each other for almost a year, we've been going out for like eight months, and I've done everything *but* try to get in your panties for at least five and a half of those months. So don't start with this 'we've been friends for too long' bullshit." Hal stood up. "If you're just not into me, then just say you're not into me."

"Okay, fine." Nikkie stuck her lip out. "I'm just not into you."

"Well, why couldn't you have just admitted that eight months ago?"

"I'm admitting it now, okay?" Nikkie looked up at him and immediately wished she hadn't. The attitude in his voice hadn't reached his eyes, which reflected the pain she knew she'd just inflicted.

He picked up the jacket he'd thrown over a chair and walked to the bedroom door. He put his hand on the knob, opened it, and then slowly turned back toward Nikkie, though his eyes stayed on the floor. "Is it something that I've said? Or something that I did, Nikkie? Is it the way I act? I mean, do you think I've been coming on too strong?" With a bitter laugh he added, "I've tried to be patient, because I know you've been through a lot, especially with the death of your parents, but damn, Nikkie, you could have told me a long time ago I was just wasting my time."

"Hal, I—"

She didn't have the opportunity to finish what she didn't know how to finish. Hal was gone, closing the door quietly behind him.

chapter twenty-one

He didn't come in the next day, or the day after that. In fact, two weeks had gone by and Hal Richardson hadn't shown up for work. The first few days he hadn't even bothered to call in, sending some of the higher-ups into a panic. It wasn't like their golden boy to just drop the ball without at least trying to hand it off. On Monday of the second week, they received an after-hours voice mail message from him saying that he had a family emergency that he had to fly out to Salt Lake City to handle.

Nikkie doubted that he'd really flown out to Utah, though. She'd gotten more than three dozen hang-ups on her home and cell phone numbers from Hal's phone, along with another dozen or so from various pay phones in Manhattan.

For her part, she'd left about fifteen messages on his voice mail: "Hal, please give me a call. We need to talk." All went unanswered, though the hang-ups continued.

She didn't just feel guilty, she felt devastated. *How can I be so busy messing up my life and everyone else's around me at the same time?*

She'd had time to think about the whole situation, and

had to admit she'd led Hal on—and done so while knowing there could never be anything real between them. And it wasn't just the fact that she was turned off by Hal physically. It was also that something told her if she crossed that line—took a white lover—she would be making a statement that she was not sure she wanted to make: this was her life, and she was white.

Hal had been nice, and, more important, he'd been convenient. Having him squire her around solidified the role she needed to play to get what and where she wanted. She'd never meant to hurt him, but she took no steps to avoid doing so. Nikkie had been to the Blessed Sacrament Catholic Church, a few blocks away from her apartment, every night that week begging Jesus to forgive her selfishness.

She felt bad about not following up with Jenice about going to Harlem to attend Sunday service at Abyssinian Baptist Church, but she hadn't really wanted to see the woman.

Lucky for her, and too bad for Paxon & Green, Jenice had been out on vacation for the past two weeks, so Hal's team actually had been down two people. She had come back two days before, but Nikkie had managed to avoid her. She wasn't yet prepared to hear Jenice celebrating her new relationship with Tyrone. There was no doubt in her mind that the two had hit it off. They probably had a lot in common. Both were young, drop-dead gorgeous, intelligent, and, most important, African-American. She just hoped she didn't get invited to the wedding.

"There you are!" Jenice's head popped into her cubicle. "How are you doing? Keeping busy?"

Now, isn't this ironic? Talk about thinking somebody up.

"Hey, Jenice. Come on in. Seems to me, you're the really busy one this week."

"Yeah, with Hal being MIA and all," Jenice said as she sat in a chair. "Of course you don't know why he's out, right?"

Nikkie said nothing.

Jenice chuckled. "Old secretive Nikkie. No problem. I'm assuming it ended between you two. I hope it didn't end badly."

Nikkie just smiled and shrugged. "So how do you like being team leader while Hal's gone?"

"Ah yes! Change the subject." Jenice chuckled. "But I'm not team leader—Vaughn Spencer has stepped into that role. But I do have more input into what's going on. People are actually asking my advice, and, more surprising, they're paying attention." She gave a little laugh. "But, listen, I wanted to talk to you about your friend Tyrone."

"Yes, I've been dying to ask how the two of you have been hitting it off," Nikkie lied while opening her desk drawer and retrieving an emery board. "So? Have I put together a love match?"

Jenice wrinkled her nose. "Maybe, but not between him and me."

"Really?" Nikkie's emery board was suspended in the air, mid-stroke. "What do you mean?"

"Well, we've actually been out twice. That first evening we went to B. Smith's, like he said, and we had a pretty good time, but he kept making it a point to tell me that I reminded him of one of his sisters. He said I looked like her, talked like her, had a lot of the same mannerisms—he just kept going on and on. I didn't know quite how to take it, you know? It's not like he said I remind him of his mother; I mean, that's an obvious no-no."

"Uh-huh" was all Nikkie could say.

"So when he took me home, and he took me home right after dinner, he told me he had a great time. Then he said we should go out again, and of course I said yes. I mean, the man is fine. So two nights later he takes me to this really fancy restaurant—One Fifth Avenue, down in the Village—and we're talking just a few minutes and then he starts saying that he feels so comfortable talking to me and that he was going to unofficially adopt me as his little sister."

"Huh? You've *got* to be kidding! What the hell is that about?"

"Girl, you tell me! I mean, I played it off, but I was shocked as all hell!"

"I know you were!"

"And then he spends the rest of the evening asking about another woman."

Nikkie's heart took a plunge. "Who?" she asked, hoping the disappointment wasn't apparent in her voice.

"You! He wanted to know how long we'd known each other, what you were like, and all kinds of crap. I was flabbergasted."

"Oh no!" *Oh yeah!* "I had no idea—"

Jenice waved her hand. "Girl, please, I know. Then it became all clear to me. He asked us out because he wanted an opportunity to be with you, not me. And then when he was stuck with me, he had to come up with some way to avoid the 'she won't go out with me because I went out with her girlfriend' syndrome you know we can put guys through. So he came up with the 'you're like a sister to me' routine.

Gotta hand it to him, though. Pretty damn slick. He even called to see if I wanted to go to a basketball game sometime this season."

"Are you going?"

Jenice huffed up. "Are you kidding? I don't want anything to do with a black man trying to chase behind some white woman."

Nikkie's eyes widened and her mouth dropped open, and so did Jenice's as soon as she realized what she'd just said. They were silent for a moment, and then they spontaneously broke out in rip-roaring laughter.

"Oh, my God! I can't believe you said that!" Nikkie managed to get out.

"Neither can I!" Jenice howled. "But you know what I mean!"

"I know!" Nikkie nodded her head. "I know!"

The women both had tears rolling down their faces by now, and Nikkie struggled to keep quiet before other coworkers started streaming by to see what was going on. She turned back to Jenice. "But you know that—"

"Yes, but he doesn't! And that's what counts, right?"

The women started cracking up again.

"Okay, okay, let's try and calm down," Nikkie finally said after a few minutes.

"All right. We can try." Jenice dabbed at her eyes with a tissue she fished from her purse. "Listen, I didn't mean to be offensive—"

"No offense taken."

"But, honestly, I do feel some kind of way about black men who go out with white women. And he made such a big deal about your being white. Saying that you are really pretty for a white woman, and you had a pretty nice butt for a white woman. It was sickening, you know?"

"Jenice?"

"Hmm?"

"Let me ask you something. You knew the first time you saw me that I was African-American. How'd you know?" Nikkie paused. "I mean, it's not like most people can simply look and tell, you know? Especially when I'm not doing anything black at the moment. You know what I mean, right?"

Jenice nodded. "Yeah."

"So how did you know?"

"Well, remember me telling you that I lived in a series of foster care homes? Well, a couple of the foster parents were white, and one had this other foster kid that was like you, and I just assumed she was white. I was like ten, and she was maybe a year older. Anyway, I made some kind of racial crack—I think I called her a redneck or something—and homegirl commenced to giving me a sho-nuff black ass whuppin'." The women started laughing again. "After being around her, I guess it just became easy for me to tell somehow."

Nikkie thought about it for a moment. "How do you think Tyrone would feel if he were to, you know—"

"Oh, I don't know. Maybe it wouldn't make a difference to him, maybe it would. I still wouldn't be able to stand him because—"

"I know. Because—"

"I mean, there he had a beautiful and intelligent African-American woman sitting across from him and all he was doing was thinking about crossing the color line. How insulting is that?"

Nikkie nodded. She knew where Jenice was coming from, but at the moment she really didn't care too much. The important thing was that Tyrone Bennett was interested in her. Now, she wondered, what was her next move? It just might be she'd found her ticket back to herself.

chapter twenty-two

It was Tyrone who made the first move, calling her that very afternoon to ask her to lunch the next day, and sending over a large bouquet of red roses when she said yes, causing a bunch of "oohs" and "aahs" from the women in the office. Then he called her home that evening. He confirmed her original thought that he had been intrigued by her since their first meeting, and would have invited her when they were outside the campaign office, but was uncertain when Hal showed up.

"You didn't have anything to worry about with Hal—"

"I know," Tyrone said, cutting her off. "I just don't care too much for the man. It's a long story, but I'll tell you about it sometime. But let's stay on a more pleasant subject, shall we? What kind of food do you like?"

They talked into the wee hours of the morning, and Nikkie arrived at Paxon & Green a little before 7:30 a.m. on Friday, determined to get all of her work done early so that no one would complain if she took a long lunch hour, or if she decided not to return to the office at all. She didn't know what to expect, but she wanted to be able to go with the flow.

It was shortly before 11 a.m. when she heard a tap on her

desk and looked up from the press release she was writing. It was Hal.

"Good morning," he said in his usual cheerful voice, though his face was drawn, and he looked a little thinner. "I see you're hard at work."

"Yeah, just trying to stay ahead of the game. You know how it is." She stood up and walked over to him. "I've been trying to get in touch with you. Are you okay?"

"Sure, sure. I just needed to get away for a little bit. I flew down to Salt Lake City to spend a few days with the folks." He smiled reassuringly. "I'm not supposed to be back in the office until Monday, but I thought I'd go ahead and pop in today so they can see I'm back on kilter."

Is that liquor I smell on his breath? When did Hal start drinking? I thought it was against his religion. And this early in the morning, and at work? "Are you sure you're okay?" she asked in a more concerned voice.

He patted her on the cheek. "Look, I'm fine. It's not the first time I've been dumped. Hopefully"—he chuckled—"it'll be the last. But either way I'll survive. And we're okay. Okay?"

She thought about asking him about the series of hang-ups, and whether there had been repercussions about his absence, and especially about the scent of brandy on his breath, but thought she'd best leave well enough alone. If he wanted to talk about it, he'd do it in his own time.

So instead, she simply smiled and said, "Okay."

As soon as he left the office, she picked up the telephone and called Tyrone's cell phone. He had said he'd pick her up at the office to take her to lunch, but now with Hal back, she thought it would be best if they met at the restaurant. When the call went straight through to voice mail, she called his office.

"I'm sorry, Mr. Bennett has already left the office and he's not expected back in until Monday."

Damn.

Nikkie put on a fresh coat of lipstick after the receptionist called to tell her that Tyrone was waiting in the lobby. She took a quick look in the mirror, fluffed her hair, and headed out the door, her heart beating fast. She gasped when she saw him. Not because of his appearance, which was impeccable, but because he was carrying a bouquet of roses even larger than the one he'd sent the day before.

"Nikkie, so good to see you." He strode over to her and handed her the flowers, then leaned in close, his lips brushing her ear, and whispered, "I hope I'm not embarrassing you. I just can't seem to walk or drive by a florist without wanting to buy out the store since I've met you."

"Well, thank you. These are just beautiful. I'll just . . ." She looked around, wondering if she should walk back to the office to drop off the flowers or if she was expected to take them with her.

The receptionist came to her rescue. "Miss Jensen, would you like me to put those in some water for you?"

Nikkie smiled gratefully. "Thanks, Sharon." She turned back around to face Tyrone just in time to see the big boss, Arthur Kadinsky, striding toward them.

"Tyrone, you old dog. What are you doing here? Come to give me some insider secrets, are you?" He pounded Tyrone on the back as they shook hands.

"No, actually I'm here to kidnap one of your employees.

I'm taking the lovely Miss Jensen out to lunch." He picked up Nikkie's hand and kissed it.

He's laying it on thick, and okay, I'm loving it. He really knows how to stake his claim.

"Well, I won't presume to impose on your luncheon plans, but I'll ride down the elevator with you. I've got a board meeting over at Rockefeller Center."

The two men talked politics and the stock market while they waited for the elevator, but Tyrone grabbed her hand and gave it a little squeeze as if to let her know that he wasn't ignoring her. He didn't let go of her hand after the squeeze, and when the elevator door opened, they walked in, holding hands, though he and Kadinsky were still chatting away. It wasn't until after she turned around in the elevator that she saw who had boarded behind him—a tight-lipped Hal Richardson and a nervous-looking Jenice Hanford.

Tyrone and Kadinsky were engrossed in conversation, and hadn't noticed them, and Nikkie prayed the elevator would make no stops between the forty-second floor and the downstairs lobby. She wanted to get out of there as quickly as possible. But it was lunch hour, and every two or three floors more people were getting on. They had made it to the thirty-first floor when Hal moved closer to her and said in a low voice, "I can't believe you ditched me for a black guy."

Nikkie blushed beet red and said nothing, but her silence seemed to piss Hal off. They'd only made it down to the twenty-eighth floor when Hal said loud enough for everyone to hear: "I said, I can't believe you dumped me for a black guy."

Mr. Kadinsky: "What?"

Tyrone Bennett: "I beg your pardon?"

Nicole Jensen: "Oh God, please!"

Jenice Hanford: "Excuse me, I'm getting off at the next floor."

"Mind your business. I was talking to the lady," Hal snarled at Tyrone.

"Hal, please! Let's not—"

"No. I think it was a fair question! And I think I deserve an answer!" Hal was shouting now. "You dumped me for him? Why didn't you just tell me you had a thing for black guys, Nikkie?"

Tyrone pulled Nikkie behind him.

"Hal, you're totally out of line, here." Mr. Kadinsky's face was turning almost as red as Nikkie's. "Tyrone, I apologize for—"

"You don't have to apologize to *him* for me! If I were sorry, I'd say so. But I'm not. And he can go straight to hell. And if he's not careful, I'll help him get there!"

Tyrone's face was impassive as he said, "I'm not a person with whom you want to tangle."

Kadinsky started furiously jabbing at the elevator buttons. "Hal, you're getting off at the very next floor."

"Is he? Then I've changed my mind. I think I'll be staying on the elevator, after all," Jenice said nervously.

"Oh, you're not a person I want to tangle with, huh?" Hal threw his head back and laughed. "What's with you people? You think all white people are afraid of you just because you're black? Well, this white boy will kick your ass."

"I wasn't planning on resorting to fisticuffs," Tyrone said coolly. "But I will sue the hell out of you. And I'm sure my lawyer can, as you say, kick your lawyer's ass."

"Get off the elevator now!" Kadinsky shouted as the elevator doors opened at the fifteenth floor.

Hal ignored him. "Why let your lawyers do your fighting for you, Bennett? Why not be a man about it?"

"You're making a fool of yourself." Tyrone shook his head in disgust. "Calm down, man."

"Don't tell me to calm down!" Hal reared back to take a punch, eliciting a large gasp from everyone in the elevator as they all tried to rush into one corner.

"Hal, please!" Nikkie shouted as Tyrone pushed her to the floor.

Tyrone ducked out of the way just in time, and Hal's punch landed on the back of the elevator wall, grazing Jenice's forehead. Tyrone pulled his fist back to land a blow of his own, but he was too late.

"Heeyah!" Jenice landed a karate chop to Hal's throat and followed up with two quick jabs to the man's face. "Hoowah!" she shouted as she brought her knee up hard into his groin. And just as the elevator doors opened, she let out with a punch to his chest that propelled him backward into three people who were waiting to board.

"Go 'head, Jenice," Nikkie said as she scrambled up from the floor. Kadinsky had grabbed the elevator telephone and was yelling for security.

"Reflexes," Jenice said sheepishly. "And I just went for my purple belt last weekend."

Tyrone whistled appreciatively. "Sista's got some skills."

Jenice looked over at Kadinsky to make sure he wasn't paying attention, then stepped in closer to Tyrone. "For the record, I'm not your sista, or your sister. Got it?"

Tyrone's face first registered shock, and then contempt. "Got it," he said brusquely.

"Security is going after Richardson. I've told them to hold

him in the lobby, and I understand perfectly if you want to press charges, Tyrone. In fact, I encourage you to do so. This is a total embarrassment." Kadinsky straightened his tie, looked over the people still on the elevator, then cleared his throat before saying: "I hope you do realize that man's views are definitely not those of Paxon and Green. Our company stands firmly behind biracial relationships."

Now what? Nikkie wondered as she and Tyrone waited to be seated. She'd let the perfect opportunity go by, two perfect opportunities actually, to let him know that she wasn't white. The first, when Hal made the statement about her liking black guys, and the second, when Mr. Kadinsky made the ludicrous statement about the company's stance on race relations. She was hoping that she'd not have to say anything at all, just start acting like her natural self, and nudge him until he got the picture. And if and when he came out and asked because of the nudging, she'd say, "Of course. Didn't you know I was black?" and then gaily laugh.

But if she let on now, he'd wonder why she hadn't said anything then. He'd know that she didn't just look white, she was passing for white. That would be much harder to simply laugh off. She'd have to wait for another opportunity to ease into the subject. She just didn't know how or when.

"I'm so sorry we had to go through all that drama back at your office," Tyrone said for the two hundredth time once they were seated and after he ordered their food. "I suppose it was my fault, I shouldn't have been so demonstrative at your workplace. And, believe me, I wouldn't have been, had I known you were previously involved with Hal."

"I should have—"

"No, no." Tyrone waved her off. "It was none of my business, of course. You're not under any obligation to tell me of your past relationships. After all, we're not exactly in a relationship. We're just going out for a friendly lunch."

"I know," Nikkie said quickly. She didn't want him to think she believed it was more than it was, although to be honest she hoped—and felt—it was definitely going to be leading to much more. "But still, I shouldn't have let you come to the office. It's just that Hal's been out for a few weeks, and he wasn't expected back until Monday." No need to tell him that Hal had been out because he was trying to get over her. Thank God Tyrone had declined to press charges, as had Jenice. But there was no way Mr. Kadinsky was going to reconsider and let Hal keep his job. Still, she reasoned with herself, it was his fault, not hers. She may have dropped him, but that didn't mean he had to act like a lunatic.

"No matter what the circumstances, he was out of line," Tyrone was saying. "I never did like him, anyway."

"Oh?" Nikkie perked up her ears.

Tyrone nodded. "From when he and I first met at the mayor's luncheon. We were seated together at a table, and he attempted to dominate the conversation. Every time I opened my mouth to say anything, he'd cut me off with some trivial remark no one was interested in. We all had those marked place settings at the table with our name and company affiliations, but you could tell he assumed that I was a nobody who was simply there because Merrill Lynch had bought a spot and filled in with one of their little people because no one in the top brass could attend.

"Then just before the luncheon ended, and everyone was milling around, he came over and introduced himself. Someone must have told him who I was." The smile on Tyrone's face was unmistakable. It was the same one she'd worn when that model, Jovanna, had been dissed by Cindy and Rachel at the nightclub, and the one she'd also worn when Sarah had seen that she was hanging out with the New York jet-setters. Of course she'd just been judged powerful because of the people she was with, whereas Tyrone's power came from who he was. That had to have been even more satisfying when Hal came running back to kiss his ass.

"I can't stand phony-ass people who only judge you by what you've achieved. People should be judged by their character or their personality, not by their position," Tyrone finished.

Handsome, successful, and intelligent; she'd really hit pay dirt with Tyrone. Or had she? The words he said earlier replayed in her mind: *After all, we're not exactly in a relationship. We're just going out for a friendly lunch.* Why would he make it a point of saying that after plying her with flowers and calling her every day to tell her how much he was looking forward to seeing her? Suddenly, she suspected that the debacle with Hal probably turned Tyrone off so much he didn't want to have anything else to do with her. *And this is just the type of man I need in my life right now,* she thought dismally.

Before she could further sink into a state of depression, they were interrupted by a short, dignified-looking African-American man in a gray Armani suit, white shirt, and red silk tie. His appearance screamed money, and his mannerisms shouted distinguished gentleman.

"Tyrone, how good to see you again." He turned to Nikkie and gave one of those almost imperceptible bows that make every woman feel like a lady. Tyrone made the introductions on cue.

"Nicole Jensen, this is Quincy Aston. Quincy is a special assistant to the mayor." He turned to the man. "How's it going, Quincy?"

"Everything is fine, thank you. I don't want to interrupt your meal," he said, moving aside as the waiter approached to serve their appetizers. "I just wanted to stop by to make sure you received your invitation to the Governor's Ball next month."

"I did, thanks. And of course I'll be there. Quite a coup getting Rudy Giuliani as the keynote speaker. Should be quite an evening." Nikkie couldn't help but notice that his tone was polite, but not as friendly as it had been with Art Kadinsky. He turned back to Nikkie. "I hope you'll consider attending as my date."

And just like that, Tyrone announced to Quincy Aston that Nikkie was not just any old luncheon date, but someone he'd better get used to seeing around. And what a coup it would be at the office if she could actually have her picture taken at the ball with the governor. *The* smile appeared on Nikkie's face again, the one that said "That's right. I am somebody." Or at least: "I'm good enough to be with a somebody, so watch out for me."

"It will be a pleasure to see both of you. Well, I'll leave you to your meal." And with that, and another one of those almost imperceptible bows, Quincy was gone.

"Shall we dig in?" Tyrone said after he left.

"He seemed very nice," Nicole said while spreading her napkin over her lap.

"Aston? Not one of my favorite people, but he has his good points. I deal with him on a business level, but I would never have anything to do with him on a personal level."

"Oh? What's wrong with him?"

"Well," Tyrone hesitated. "Do you know what 'down low' means? As in, he's on the down low?"

Nikkie nodded, but Tyrone continued as if he hadn't noticed.

"It's a term, usually used in the African-American community, to refer to a gay man who is not only in the closet, but goes to great lengths to hide his homosexuality by squiring around beautiful women, getting married and having children, and doing everything he can think of to appear manly—"

"I know what you're talking about," Nikkie interrupted.

"Oh, good," Tyrone said absently.

Oh God, and he seemed like the perfect man. Don't tell me Tyrone is homophobic. "So you don't like homosexuals," she said casually. "Oh, the shrimp cocktail is delicious."

"That's not it at all." He suddenly laughed. "I almost said some of my best friends are gay. But that would have sounded as phony as the white people who say *some of my best friends are black*, wouldn't it?" He smiled.

"No, it doesn't matter to me at all that Quincy is gay," he continued. "What bothers me is that he's on the down low. I find that deceitful. Downright despicable, in fact. And most openly gay people, even those who have no issue with gays who are in the closet, consider men on the down low as traitors. I think people should be what they are, and be proud, even if they don't go around announcing it. Don't you agree?"

The stone that had been in her stomach for the past year was suddenly making its way up her throat. "Would you excuse me for a moment?" She jumped up from the table without waiting for an answer and barely made it to the bathroom stall before she emptied the contents of her stomach into the commode. When she finally stood up and wiped her mouth, her brother's words echoed in her ears: "Turn your back on your race if you want to, but you'd best remember, when you burn bridges like that, you're going to have a helluva time trying to cross back over to the other side when you need to do so."

chapter twenty-three

"Okay, I was going to ask how you're doing, but you look so miserable I see I can save my breath," Jenice said as she took a seat in Nicole's cubicle. "Is Mr. Kadinsky blaming you for Hal's meltdown on Friday?"

Nikkie shook her head. "No, I don't think so. In fact, he called me over the weekend to make sure I was okay."

Jenice laughed. "Probably trying to head off some kind of sexual harassment lawsuit against the firm or something."

"More than likely. He also told me that the police had to let Hal go with a warning, since I convinced Tyrone not to press charges against him for attempted assault, and suggested I consider taking out a restraining order against him."

Jenice whistled. "Are you going to?"

"No. I got a call from Hal's mother on Sunday. He asked her to call to let me know he's checked himself into a sanatorium in Salt Lake City. She told me he wanted to apologize and assure me he wouldn't be bothering me further." Nikkie shrugged. "I believe him."

"Well, you've had a wonderful weekend, huh?"

Nikkie rolled her eyes. "Simply outstanding."

"Well, what about Tyrone?"

"What about him?"

Jenice sucked her teeth. "Go ahead and play stupid."

Nikkie sighed. "We went ahead and had lunch on Friday; then we met for brunch on Sunday. Pier 2110, ever heard of it?" She didn't wait for Jenice to answer. "We had a nice time. He's a nice guy. But I don't think I'm going to see him again."

Jenice shot her a puzzled look. "Why not?"

Nikkie shrugged and started shuffling around papers. "It's only bound to make things even more complicated, Jenice. I mean, I thought I was going to be able to be truthful with him, you know? I thought he might even actually be my ticket out of all of this. But he's not." Nikkie explained to Jenice the meeting with Quincy Aston at the restaurant. She finished by saying, "He made it clear what he thought about people passing for something that they're not. Not exactly the person I can come out to, now is he?"

Jenice strummed her fingers on Nikkie's desk. "I see your point."

"The thing is, I really like him," Nikkie whined. "I mean, he's so nice, and he's so into me already. And he's handsome. He's got money. He's the perfect man."

"Well," Jenice said slowly, "why not go ahead and keep him? I mean, like you said, he's into you. Maybe it's because he thinks you're white, but maybe it's because he really likes you. Why throw that away? Go ahead and get to know him better. Maybe as time goes by, you'll figure out a way to tell him." She paused. "Or . . ."

"Or what?" Nikkie said expectantly.

"Or go ahead and tell him now and get it over with. I mean, why not? If he doesn't want you because of it, then so be it. You just said you were going to drop him, anyway. But why not just give him a chance? You said you like him."

"Jenice—"

"Look." Jenice threw up her hands. "Either you don't tell him yet and see if it's going to go somewhere and then take a chance and tell him, or tell him now and get it over quickly. All I'm saying is that I don't think you should dump someone just because of what you think they might do. It doesn't seem fair."

Nikkie sighed. "I don't know, Jenice. I don't know."

"Just think about it." Jenice stood up. "Wanna have lunch later?"

"Sure."

Jenice walked to the door, then hesitated. "One more question before I go."

Nikkie looked up expectantly. "What's that?"

"Well . . . I mean . . . just how long do you plan on passing, anyway? Is this going to be a lifelong thing?"

Nikkie grimaced. "I don't know that, either. I mean . . . Oh God, Jenice. I'm so tired of all this. But I don't know how to get out. For Christ's sake! How do I come out now and tell everyone I've been lying all this time?" She looked up at Jenice quickly. "Not that I've actually lied. I mean, I never told anyone that I'm—"

"Do me a favor and spare me *that* bullshit, Nikkie."

"Yeah, yeah, I know. Sorry. But that's just what I'm saying. How do I just come out now and admit to everyone I've been living a lie? I mean, I have a hard enough time admitting it to myself."

"Just go ahead and do it."

"That's easy for you to say," Nikkie grumbled. "You don't have to go ahead and tell everyone you're a fraud."

"Well," Jenice said as she got up again, "I suggest you pray on it. You didn't make it over to my church on Sunday, but there's always next."

"Yeah," Nikkie said absentmindedly. "Maybe I'll do that."

chapter twenty-four

May 2008

"It's a pleasure to meet you, Mrs. Bennett. Tyrone's told me so much about you." Nikkie folded her hands in her lap, and started to cross her legs, but thought better of it. She wanted to make a good impression on the Bennett family—and especially the matriarch, Tyrone's mother. She smiled at Tyrone, who was hovering next to her chair.

The small woman with the wizened face looked over her from foot to head before answering. "Has he? Well, he's told us quite a bit about you, too. He said you're from Detroit."

"Yes. But I've been in New York for a year now. I truly love the city." Nikkie folded and refolded her hands. "I understand you're originally from Trinidad. I've always wanted to visit. Do you go back often?"

"She goes every couple of years—"

Mrs. Bennett shot her son a disapproving look. "I think I can speak for myself." She turned back to Nikkie. "Once every few years only. Most of my family moved to the States years ago. My husband—God rest his soul—and I have been in this same neighborhood going on forty years. All of our children were born here in Harlem."

"That must be why you have no accent. If Tyrone hadn't told me you were Caribbean, I'd never have known."

"Oh, get her mad or excited." Tyrone chuckled. "Then her accent comes out hot and heavy. Emphasis on hot."

Mrs. Bennett ignored him. "What about you? Do you go back to Detroit often to visit your family?"

Nikkie looked down. "Well, I did, but my parents died earlier this year . . ."

"Mom, I told you that." Tyrone rubbed Nikkie's shoulders.

"Oh, I'm so sorry, child." Mrs. Bennett put her hand over her mouth. "Tyrone did tell me, forgive me for forgetting." They fell into an awkward silence.

"What about your other family?" Mrs. Bennett asked finally. "You have no brothers or sisters? Or aunties? Cousins?"

"My mother was an only child, and my father's family has all passed," Nikkie lied. "I do have one brother. But he's thirteen years older than me, and we're not close."

Well, the latter part of the statement was the truth. Joseph had hit the roof when she first told him that she was dating Tyrone.

"He's black, and you still can't tell him? What kind of craziness is that?" Joseph had demanded over the telephone.

"Joseph, it's just complicated. I'm going to tell him, but I'm waiting for the right time," Nikkie tried to explain.

"When is the right time? You know what? Don't even bother answering that. I don't have anything else to say." And with that, Joseph had hung up, leaving Nikkie once again in tears.

"Thirteen years or not, he's still your blood. You should

try to get close. Especially since you're all the two of you have."

The tears that had sprung to Nikkie's eyes were real, and she lowered her head and tried to blink them back before anyone noticed.

"Mom, you're giving Nikkie the third degree. You—"

"I am not," the woman huffed up. "I'm making pleasant conversation. And it's natural for me to ask questions. You bring her here to meet your mama, I can ask a few questions, I think."

"Yes, ma'am," Nikkie said hurriedly. "Of course you can. I certainly don't mind."

"Well, you must be thirsty. Denise," Mrs. Bennett said to a young woman who was passing through the living room, "would you bring your brother and his lady friend something to drink?"

"Okay," Denise said, making a face.

"What's that?"

"Yes, ma'am." The girl sighed as she disappeared into the kitchen.

Mrs. Bennett turned to Tyrone, who was still massaging Nikkie's shoulders. "Give the woman some breathing room. Come. Sit on the couch next to me."

It was easy, now, to see where Tyrone got his imperious manner. Mrs. Bennett was a woman who liked being in charge, and even her son—who had the same commanding quality—didn't question her authority.

But yet there was nothing cold or snobbish about her. In fact, Nikkie thought, she was probably a very warm woman, once she decided to let you in her inner circle. And Nikkie knew she was now on trial to see if she was worthy or not.

She looked around the room. The beige walls were filled with framed photographs of family members, certificates, and diplomas. The furniture was old, but well-kept and expensive. The couch was brown tweed, with a matching love seat and recliner. Although the room had wall-to-wall carpeting, there was a multicolored throw rug under the end table and another in front of the couch where Mrs. Bennett and now Tyrone were seated. The two wood end tables and the nineteen-inch console television were cluttered with more framed pictures, and there was not a speck of dust to be found anywhere.

"This is such a lovely home."

"Thank you. We've been here thirty-seven years. We bought this house for thirty-five thousand back in 1970. Now they just sold one of the brownstones for almost three-quarters of a million dollars. We've had many, many offers to sell since the white . . . since the neighborhood became more mixed. We're not moving, though," Mrs. Bennett said firmly. "This is our home."

Nikkie blushed. Mrs. Bennett hadn't brought up the so-called interracial relationship, but Tyrone had warned her they weren't pleased at the prospect of their only son dating a white woman. "They'll get over it," he had assured her. "I know my mother. Once she meets you, she'll love you. And if she loves you, the rest of the family will, too, or she'll beat them until they do."

So far, things were going politely, but she didn't feel the love as of yet.

"It took you long enough to get these," Tyrone was saying as his sister handed him a glass of brown liquid from a silver-plated tray.

"Be glad you didn't have to get them yourself," the woman replied. She handed her mother a glass, then walked over to Nikkie. "I hope you like iced tea."

"I love it." Nikkie gratefully took a sip. *Oh, my goodness! Sugar!*

Tyrone must have mistaken her surprised look for displeasure. "It's too sweet, isn't it? My mother loads her tea down with sugar. I keep telling her she'll get diabetes." He stood up and reached for Nikkie's glass. "Let me get you something else."

Nikkie pulled the glass away from his reach. "No, this is fine, actually. I happen to like sweetened tea."

She took a greedy swallow. "This is actually very good." Tyrone gave her a smile that she read as "thanks for saying that." *Hah! Let him think I'm only trying to be nice. This stuff is delicious.*

"Well, Mom, Nikkie and I have to go." Tyrone gave his mother a kiss. "I'll call you tomorrow, okay?"

"What do you mean? You just got here! Sit back down, we're going to eat dinner in just a bit. I have smothered chicken, red rice, and greens waiting in the pot." She turned to Nikkie. "I think you two should stay and have dinner. It'll give us a chance to get to know you better."

Nikkie's mouth had started watering as soon as Mrs. Bennett had ticked off the menu. Real food! She and Tyrone had agreed that they would only stay for a half hour or so and then head out to an Italian restaurant. But, heck, smothered chicken beat lasagna in her book any day.

"Tyrone, couldn't we stay?" she said quickly. She smiled, ignoring the surprised look on his face. "I mean, I don't mind if you don't."

Dinner was simply heaven, and the best meal she'd eaten since moving to New York. The smothered chicken and red rice were seasoned to perfection, and the greens were actually cooked all the way through. Mrs. Bennett had even made fried plantains and had baked a pound cake for dessert.

"Bet you never had food like this before." The woman chuckled as Nikkie wolfed down her food. "Black people cook food different than white, eh?"

Nikkie nodded as she finished the last bite of cake. "They do, but I can tell you I truly enjoyed this meal." She moved her chair slightly from the table and rubbed her stomach. "I'm sure I gained a good ten pounds."

Mrs. Bennett looked at her approvingly. "Tyrone, you have to bring her to eat every week. We've got to get some meat on your girl's bones. Fill her out some."

"I like her just the way she is, Mom." Tyrone reached down and grabbed Nikkie's hand under the table and gave a quick squeeze.

"You don't know nothing, boy. Mom's right. She could use some filling out," Denise said as she wiped her mouth with a blue paper napkin. "Nikkie, why do white women always think they have to starve themselves to look good? Don't they know that no man wants a bone?"

"And don't you know not to be rude at de dining table, girl! Act like you raised, eh," Mrs. Bennett said before Nikkie could reply.

"Yes, ma'am," Denise said quietly.

"Now help me get dese plates off de table."

There goes that accent Tyrone was talking about. "Here, why don't you let me help you," Nikkie said, standing up.

"No, don't worry about it." The woman waved Nikkie off. "Denise and I can handle it. Can't we, Denise?"

"Yes, ma'am."

"I insist." Nikkie picked up a couple of plates. "It's the least I can do to repay you for that delicious meal."

"Well, let me get you an apron, then," Denise said as she rose from the table. "I don't want you to dirty up that nice dress." She paused, then looked at Nikkie sheepishly. "I'm saying that because it's really nice. I like it. I really do."

Nikkie smiled at the girl's peace offering. "Thanks," she said as she followed her into the kitchen.

Mrs. Bennett washed, while Denise and Nikkie dried the dinnerware as strains of upbeat music drifted from the radio. All three women swayed their shoulders and hips to the tune as they worked.

"Is that reggae?" Nikkie asked as she wiped the last glass.

"No, calypso. Hear the steel drum?" Mrs. Bennett reached over and turned up the volume. "That's the music of Trinidad." She started humming along to the song.

"It's nice. I can't understand the lyrics, though. They sing them too fast."

"Don't worry, most African-Americans can't even pick up the words, unless they're from the islands," Denise said as she did a little twirl. "Come on, Mom. Dance with me."

Mrs. Bennett wiped her hands on her apron and joined her daughter in the middle of the kitchen floor. "You watch now, Nikkie. You're going to have to learn to calypso if you're going to be in the family."

They sang as they danced together and then apart, and Nikkie was able to pick up some of the words.

Anytime you goine to cook an ole cowhead,
Get the hammer, tie yo head wid coolie red.
For it mek a poor man nearly lose 'im life,
Lef 'im house an make 'im run and left 'im wife.

De cow get up, raise up 'im horn,
Open 'im mout', and start to gwan.
De poor man holler until 'im hoarse,
Run from Clarendon down to Racecourse.

Nail, nail, ten penny nail
Get yo hammer and a' ten penny nail.
Nail, nail, ten penny nail
Get yo hammer and a' ten penny nail.

After a few minutes, Nikkie was able to pick up the chorus and sing along with them.

De cow get up, raise 'im horn,
Open 'im mout', and start to gwan.
De poor man holler until 'im hoarse,
Run from Clarendon down to Racecourse.

"Hey, de girl gwine Trinidadian," Mrs. Bennett shouted with glee. She grabbed Nikkie's hand. "Just watch my feet and do de same ting."

It didn't take long for Nikkie to master the steps, and soon all three women were twirling around the kitchen.

"Look at her, Mom! The girl must have some black in her," Denise shouted over the music, which they were now blasting.

"Oh, Denise, please."

Nikkie looked up to see Tyrone smiling in the kitchen doorway.

"Not all white people dance like they're having seizures," he said.

"Don't worry." Nikkie threw back her head as she danced, then raised her hand in the air and twirled it as if she were ringing a bell the way Mrs. Bennett taught her. "I take it as a compliment." She started singing again, and Mrs. Bennett, Denise, and even Tyrone joined in.

Nail, nail, ten penny nail
Get yo hammer and a' ten penny nail.
Nail, nail, ten penny nail
Get yo hammer and a' ten penny nail.

"I *love* your family," she said after they were back at Tyrone's Brooklyn brownstone.

He smiled. "I thought you would. And I kind of think they love you, just as I said they would."

"I have to admit I was worried there for the first few minutes, but they seemed to warm up after a while," she said as they headed to the bedroom.

"That's because"—Tyrone took her in his arms and kissed her on the throat—"they saw you weren't stuck-up or standoffish. You were willing to try new things. Bet you never had collard greens cooked with salt pork before, huh?"

Not since my mother cooked a pot. "It was really good. I'm going to have to get some recipes from your mother so I can cook for my man."

Tyrone held her at arm's length, then pulled her back into an embrace. "See, that's what I'm talking about. You don't have a problem with cultural differences. You're just . . . just so accepting.

"It's going to take my mother some time to get used to me dating a white woman, and I hope you're patient with them, especially Denise. She's young and says stupid things, but she doesn't mean them."

"Um-hm, she was actually really sweet after a while." Nikkie unbuttoned Tyrone's shirt as she spoke.

Tyrone nodded. "She really is." He was quiet for a few moments. "I had to explain to them that I didn't mean to fall in love outside my race, but it just happened. I think at first they felt it was some kind of betrayal, but, you know, black women are like that. They hate seeing black men with white women. I'm sure you've seen the dirty looks they give us when we're together—even your friend Jenice. They automatically think that the man hates black women or something."

He shrugged. "That's not the case with me, of course. And my mother knows I've gone out with plenty of black women, Puerto Rican, and Asian, too. It just so happened I fell in love with a white woman."

He pushed her down on the bed and lay down next to her, cupping her breast in his hands. "And now that I have, I find that I've been missing out all my life. God forgive me for saying this, and I trust you'll never repeat it, but you're so much gentler and sweeter than any black woman I've known." He caressed her face, then kissed her on the lips, then down her torso, stopping just above her panties. "Your skin is so soft, and you smell so good." He started kissing her panties. "Especially down here."

A lump developed in Nikkie's throat and she gently pushed him away. "I'm sure black women have soft skin and smell good down there, too."

"I haven't run into any as soft as you." He seemed unperturbed as he slipped his hand into her underwear and began fingering her clitoris. "And I've never run into any who taste as good as you." He licked his lips.

You're not dipping into the honeypot tonight! Nikkie wanted to scream, but instead she calmly removed his hand. "So you're trying to say that white women smell and taste better than black women?"

Tyrone propped himself up on his elbow. "What's wrong with you?"

"Nothing. I guess I'm just not in the mood. In fact"—she stood up and grabbed her skirt—"I think I want to go home tonight. I have a big day in the morning."

"Hey!" Tyrone sat up. "What are you getting an attitude about?"

"To be honest? I'm just uncomfortable hearing you talk so negatively about black women."

"What are you talking about? Just because I said I'm into you, you think I hate black women? Give me more credit than that."

Nikkie turned to face him as she buttoned up her blouse. "Didn't you just say that white women smell and taste better than blacks?"

"Nooooo. I just said that you smell and taste better than any woman I've ever been with. But then I haven't been with every black woman in America, you know." He grabbed her hand and pulled her back in the bed.

"Tyrone," Nikkie said as he pushed her back into a lying position, "tell me you don't like me just because of my color."

"Don't be ridiculous," he said as he undressed her again. "I love you because you're Nicole Jensen. Your race makes absolutely no difference."

God, she thought as he started nibbling her breast, *if only I could believe that was true.*

chapter twenty-five

June 2008

"I don't know why I let you drag me here," Cindy said to Nikkie after Tyrone walked away from their table to refresh their drinks. "This place is just boring." Cindy made a face as she looked around the small, crowded club. "When your boyfriend said he wanted to go to a club in Harlem, I thought he was talking about some swinging spot. I don't even like jazz."

"Give it a chance, Cindy," Rachel said reprovingly. "We've only been here a few minutes."

"And I'm only going to give it a few more," Cindy said with a sniff. "They don't even have a VIP section."

"Well, here's your chance to mingle with the common people," Nikkie said with a giggle.

"I can't believe no one's recognized me," Lucia said, looking around the place.

"That's because you've never starred in a Spike Lee Joint," Cindy said with a laugh. "Good Lord, what the hell am I doing here?"

"Sorry, superstar. Uptown you're just another white girl," Tyrone said as he rejoined the four women at the table. "Don't worry. Once the show starts, the gentrification folks will start coming in. I'm sure some of them will ask for autographs."

"Whatever," Cindy said in a bored voice.

Lucia took a sip from her drink and waved her hand. "I was just kidding. I don't want anyone asking for autographs while I'm out having a good time."

Tyrone grinned. "You're such a liar."

The table burst out in laughter.

"So, Tyrone, how did you find this place?" Rachel asked. "I've been to Harlem before, but I've never been to this club."

"I was raised not far from here," Tyrone answered as he looked toward the bar. "See that guy over there? He's the owner, Lloyd Watson."

Nikkie craned her neck to get a look. "Really? I'd like to go over and talk to him."

Tyrone patted her hand. "Don't worry. I'll handle it." He got up from the table again.

"Ooh, Nikkie," Cindy said when he was out of earshot. "Not only did you hook up with a black guy. You hooked up with a black guy from Harlem. You get extra points for that."

"Just ignore her, Nikkie," Rachel said quickly. "I'm glad you and Tyrone are together. I've never seen you happier."

"Don't worry, I'm not paying her any mind," Nikkie said as she downed her drink. "I'm having a great time myself."

"I bet you are," Lucia said with a laugh. "Your boyfriend seems to be quite a guy. And you two make a cute couple.

I'm glad you dumped that Hal guy. I told you he wasn't your type."

"Oh," Nikkie said, turning to Lucia. "And what do you know of my type?"

"Well," Lucia said with a twinkle in her eye, "I know that it's the Tyrone type and not the Hal type." She gave Nikkie a wink. "Dig, girlfriend?"

Nikkie's eyes widened. *Lucia knows!* No, it couldn't be. She pushed the thought out of her head. *If Lucia knew, she would have let the cat out of the bag before now.*

"Damn, Lucia. Now you're beginning to sound like Tina. Just because we're in Harlem doesn't mean you have to talk like the natives."

"Shut up, bitch," Lucia answered. "I'm just having a good time."

"What the hell is it you and Lucia are drinking, anyway?" Cindy asked Nikkie.

"Harlem mojitos. It's a mojito made with cognac, instead of rum."

Lucia grinned and raised her glass. "When in Harlem, do as the Harlemites do."

"Well, you don't have to overdo it," Cindy grumbled.

"Shut up, bitch." Lucia giggled. "I can't believe you made me repeat myself."

"Bitch, please," Cindy snapped.

"Now, now, ladies," Tyrone said soothingly, sitting back down. "Can't we all just get along? Now all of you be quiet a moment. I believe Lloyd is going to make an announcement."

Sure enough, Nikkie saw a tall black man with slicked-back salt-and-pepper hair mount the empty bandstand and grab the microphone.

"Ladies and gentlemen," he said after he had everyone's attention. "It's just been brought to my attention we have a celebrity in our midst. Ms. Lucia Silver, star of the upcoming Woody Allen movie, *Lake Oh She's Gone*. Ms. Silver, please stand up and take a bow."

Lucia smiled and put her hand on her chest in a "who me?" gesture, then graciously got up and nodded at the crowd, which had broken out into applause. She blew a kiss to Lloyd before sitting down again.

"You didn't have to do that, Tyrone," Lucia said out the corner of her mouth as she smiled at the people taking pictures with their cell phone cameras.

Tyrone grinned. "Oh yes, I did. Nikkie gave me my marching orders right after we got here."

"Always on the job, huh, Nikkie?" Lucia reached over and patted her hand, then leaned and whispered in her ear, "I'm serious. This guy is a keeper. Don't blow it, okay?"

Nikkie smiled and whispered back, "Don't worry. I have no intention of doing so. Watch. I'm going to marry this guy." She straightened up and grabbed Tyrone's hand under the table.

"You ladies are in for a treat," he said, giving her fingers a quick squeeze. "Lloyd told me that the guy who usually plays sax with the jazz trio appearing tonight is sick, and Julian Meyers is sitting in."

"Who's he?" Rachel asked.

"He's played with some of the jazz greats, like Dizzy Gillespie and Michael Raye, but he's just beginning to get some notice around Harlem. I've seen him perform at a club down the street. Believe me, you'll enjoy him." He leaned over close to Nikkie's ear. "By the way, I heard what you and Lucia were whispering. Glad to hear you plan on keeping me around for a while."

Nikkie blushed. "Oh! I, uh, um—"

Tyrone laughed and grabbed her around the shoulders, pulling her close to him. "Don't worry. I'm not planning on letting you get away, either." He planted a soft kiss on her lips.

"Aw, isn't that sweet," Lucia said.

"Isn't it just?" Nikkie said as she looked up into Tyrone's mesmerizing eyes. "Isn't it just?"

chapter twenty-six

July 2008

So you actually signed Ruta Savage as a client, huh?" Tyrone said as he and Nikkie strolled down Amsterdam Avenue, hand in hand, toward her apartment building. "Pretty impressive. They did a write-up on her in the *Village Voice* just last week."

Nikkie nodded. "I know. She's actually a PR person's dream. She's so gorgeous, sweet, and talented, it's not going to be hard getting her press, or getting her into the right events. And she's so focused and dedicated to her acting career that I really don't think I'm going to have to worry about her getting into some scandal that can't be handled with an easy spin. I really lucked up with this one."

Their walk was slow, allowing her to take in the Saturday-afternoon sights and sounds of the Upper West Side, where she'd been living for almost a year now.

"How did you meet her?" Tyrone asked.

"Through Lucia," Nikkie answered. "Ruta had a bit part in the film that Lucia just finished shooting and the two became friends. When she found out that Ruta didn't have a PR person, she recommended me. I jumped at the opportunity, of course. Ruta doesn't have a lot of money now, but it's obvious the girl is headed for big things."

"Let's go to the movies."

"Hmm?"

Tyrone pointed to a movie marquee a block down from where they were. "Let's go see a flick. That movie house always has old films from the thirties and forties. I'm in the mood for an old flick, how about you? We're not doing anything, anyway."

"Sure."

"So how many clients do you have now?" Tyrone said as they crossed the street.

"Well, I have four personal clients, whose accounts I work on personally, and then there's another five that I work on alongside the team." Nikkie smiled. "I have just enough to keep me busy."

"And to keep you at parties or in the clubs every night," Tyrone deadpanned.

Nikkie squeezed his hand. "Come on, not every night. Maybe two or three times a week. Just looking out for my clients, though. Making sure that they're on point, and that they're being seen with the right people, and the photographers only get their good sides. And you know you're always welcome to come along. I've told you that."

Tyrone shook his head. "I'm sure Merrill Lynch wouldn't be quite as understanding as Paxon and Green about me strolling in at twelve-thirty in the afternoon, saying I was up all night partying. No, dear, I'll leave the club scene to you." He stopped at the ticket booth outside the movie theater. "What time does the next show start?"

"In fifteen minutes," the clerk, an older man with a liver-spotted face and long gray ponytail, answered.

"Two tickets, please." Tyrone pulled out his wallet and pushed a twenty-dollar bill through the slot at the box office booth.

"Well, I don't complain when you spend twelve- or fourteen-hour days at your office," Nikkie said.

"Yes, you do."

"Well, okay. But I don't complain all the time."

"I don't think I complain all the time about your spending all your evenings in the clubs," Tyrone said as they walked over to the concession stand and ordered their popcorn and sodas. "But I'm a man, and no man likes his woman out every night at a club, unless he's with her."

"Tyrone, it's all work-related."

"I thought I already said I understood that."

"Then why are you still bringing it up?" Nikkie said irritably. They walked into the dark, almost empty auditorium, and settled into seats near the back of the theater. "What movie are we seeing, anyway?"

Tyrone shrugged. "Hell if I know."

They both laughed. Nikkie's mirth turned to horror, though, when she saw the movie begin to play.

Lana Turner, John Gavin, Sandra Dee, and Juanita Moore playing in the 1959 version of *Imitation of Life*—a film about two women, one white and one black, and their difficult relationships with their daughters. The white woman, played by Lana Turner, is a struggling actress who finally makes it big, but whose daughter falls in love with the mother's boyfriend. The black woman, played by Juanita Moore, acts as an unofficial maid for the white woman, and the difficulty with Moore's daughter is that she looks white, and, to her mother's horror, decides to pass.

"I don't want to see this," Nikkie said, jumping up from her seat, and almost upsetting her soda.

"Why? What's the matter?" a startled Tyrone asked as he caught her by the arm.

"I've just . . . I've seen it before. And I don't want to see it again. I didn't really like it."

"You're kidding? How can you not like this film?"

"I just don't."

Tyrone shook his head in puzzlement. "Yeah, well, how about you just do me a favor and just sit down and watch just because I want you to? Can you do that for me? This happens to be one of my mother's favorite movies, but I haven't seen it since I was a kid." He gently pulled her back into the seat. "Besides, it's going to be different for you to watch the movie now that you know more about black culture. I bet you'll have a whole new perspective. Come on, Nikkie. Let's just stay."

Nikkie managed to control herself throughout the film, but it was the funeral scene that was finally her undoing. The mother dies of a broken heart after the daughter moves to another state to pass for white. In the church, gospel great Mahalia Jackson sings her solo, "Trouble of the World," wailing about wanting to see her ma, wanting to see her mother. Then afterward, when the undertaker is about to shut the door of the horse-drawn hearse once the coffin is placed inside, the daughter runs up and flings herself across the casket, saying, "Mama, I'm so sorry. I didn't mean it, Mama."

Suddenly, it wasn't Juanita Moore in the casket, but Rina Jenkins. And it wasn't Susan Kohner berating herself for hurting her mother, but Nicole. Hadn't Rina also gone to her grave under the same circumstances? Hadn't she gone to her grave grieving because Nikkie had turned her back on her race, and, in doing so, had turned her back on Rina and the rest of her family?

At first, Tyrone thought the tears and sniffles were cute, even endearing. But when she started all-out sobbing, and finally went into near hysterics, he hurried her out of the theater.

"Nikkie, sweetie, come on. I know the movie was sad, but you have to get ahold of yourself," he said once they were on the sidewalk. "It's only a movie."

"It's not just a movie!" Nikkie yelled.

"What do you mean?"

"I mean, it's . . . it's . . . okay, it's just a movie, but I told you I didn't want to see the damn movie! Why did you make me?" She started sobbing again.

Tyrone looked around hopelessly, then pulled Nikkie into his arms. "Okay, baby, I'm sorry. I knew it was a sad movie, but, God, I didn't know you were going to act like this."

Nikkie continued sobbing in Tyrone's chest.

"You know, you've been really emotional lately," he said, gently pushing her away and lifting her face up, and kissing her on her tearstained face. "You need to get more sleep. See, that's what happens when you're out in the club partying all night, instead of snuggled up with your man in bed."

Nikkie managed a smile. "That must be it. Maybe I will slow down a bit." She squeezed his hand.

"Come on, let's go home."

I only wish I could, Nikkie thought as she docilely followed him. *I only wish I could.*

chapter twenty-seven

"Nikkie. Nikkie." Lucia snapped her fingers, trying to get the woman's attention. "Did you even hear what I just said?"

"Huh?" Nikkie snapped out of her reverie and frantically tried to replay Lucia's word in her head. It wasn't often that her star client invited her to her home for brunch, so it had to have been important. She should have been listening intently rather than drifting off thinking about her own problems. She put down the unbuttered biscuit she'd been holding in midair.

"Yes, of course I heard you. You were saying you're on your way back out to Hollywood?" She pushed her untouched plate of French toast and sausage away from her. "When are you leaving? Do you need me to make your plane reservations?"

Lucia rolled her eyes. "And why did I say I was going back out to Hollywood?"

"Because . . . um . . . uh, I guess my thoughts must have drifted off," Nikkie admitted sheepishly.

Lucia sighed and shook her head. "Okay, you're obviously not interested in what I'm saying, so what the hell is going on in your life? And it better be good."

Nikkie shrugged. "Nothing, I guess. Sorry."

"Come on, you can do better than that, girl."

"Really, it's nothing. I just had a bad weekend." Nikkie's eyes brimmed with tears. "Just stressed, I guess."

"Anything to do with that new boyfriend of yours? What's his name again?"

"Tyrone."

"Right, that very handsome, dashing, and charming Tyrone. How is he?"

"He's fine." Nikkie looked away so that Lucia wouldn't see the tears brimming in her eyes. "Well, we had kind of a row this weekend, but nothing we can't get over." The tears she tried to hide spilled over, and she quickly brought the napkin in her lap up to dab at her eyes. "You have to excuse me. I don't know why I've been so emotional lately."

Lucia's brow furrowed. "What were you two arguing about? Or is that too personal?"

Nikkie's shoulders sagged. "Not really. It was stupid, really. He got upset because I cried while watching a movie."

Lucia looked at her quizzically. "Why would he get mad about that? A lot of people get mushy when they watch movies. What film was it?"

"*Imitation of Life.*"

A strange look appeared on Lucia's face. "Oh. Well." She paused. "Well, now that's exactly the kind of movie people cry over. I mean, who can help but tear up when Mahalia Jackson starts belting out that song at the funeral?"

Nikkie tried to sniffle back the additional tears forming.

"And then when the daughter rushes up and throws herself at the hearse and tries to climb on top of the coffin . . ."

Nikkie's chest began to heave.

". . . but then I guess some people would find it hard to feel sorry for the girl, huh?" Lucia continued. "I mean, her being so mean to her mother and all. Not only denying her heritage, but denying her own mother—that's gotta be some hard guilt to live with. Wouldn't you think?"

Nikkie managed to nod her head before breaking out into deep sobs. She bunched the napkin into a ball and held it against her mouth to muffle the sound. To her surprise, Lucia immediately got up from across the table and sat next to her.

"Look, you go ahead and let it out," she said, patting Nikkie on the back. "That's the only way you're going to feel better."

Nikkie shook her head miserably. "I've been crying all weekend," she said in between sobs. "Believe me, I don't feel any better."

"Yeah, well, now you're crying to someone who understands why you're crying. And it wasn't because of some damn actress up on some movie screen."

"What do you mean?" Nikkie said as she attempted, once again, to wipe her eyes.

"I mean, I know your little secret, silly," Lucia said as she picked up the water glass from the table and offered Nikkie a sip.

"What secret?" Nikkie asked, ignoring the glass.

Lucia sighed, then leaned into Nikkie's ear. "The secret. The fact that you're black and passing for white."

Nikkie's face contorted with horror.

"And my guess is that your mother died knowing you were passing, and not feeling too good about it. Am I right?"

Nikkie looked at Lucia, not knowing how to react, then finally collapsing into her arms, no longer trying to stifle her sobs. "She begged me to stop, and she died knowing I let her down. How could I hurt my mother like that? Oh God, I know I hurt her so bad. I hurt her so bad!"

"It's okay, Nikkie," Lucia said soothingly, while rocking Nikkie back and forth. "Let it out. Let it all out."

"I never invited her to New York because I didn't want anyone to see her. I never told her that was why, but I know she knew." Nikkie wailed. "She must have thought I was ashamed of her. She died thinking I was ashamed of her, Lucia. And I never got the chance to tell her any different."

"I'm sure she knows, sweetie. Mothers always know." Lucia stroked Nikkie's hair as she talked. "I'm sure she's looking down from heaven right now, wanting you to know she understands and that she forgives you."

Nikkie shook her head. "I can't forgive myself." Her sobs increased in volume. "I'll never forgive myself."

Nikkie continued to cry for another five minutes, and Lucia continued to murmur that it was okay, and to let it all out.

"I can't believe I'm sitting here acting so stupid," Nikkie said finally. She gulped down the water Lucia offered her. "You must think awful of me." She paused, still holding the glass midair. "Oh, my God, you must think awful of me!" She buried her face in her hands and started sobbing again.

"Nikkie, come on!" Lucia's sympathetic tone turned to one of exasperation. "Do I act like I think awful of you?"

Nikkie hesitated, then shook her head. "But how did you know? I mean, about me, you know—"

"About you passing?" Lucia chuckled. "Come on. I'm an actress. I know when someone's putting on an act. I'm trained to be observant."

Nikkie cocked her head and looked at Lucia suspiciously. "So you've known from the beginning?"

"No. It was right after the magazine shoot, remember? When you, Hal, and I went to lunch. After I kind of burst his bubble about the affirmative action thing, I noticed the look on your face. You were really happy." Lucia smiled. "At first, I simply put it down to you being glad that I had put Hal in his place, but then when I studied your face more, I thought I saw relief. Then when studying your face more, I began to think, 'Well, if she's glad he was put in his place, why didn't she say something to that effect?' I mean, it was obvious you wanted to. So why didn't she? That's when I began to really look at you, Nikkie. And if someone is really looking, they can see it. At first glance you look like you have a really good tan, but damn, that's the best tanning I've ever seen. And of course, you have an ass." She laughed. "I don't know, I just started putting a whole bunch of different things together, and I just knew."

"So then, I mean, how come you didn't, or did you . . ." Nikkie pulled back a little in her chair. "Have you said anything to anyone?"

Lucia waved her hand. "Please. It's nobody's business. Why should I care what you do?"

Nikkie looked at her for a moment, then nodded. "Well, so then you know. Cool. I mean, what the hell, you know?"

"But Tyrone doesn't know, huh?"

Nikkie shook her head. "No, not at all."

"And he doesn't know you're pregnant?"

Nikkie's eyes widened. "I'm not pregnant."

Lucia sucked her teeth. "Oh please."

"No, I'm serious. I'm not," Nikkie insisted.

"Oh, so it's just a coincidence that all of a sudden you've become—as you say—overly emotional? And here my cook fixed this wonderful breakfast and all you're doing is nibbling on a biscuit? And unbuttered at that?"

Nikkie shrugged. "I'm not really hungry. And my stomach's been a bit upset lately. I've been a little nauseous, and . . ." Her mouth dropped open. "Oh, my God, I'm pregnant!"

Lucia laughed. "You really didn't know, huh?"

"No, no," Nikkie said slowly. "But what's today, the tenth? I should have had my period a week ago. I didn't even realize I was late."

"Well, congratulations. Looks like you're going to be a mommy."

"Yeah, I guess I am," Nikkie said incredulously. "I mean, I guess I am." She jumped up from the chair. "Oh, my God. I've got to get one of those drugstore pregnancy tests. And then I have to figure out how to tell Tyrone!"

"So I take it you're happy about it? Or at least the possibility of it?"

"You know, I think I am." Nikkie clasped her hands together.

"And you think Tyrone's going to be as happy about it?" Lucia said skeptically. "You've only been together a few months, and he seems to be a very practical guy—not the type to be rushed into anything."

"You'd be surprised," Nikkie said, waving her hand. "He's been hinting about marriage since almost the day we met. And he's one of those people who are really big about family values. Once I tell him about the baby, he'll insist we get married right away. And I know he's going to be a great father, and a wonderful husband."

She grabbed her purse, but as she did, tears once again pooled in her eyes.

"Hey, now what's wrong?" Lucia stood up and pulled her into a loose hug.

"It's just that, well, I wish I could tell my mother," Nikkie said with a watery smile.

"I'm sure she knows."

Nikkie nodded. "You're right. And it's like I may have lost one family, but now maybe this is my opportunity to start another." She kissed Lucia on the cheek. "Thanks for everything. I hope you don't mind me rushing out like this."

"Not at all. We'll talk tomorrow before I leave for the Coast, okay?"

Nikkie was almost at the door when she suddenly swung around to face Lucia. "Oh, wait a minute, you never did say why you were heading for Hollywood."

Lucia grinned. "Actually, I did, but you just weren't listening. I'm going out for a screen test."

"Wonderful!" Nikkie clasped her hands together. "I'll get a press release together immediately!"

"Well, let's wait to see if I get the part," Lucia said with a laugh.

"Of course you'll get it. What's the name of the movie?"

"Guess."

"Guess?" Nikkie shrugged. "How am I supposed to guess?"

"You're not going to believe me."

"What do you mean?" Nikkie looked at her quizzically.

Lucia reached over and picked up a bound script that was lying on an end table and handed it to Nikkie.

Nikkie gasped when she read the title. "*Imitation of Life*? Are you serious?"

Lucia nodded. "And would you believe I'm reading for the part of the black girl who decides to pass for white?"

Nikkie sunk down into a nearby chair. "I don't believe it."

Lucia giggled. "I told you that you wouldn't."

"But, well," Nikkie said as she gathered her thoughts, "you don't think there's going to be an outcry in the African-American community about them getting a white girl to play the part? I mean, shouldn't they find a light-skinned black for the role?"

"Yeah, and I'm sure they're going to test some for the part," Lucia said nonchalantly, "but I'm also sure that if I get the role and there's some flack, I have a very good PR agent who I *know* can manage to put a positive spin on it."

Nikkie chuckled in spite of herself. "There's probably not anyone more qualified."

"Nope," Lucia said. "Not many."

"And, honey"—Nikkie put her hand on Lucia's shoulder—"if you need any help in learning how to act black, you know you can count on me."

Lucia looked at her and started laughing. "Well, I'll just have to keep that in mind."

"You do that," Nikkie said as she opened the door to leave. She turned back to face Lucia one last time. "Just think. I have to act white, and you have to act black."

"As they say," Lucia said with a grin, "all the world is a stage."

chapter twenty-eight

September 2008

"All this for me," Nikkie said as she looked around the large gathering in the grand ballroom. "Well, for me and Tyrone, mostly for me. Even if most of the guests are friends of his."

"All for you, honey." Cindy drained the last drop from her champagne glass. "Aunt Helen and your new bridegroom might be on a couple of boards together, but she wouldn't have offered to host the wedding reception for him. There's got to be some benefit to being an orphan, huh?"

"Cindy!" Rachel slapped her cousin on the wrist. "Sometimes you are just too damn outrageous." She turned to Nikkie. "I apologize for her. Too many martinis and she says the stupidest things."

"Oh, be quiet. I'm drinking champagne."

"Don't worry about it," Nikkie said cheerfully. "Nothing can ruin all of this for me. Just think! I'm a bride!"

"Yes, you are, dear. And you're a lovely bride, indeed," Mrs. Riverton said as she joined their little gathering in the corner of the room. "I just wish you hadn't decided to get married in City Hall."

"We just wanted something quiet," Nikkie said demurely.

"I still can't believe you married after only dating Tyrone like six months." Rachel shook her head. "But they say it's the whirlwind romances that last the longest."

"That's certainly the way it was for your father and me," Mrs. Riverton said wistfully. "He proposed on our second date, and I only made him wait three days for my answer. And we lasted twenty years. Twenty very happy years." Her voice caught. "I never even thought about being with another man after he passed. No one could ever replace him."

Rachel put her arm on her mother's arm. "Mother? Are you okay?"

"Oh, child, I'm fine. Don't worry." She turned to Nikkie. "I only hope you and Tyrone find half the happiness that Charles and I had, and I hope you're together twice as long."

"Thank you," Nikkie said.

Truth be told, Nikkie was sure that she and Tyrone were going to have a long and successful marriage. Their time together had been nothing short of bliss. He was attentive, generous, and he was simply delighted that she had "devoted so much time and energy into learning" his culture. What he didn't realize was that he was giving her the opportunity, and the excuse, to reembrace her own. He thought it was because of him that she learned how to cook soul food and started listening to black music. She was even able to watch her favorite television shows again—not that he was interested in watching them, but he thought she did so to impress him, and he was appreciative of her efforts.

Yes, marrying a black man helped complete her disguise. Even the six-week-old fetus she was carrying in her stomach wouldn't give her away. If it came out light, everyone would attribute it to her being white. If it came out dark, it would be attributed to the fact that Tyrone was black. All in all, there was no motivation to cross back over at all. No reason except for her estrangement with Joseph. But, she rationalized, he would never truly forgive her for ever passing in the first place. Their relationship could never be the same.

She made her bed, and damn if she wasn't going to make the best of lying in it.

"Ah, there's the missing groom," Mrs. Riverton said as Tyrone grabbed Nikkie by the waist.

"And why is the new Mrs. Bennett hiding here in the corner?" He planted a big kiss on her lips. Like always, it took Nikkie's breath away. God, how good it was, she thought, being with such a man; being married to such a man.

"Just chatting," Nikkie said, nibbling his ear. "I hope you don't mind."

"You're being neglectful, Nikkie." Cindy pressed her champagne glass against the nape of her neck and smiled wickedly. "Your husband wants to dance, mingle, and show off his new bride. I know I would never abandon a man like Tyrone, especially on his wedding night." She gave Tyrone an up-and-down glance, lingering more than just a few seconds at his groin region. She licked her lips appreciatively.

"Ahem." Mrs. Riverton cleared her throat. "Rachel, dear, why don't you take your cousin Cindy out on the balcony to get some fresh air. She looks a little flushed."

"Oh, Aunt Helen, I'm fine." Cindy tossed her long red hair. "I just need another drink. Is it okay if I ask Tyrone to get me a drink? No? Well, then I'll hunt one down myself. Bye!" she said in one long breath. And with that, she strode off without looking back. Mrs. Riverton sighed and walked away in the other direction. Rachel and Nikkie laughed, and Tyrone just shook his head.

Rachel whispered into Nikkie's ear, "And *this*"—she made a sizzling sound—"is your brain on drugs."

"What's she on now? That doesn't even seem like E," Nikkie whispered back.

"Don't know. Maybe meth?"

"Whatever it is, I don't appreciate her coming to my wedding reception high," Tyrone said, obviously having overheard them. He grabbed Nikkie again. "What say we go ahead and tell our guests good night and then make our exit?"

"Wait, give me a minute to tell everyone to grab their bags of rice!" Rachel hurried off.

Tyrone pulled Nikkie to him. "So how does it feel to be Mrs. Bennett?"

"Feels very good." Nikkie nuzzled his neck. "And I can't wait to see what married sex is like."

Tyrone grinned. "That's my girl."

"Ahem." Ritchie, Cindy's brother, stood in front of them. "I just wanted to give my congratulations again and my sincerest wishes for a happy life."

"Why, thank you, Ritchie!" Nikkie said, nestled in her husband's arms.

Ritchie shifted his weight from one foot to the other. "Uh, Tyrone, do you think I might be able to speak to you for a moment?" He smiled at Nikkie. "I promise I won't keep him long."

Nikkie leisurely strolled toward the dais while Tyrone and Ritchie walked out onto the balcony. She wasn't half-way across the ballroom floor when Tyrone roughly grabbed her by the arm.

"Come on. We're getting out of here now before I hurt somebody," he said gruffly as he propelled her toward the door. "We'll call and give our regrets tomorrow."

"What happened?" Nikkie asked when they were outside and they were waiting for the valet to retrieve their car.

"I don't want to talk about it," Tyrone said brusquely.

Nikkie put her hand on his shoulder. "Was it something Ritchie said or did?"

"Didn't I just say I didn't want to talk about it?" Tyrone snapped.

It was only when they were in the car and a mile away from the Riverton mansion that Tyrone spoke again. "That little white bastard had the nerve to ask me if I knew where he could score some heroin because his connect was dry."

"Oh, my God," Nikkie said breathlessly. "Ty, I'm so sorry."

"See, to people like him, all blacks are just a bunch of drug-using, drug-pushing niggers," Tyrone continued as if he hadn't heard her. "It doesn't make any difference how much money a black person has, or how successful a career he has. We're just a bunch of niggers." Tyrone hit the steering wheel with his fist. "That's why I can't stand white people. Even when I marry a white woman, I'm still nothing but a nigger to them."

Nikkie couldn't think of anything to say, so said nothing. They drove on in silence.

"I'm sorry," Tyrone said when they pulled up in front of his Brooklyn brownstone. "You know I didn't mean I can't stand all white people, right? I hope I didn't hurt your feelings."

Nikkie shook her head. "No, I'm okay."

Tyrone sighed. "And I didn't mean to imply that I married you to gain some kind of acceptance, or to prove that I'm just as good as a white man. I swear I don't care about those people."

"I believe you," Nikkie said simply. She hoped she did.

chapter twenty-nine

May 2009

Nikkie's labor had been long and hard, but the twenty-eight hours of intense pain were nothing compared to the joy she felt as she nestled her newborn daughter, Elizabeth Ann Bennett, to her breast.

"How many times are you going to count her fingers?" Jenice asked as she poured herself a glass of water. "If there were ten the last time, there's not going to be eleven this time."

Nikkie smiled. "I know, I know. She's just perfect, isn't she?"

"And just the most beautiful baby in the world," Mrs. Bennett said. "When I went down to the nursery to see her this morning, everyone was pointing to her, saying how lovely she was. I told everyone, that's my grandchild laying there—of course she's lovely."

"They say blacks and whites make the best-looking babies, and I guess it's true," Denise added. "I might have to marry a white man so I can have a baby this pretty."

"Stop talking nonsense, Denise."

"Yes, ma'am."

Nikkie traced her fingers over her daughter's face. Unlike many babies whose faces seemed blotted with little color dots, Elizabeth Ann's face was smooth, and the color of cream. Her brown eyes were already framed by thick eyebrows, and her head was covered in long silky brown curls.

"So where's the proud papa?" Jenice asked.

"He went to his office to hand out cigars. He was here with me the whole time I was in labor, though, and the doctors let him cut the umbilical cord. I'm sure he'll be back soon."

"Here, let Nana hold her grandchild for a moment, won't you?" Mrs. Bennett reached for the baby.

Nikkie leaned back and closed her eyes. She'd done it. She'd become a mother, and had not threatened her secret in doing so. Elizabeth Ann's black features could have been inherited from either her or Tyrone, but everyone would just assume it came from the father's side of the family. The same would be said of any other child they may have. She would forever regret that her children would never get to know Joseph and his family, but there was nothing she could do about that at this point. The die had been cast. There was no longer any turning back. She opened her eyes to see Jenice staring at her intensely. Something told her the woman was thinking the same thing. She'd actually been able to pull it off.

"Well, I'm going to head on back to the office myself." Jenice bent down and kissed Nikkie's cheek. "I'll try and stop over and see you tomorrow."

"Actually, I'll probably be going home tomorrow."

Mrs. Bennett shook her head. "Isn't that something? Have a baby one day, send the mother home the next. I stayed in the hospital three days when I had my children."

"Well, I'm not going to stop by the house, because I know you're going to need time to get your rest, but I'll call you tomorrow or the next." Jenice got to the door just as Tyrone appeared with a six-foot pink teddy bear.

"Here, Jenice!" he said grandly as he placed the teddy bear on a chair and pulled a cigar out of his breast pocket. "Have a cigar! It's a girl!"

"I know that, you fool." Jenice gave a little laugh as she left the room.

Tyrone walked over to Nikkie's bed. "Hello, my lovely wife, my dear sweetheart, my wonderful mother of my very beautiful child!" He bent down and gave her a big kiss on the lips.

"Tyrone, you've been drinking!" Nikkie said reprovingly.

"Well, I had a couple of toasts with some of the boys at the firm, but I'm all right, don't worry." He turned to his mother. "So how does it feel finally to be a nana? You feel old?" He held his hand out to take hold of the baby, but Mrs. Bennett turned the other way.

"I be feeling fine, boy. And toast, or no toast, you shouldn't be come to the hospital with de liquor on your breath. And don't you t'ink about holding this li'l angel in your arms with you be drinking."

"She does look like an angel, though, doesn't she?" Tyrone looked down at the child sleeping in his mother's arms. "I think she's got my eyes, but her nose and lips are definitely those of her mother."

"I think she has my ears," Denise piped in. "See. She has thick earlobes just like me. She's going to have a hard time getting them pierced."

"Well, she's got her nana's temperament," Mrs. Bennett

said. "The baby don't hardly cry 'cept when she ready to feed. Otherwise, she don't do no fussing."

"But, Lawd, when she fusses, she fusses really loud," Nikkie said wearily. "The nurses say she has the strongest lungs in the nursery."

"Now, that she got from her nana," Tyrone said, causing the whole room to burst into laughter.

"Knock, knock. Mind if I come in?"

"Dr. Rheingold. Here"—Tyrone pulled another cigar out of his breast pocket—"have a cigar!"

"Thanks. I'll save it for later, if you don't mind." The doctor put the cigar in his coat pocket. "So we have mama, papa, and grandmama here?"

"And auntie," Denise piped in.

Dr. Rheingold smiled. "And auntie." He sat down in a chair in the corner so that he faced everyone. "Actually, I'm rather glad. Because I need to talk to you about a serious matter."

Nikkie sat up in the bed. "Is there something wrong with Elizabeth Ann?"

"Unfortunately, yes." The doctor's voice was solemn. "While running the normal battery of tests we do on newborns, we found that Elizabeth Ann has sickle-cell anemia. I'm sorry."

"What?" Tyrone abruptly sat down on the night table, knocking over a glass of water. "How can that be?"

"Oh, my dear God," Mrs. Bennett whispered.

"But how can that be?" Tyrone said again.

"Mr. Bennett, it seems that your daughter inherited one sickle-cell hemoglobin gene from both you and your wife. Probably neither of you even knew you had the gene, because people with just one sickle-cell hemoglobin gene don't usually develop the disease, they simply have what's called sickle-cell trait—which usually has no symptoms."

The doctor turned to Nikkie, who lay in the bed with unshed tears in her eyes. "But anyone who has the trait has the ability to pass on the gene, and when the baby inherits the gene from both parents, it results in the baby getting the disease."

"I don't understand." Tyrone slowly shook his head, then looked at Nikkie, who averted her eyes. "How—"

"Maybe you need to do another test. Maybe you got the results mixed up with another baby's," Mrs. Bennett said frantically. "I thought only black people could get sickle-cell anemia. The baby couldn't possibly have sickle-cell disease. Her mother's white."

The doctor cleared his throat. "Well, actually—"

He's going to say it. He's going to say, "Well, actually, the mother couldn't be white." He's going to out me.

"No, I'm not. I'm African-American." Nikkie couldn't believe she uttered the words, but what did it matter now? There was no use in trying to dispute biology. After all, how could a white woman give her child a gene that only blacks have? "I'm black."

"Doctor, are you sure there's not some . . ." Tyrone swung to face Nikkie. "What?"

"I'm African-American, Doctor. God believe me, I didn't know I had the trait, but I'm black. My mother was black, my father was black, and I'm black."

"Nikkie, w-what?" Tyrone stammered. "What are you saying?"

"Tyrone, I'm saying I'm black. Just like you. Just like your mother. Just like your sister," Nikkie said, waving in his family's direction. She couldn't keep the hostility out of her voice. She wasn't mad at Tyrone, or even at herself for that matter—not for the moment at least. But she was pissed as hell at the situation. In fact, she was furious. "I'm just light-skinned is all."

"But I thought . . . we all thought—" Mrs. Bennett started.

"Mama Bennett, I know what you thought," Nikkie said in a tired voice. "But I've been passing all this time."

"Mom!" Denise reached out just in time to catch the baby, which fell from her mother's arms.

"Dear sweet Jesus," Mrs. Bennett said as she struggled to a chair.

"Oh, my God!" All eyes turned to Cindy and Rachel, who were standing in the door with Bloomingdale's shopping bags brimming with toys and baby clothes.

"You're black?" Cindy asked incredulously.

"Please git out," Mrs. Bennett said abruptly. "Dis be a family matta."

"Um, perhaps I should leave, too." The bewildered Dr. Rheingold slowly stood up. "I can see that your family has some issues to work out, but please just page me when you're ready to talk about your daughter's disease." He walked to the door, and then paused and turned toward Nikkie. "What I was going to say, though, was that African-Americans are not the only people with the sickle-cell gene. Caucasians of Mediterranean descent can also be carriers. I just thought your family might have been Greek or Italian."

"How can you be black?" Tyrone stood in the middle of the room, looking from his mother and sister to Nikkie, the color drained from his face.

Her first instinct was to look away, but she gathered her

strength to look Tyrone in the eye. "Tyrone, I'm sorry. I've wanted to tell you so many times, but I didn't know how."

"You didn't know how to tell me? What the hell does that mean?" Tyrone asked, his voice now rising.

"Tyrone, I swear I'm so sorry." Nikkie began crying. "It just kind of happened. I went up for the job at Paxon and Green and didn't get it because it was set aside for a black and I wasn't black enough. So the next time I went up, I made believe I was white and I got it. I never meant for it to go on as long as it has, but it just seemed as if I were trapped."

"All you can say is you're sorry?" Tyrone slowly approached Nikkie's bed, his hands balled up into fists. "You made a fool of me in front of my family and my friends, and all you can say is you're sorry?"

Mrs. Bennett threw herself in front of her son. "Tyrone, no."

"Tyrone, please." Nikkie was now crying hysterically. "I know you hate me, but please try to at least understand."

Tyrone stood stock-still for a moment, shook his head, and hissed, "You no-good nigger bitch," then stomped out the door.

chapter thirty

I still can't believe it. Nikkie is black? How did she hide it all this time? You didn't know?" Ritchie dipped a hundred-dollar bill into the packet of white powder and brought it up to his nose, then took a long sniff.

"I know," Cindy told her brother as she popped her second ecstasy pill and swigged it down with a glass of bourbon. "I thought she was one of those damn liberals, you know hooking up with a black guy, but all this time she was a fake. Damn, I should have known. She was the best dancer in the group."

"All this time I could have been scoring at a discount, and I didn't even know." Ritchie dipped the hundred-dollar bill back into the white powder. "Bet her stuff would have been better than this whack shit."

"You've got to be kidding! So all that time I was living with a black girl? She didn't smell black."

"Sarah, stop acting silly," Yanna said reprovingly into the telephone. "Blacks don't smell any different than anyone else."

"Maybe not out in the open, but their homes are supposed to smell different."

"How do you know that? Have you even been in a black person's home?"

"No, but I just assumed—"

"God, I don't believe you can be so stupid. You'd think as a Jew you might be more sensitive."

"Man, I wish I could remember where she got her hair done. They say that black beauticians straighten hair better than anyone else, and you know how frizzy my hair is."

"I'm going to hang up."

"Come on, Yanna. I'm only kidding," Sarah said with a laugh.

"No, you're not," Yanna said stiffly.

"Yes, I am. I'm just shocked, is all. I mean, well, what do you think about it? She fooled you, too."

Yanna hesitated. "I used to like her. Not so much anymore, I suppose."

"Why not?"

"For the same reason I despise the women in the synagogue who get nose jobs. I think people should be proud of their heritage."

"There you go with that 'Jewish pride' thing again."

"Okay, now I'm hanging up for real."

"But what I can't understand is why she would want to pretend to be white," Rachel told her mother as they sat out on the balcony sipping tea. "It's not like back in the thirties and forties where blacks couldn't get an education or jobs."

"The poor dear," her mother said simply, shaking her head. "I feel so guilty."

"Why, Mother?"

"Well, I reprimanded her for using the word 'nigger.' But you know blacks use that word all the time when they're referring to each other. It's like a form of endearment or something. I hope she didn't think I was a prude."

"I tell you I was shocked when Helen Riverton told me. But I can't say the girl ever told me she was white. I just assumed." Henry Finch took a leisurely puff of his cigar, then motioned for the butler at the gentleman's club to come over. "Another bourbon, Walter. And not as much ice this time."

"Yes sir, Mr. Finch, right away." The mahogany-skinned butler bowed his graying head and walked off.

"So you say no one at your firm knew, Art? What about her job application?"

Mr. Kadinsky shook his head. "I pulled them as soon as you called me this morning. You know the racial part of the form is voluntary, and she never filled it out. I asked other members of the firm, and her teammates, but they all said they assumed she was white, although she never came out and said so." He tinkled the ice in his glass. "I just hope none of them made any racial remarks in front of her. You know how touchy those people can be."

"So what are you going to do?" Henry asked.

"There's nothing I can do. She was a good worker, and as soon as she comes back from maternity leave, she'll find her position waiting for her as promised. We were going to give her a bonus for all of her good work, but I've already told Human Resources to cut it in half. Those people are always demanding raises, so we can't just give them the same bonuses willy-nilly. We'll give her the other half once she comes in and asks for more money."

chapter thirty-one

October 2009

"So how are you holding up?" Mrs. Randolph said as she daintily dabbed at the corner of her mouth with her napkin at Morton's Steakhouse in midtown Manhattan. "I know the last few weeks must have been hell."

"About as well as anyone whose life has come crashing down on them. Twice," Nikkie said dryly.

Mrs. Randolph's eyebrow shot up. "Twice?"

Nikkie nodded. "First my black life, and now my white."

"Well, you can always go for Asian and see how that works out."

Nikkie rolled her eyes. "Very funny," she said dryly.

Mrs. Randolph sighed. "I have to admit I feel guilty about this whole thing. After all, it was my idea for you to pass in the first place. But God knows I had no idea you were going to take it as far as you did. Marrying a black man and letting *him* think you were white? Nikkie, what were you thinking?"

Nikkie rubbed her hands over her face. "I don't know. I don't think I was thinking. In fact, I don't think I've done any thinking at all since this whole thing started. I just kind of was telling myself I was going with the flow. I just didn't realize I was swimming against a tidal wave of my own making."

Mrs. Randolph took a sip of her drink and said nothing.

"Now," Nikkie continued, "my husband, whom I truly love, is divorcing me, I'm suddenly a single mother of a child with a serious disease, and I'm the laughingstock of New York."

"I'd say that last little bit is an exaggeration," Mrs. Randolph said, and sliced into her extra rare prime rib.

"Well, at least among my circle of friends."

"Really? All of your friends have turned on you?"

Nikkie shrugged. "Well, Jenice is still in my corner. I don't know how I would have survived this fiasco without her, in fact." Nikkie smiled. "And she was the one I thought was my sworn enemy in the beginning, remember?"

Mrs. Randolph nodded. "I remember."

"She's even got me going to church now. It's kind of late in the game, but God knows I have a lot to pray about lately.

"You know, Jenice never got on me about passing, but I knew she didn't approve. Hell, nobody approved. And I knew it was wrong. And I felt guilty and ashamed of myself the whole time. So why the hell did I do it? Like you said long ago, it was one thing to pull it off to get the job, but why did I continue?"

Mrs. Randolph put her napkin down on the table. "I'm listening."

"What do you mean?"

"You just asked why did you continue, and you're the only one who knows, Nikkie. And I'd love to hear the answer." Mrs. Randolph took a sip of her red wine. "Please go on."

Nikkie bit her lip. "I've been thinking about that ever since it all blew up in my face, and I honestly don't have a good answer. Except maybe . . ." She paused. "Maybe it was because I just wanted to see what it would be like. I wanted to see how the other half lived."

"The other half?"

"Whites. I just knew their lives were so much different than ours, and I wanted to live that difference, even though I wasn't sure what it would be. And I kept chasing the difference."

"What do you mean?" Mrs. Randolph's fascination was evident in her tone and her face as she egged Nikkie on.

"Well, you see, once I was, you know, white, I thought somehow I'd see what the difference was between blacks and whites. But I couldn't find it. I mean, Cindy and Rachel were different than any blacks I've known, but then I haven't known any blacks who were that rich. But then the whites like Yanna and my roommate, Sarah—who were working-class whites—were just like the working-class blacks I've known. Passing for white let me hear some of the bigoted statements that whites make about blacks, but being black, I've always heard bigoted statements about whites. It was all the same! All I really learned was that whites had all the same desires, the same fears, the same wants, the same struggles, that we have. But I couldn't accept that. I just knew whites were different, and I wanted to experience that difference. I couldn't stop until I did."

Mrs. Randolph leaned back in her chair. "Wow," she said finally.

"Yeah, I do think that whites may have more of a feeling of entitlement than most blacks—but I think they're born with that, you know? And passing for white is not the same as being born white, so there was no way I was ever going to obtain that. But I wanted to! Even though I knew it wasn't going to happen, I wanted to. I wanted to just assume like I could do anything, instead of hoping I'd get the chance. But it never happened."

Nikkie started chewing her lips again. "And there's the self-hatred aspect of it."

Mrs. Randolph's eyebrows shot up.

Nikkie shook her head. "No, I don't mean what you think. I don't mean that I hated being African-American and so I wanted to be white. I mean that deep down I didn't like myself. I didn't like *me*. I didn't like my superficiality, my shallowness . . . my everything. I'm sure I thought by reinventing myself I'd like my new self more. But being white didn't change anything. The only difference between black Nikkie and white Nikkie was that white Nikkie was always looking over her shoulder, waiting for someone to find out her little secret. Black Nikkie didn't have that stress. But I was still the same screwed-up person—not caring enough about the people around me to worry about the hurt I might be causing them, just wanting to get what I wanted, and disregarding the pain I caused people in the process."

"God," Mrs. Randolph said with a little laugh. "Now I'm not sure that I even like Nikkie."

"Yeah, well"—Nikkie picked up her glass of wine and downed it in a gulp—"join the club."

"I still think you're crazy. Tyrone said he'd let you keep this place. Why do you want to move back to Detroit?" Jenice said as she wrapped a goblet in newspaper and placed it in a box marked GLASSWARE.

"New York hasn't been good for me, and it would be even worse for me now," Nikkie said simply. "Tyrone hates me, and even though I'm sure he's not going to go around spreading what happened, there's just going to be too many questions asked that I won't be able to answer. Better to just go back to Detroit and start all over again."

"So, are you going to be Nicole Jensen or . . ." Jenice wrinkled up her nose. "What did you say your real name was, again?"

"Shanika Jenkins. I haven't decided yet, but I'll probably stay Nicole. I'm going to have to get a job, you know, and all of my work achievements have been credited to that name."

The women were interrupted by the sound of a baby crying. "Oops! Feeding time!"

Nikkie walked into the nursery, with Jenice following closely on her heels.

"So you're still going to pass, then?" Jenice said after Nicole settled into a rocking chair and began nursing the baby.

"Oh, good Lord, no. I'll be Nicole Jensen, but I'll be a very proud black Nicole Jensen." Nicole gave a sad chuckle. "Believe me, I've learned my lesson."

"I know that will make your brother happy." Jenice sat down in a chair across from Nicole.

Nikkie sighed. "I don't know that anything I do will make my brother happy at this point. I'm sure he's glad that I'm no longer passing for white, but at the same time, I don't think that he'll ever forgive me for having done so. Especially after I went and got married as a white woman, because that meant I was renouncing him as my family. So how can I now be angry with him renouncing me?" Tears sprung to Nikkie's eyes.

"He'll come around again," Jenice said soothingly.

"Well"—Nikkie shrugged—"I hope he does, but my going back to my roots really doesn't have anything to do with him. I'm doing this for me and my little Elizabeth Ann. She's not going to grow up having to live a lie her mama told, that's for sure." She began to hum a lullaby as the baby nursed at her breast. In ten minutes her daughter was asleep, and she placed her back in the bassinet. She was so focused on her infant that the ringing of her cell phone startled her.

She rushed to answer it, hoping against hope that it was Tyrone, and he had finally come to his senses and realized that he wanted to make the marriage work. The disappointment on her face was apparent when she looked at the caller ID and saw that it was just Lucia.

"Hello."

"Hey, have you gotten used to being black again?" Lucia asked in a jovial voice.

Nikkie chuckled. "It's like riding a bike. You never really forget."

"Good. Now, did you quit your job at Paxon and Green yet?"

"I've still got another three weeks' maternity leave, so I haven't turned in my notice yet. I mean, what's the rush, right? I'll probably sneak in like four forty-five on a Friday, when most of the people are gone. I don't want to have to face them."

"Uh-huh, yeah, whatever," Lucia said as if not really caring. "Look, you can't quit just yet. I need you."

"Why? What's going on?"

"I think I have that role in *Imitation of Life*. And I really, really want it. I know that at least one of the producers is having some doubts because he thinks there might be some stink in the black community, like you said. So you have to fix that for me."

"Oh? And how am I supposed to do that?" Nikkie asked as she settled down into a chair next to Jenice.

"We've got to get it into the papers that I'm actually black."

"*What?*"

"What's going on?" Jenice whispered, nudging her. "What happened? Is that Tyrone?"

Nikkie quickly shook her head and held up her hand to signal Jenice to hold on.

"I'm serious. I am. Well, biracial, anyway. My mother's Italian, but my father is Brazilian. You know, as in the country that has more blacks than any outside the continent of Africa. I'm half-black."

"And you never told me?"

Lucia giggled. "You never asked. In fact, no one has. Let's face it, all of the roles I've had up until now have been good, but small. No one's ever taken any notice of me, or really worried about my bio. And it's not like my bio contains any lies. I was born right here in Manhattan. I look white, and no one's ever questioned my ethnicity. I'm sure *you* know what I'm talking about."

Nikkie grinned. "I'm sure I do."

"My father died when I was a kid, all of his family is still in Brazil, and I'm an only child. So all anyone saw was my mom. But now—"

Nikkie nodded. "Now it's to your advantage to make sure people know."

"Exactly!"

Nikkie's brow furrowed, "But, well, why now? I mean,

what about the Spielberg movie? You lost that part because you weren't black; why didn't you speak up then?"

"Oh, please. For that little part? A chambermaid? I wasn't going to blow my cover over that, even if it was a Spielberg movie. But this . . . come on, this is a starring role. The kind that can really make my career! For this, I'll be black."

"You sure about this?" Nikkie asked.

"Positive. But you have to spin it just right, Nikkie. Don't make it like I was pretending to be white before, but that as an actress I was just playing roles I was asked to play. You know how to do it, girl."

"Don't worry. I'll get on it immediately. I'll call into the office and let them know I'll be taking care of this personally, from home, of course. Do you have any pictures of your father?"

"I'll have my mother send them over to your house by messenger this afternoon."

"Good. I know just the person at the *New York Times* to bring in on this. Very compassionate, but always looking for a scoop. Don't worry, girl, I got you covered. But, listen, this is likely the last thing I'm going to be able to do for you."

"What do you mean?"

"As I said, I'm going to be giving my notice to Paxon and Green in a few weeks, and I'm moving back to Detroit."

There was silence at the other end.

"You still there," Nikkie asked nervously.

"Is my contract with Paxon and Green or with you?"

"With Paxon and Green."

"And you won't reconsider your decision to move back to Detroit?"

"Absolutely not."

"Well," Lucia said after a pause, "how about I insist that Paxon and Green keep you on as a subcontractor or something even though you're in Detroit? I mean, they're not stupid. My career is definitely on the upswing, and they're going to want to keep me happy."

Nikkie looked at Jenice. "I have a better idea. I really want to cut all my ties with Paxon and Green and this whole mess I've made of it in New York, but I'll turn you over to one of my colleagues who would be perfect for you. Wait. Hold on." She took the phone away from her ear and hit the mute button.

"Jenice. What's your workload like?"

Jenice grimaced. "Please. Overloaded as usual."

"Really? You don't think you can take over another account?"

"Really, and absolutely no way."

Nikkie grinned. "Not even the Lucia Silver account? And by the way, she's up for yet another major role, which is sure to land her an Oscar."

Jenice's eyes widened and she jumped up from the chair. "Are you serious? Oh, my God, I'd love that account! But do you think the powers that be would let that happen?"

"I'm sure they will if Lucia insists. And I'm sure that she will. Consider it my parting gift to you. From one sista to another."

Jenice raised her fist in the old Black Power salute. "My sista!"

Nikkie laughed and took her finger off the mute button. "Lucia, listen . . . have I got a deal for you . . . !"

Nikkie hung up, looked at Jenice, and started laughing.

Discussion Questions

1. If you think there was just one real reason why Shanika decided to pass for white, what would it be? Is self-hatred the main reason that most people pass?
2. Most African-Americans are familiar with the issue of passing, but most think it's something that was only done before the Civil Rights and Black Power movements, when black people faced overt prejudice and discrimination. Do you think there would be any reason for a black person to pass for white in the twenty-first century?
3. How would you react if someone in your family told you they were considering passing for another race?
4. How would you feel if you found out someone you knew to be white was actually black? Would you tell anyone? Why or why not?
5. Is passing for another race morally wrong? What about other ways of passing, such as gay/straight or Jewish/gentile?
6. Do you think Tyrone fell in love with Shanika/Nicole because he thought she was white, or in spite of the fact?
7. Was Lucia right? Have other white people benefited from affirmative action? If so, in what way(s)?
8. Would you consider Hal, Rachel, Cindy or Mrs. Riverton to be prejudiced? Why or why not? What about Joseph? Do you think whites tend to be more prejudiced than blacks, or vice versa?
9. At what point do you think Shanika should have let people know that she was African-American? Do you think it was as difficult as she said, or was she making excuses?
10. Do you think Joseph should forgive Shanika? What about Tyrone?

Author's Recommended Reading List

Nonfiction

Passing: When People Can't Be Who They Are by Brooke Kroeger

Noted journalist Brooke Kroeger profiles six people who are passing for other than what they are (black passing for white, white passing for black, gay passing for straight, etc.) and explores their reasons for doing so.

The Black Notebooks: An Interior Journey by Toi Derricotte

African-American poet and college professor Derricotte details her experiences and struggles with being light enough to be mistaken for white.

Fiction

Passing by Nella Larsen

This classic novel published in the mid-1920s explores the lives of two African-African women who are light enough to pass for white, and how their decisions to pass or not changes their lives.

An Autobiography of an Ex-Colored Man
by James Weldon Johnson

Another African-American classic, this novel follows the journey of a biracial man in the 1920s who was raised by his African-American mother but could easily pass for white. He switches back and forth between the races at will, and begins to lose his identity in the process.

The Human Stain by Philip Roth

A college professor is labeled a bigot and forced to resign after a joke he makes in class is deemed racist against African-Americans. The irony is that the professor is himself African-American, but has hidden the fact from friends and colleagues for almost fifty years.

Acknowledgments

I would like to start off by thanking my brother and sister-in-law, Joseph and Ayoka Quinones. They were, as usual, wonderfully supportive of me while I was working on *Passin'*.

I'd also like to thank all of the people who were kind enough to talk to me about their experiences in passing.

I'd also like to thank Zemoria Brandon, who was kind enough to give me some medical information I needed to include in this book.

As always, I have to say that my agent, Liza Dawson of Liza Dawson Associates, and my editor at Grand Central Publishing, Beth de Guzman, are simply the best in the business! I'm so happy to working with you ladies!

A big thank-you to my fellow authors, Daaimah S. Poole, Miasha, Gloria Mallette, Shannon Holmes, Tracy Price-Thompson, Zane, Eric Pete, Kwan, T. Styles, and Terrance Dean—I so appreciate your support and comments!

A special shout-out goes to my daughter, Camille R. Quinones Miller, who not only helped me by reading chapters as I went along, but also producing and directing a trailer for *Passin'*. And she did an outstanding job!

My niece, Takia Miguel, aka "Chocolate—Princess of Harlem," also did her thing. She wrote the lyrics for a soundtrack for the trailer, then went in the studio to record the title song. Takia, I always knew you were talented, but you really managed to blow me away with this one! Hey y'all . . . check her out at www.myspace.com/chocmusik.

And I would be truly derelict if I didn't thank *you*! I'm ever so grateful for the support I've been given by readers. I hope I never let you down!

About the Author

Karen E. Quinones Miller, a former reporter for the *Philadelphia Inquirer*, is the *Essence* bestselling author of several novels, including *Satin Doll* and *I'm Telling*. Her daughter, Camille, is a junior at Clark Atlanta University. Karen lives in Philadelphia and is working on her next novel and a screenplay. You can visit her Web site at www.karenequinonesmiller.com.